EVERYO

(finalist for the 20~~~~~~~ .....aru in Fiction)

"B.K. Troop is that rarest find: an unexpected and entirely engaging new character. It is B.K.'s voice—his allusions, fulminations, deprecations, and ultimately his hapless, hopeless romanticism—that makes this fine first novel such an enjoyable romp."
Seduced by a Literary Original by Robin Russin, *Los Angeles Times*

"Burnett captures perfectly both the mid-1980's setting and the feelings of both the lovable, predatory narrator and his elusive quarry. B.K. is both hilariously outlandish and utterly touching."
***Booklist*, the American Library Association magazine**

"At times both acid-tinged and unbelievably sweet, a hopeless love's lament."
Kirkus Reviews

"A genuinely touching and unexpected love story."
The Hollywood Reporter

"Through his flamboyant character of Troop, Burnett offers one page after another of witty, outrageous, raunchy, insightful, tender and romantic prose."
Chicago Free Press

Praise for *The House Beautiful*

"The Greenwich Village demimonde never seemed so demented . . . The plot here is dandy, mainly along the lines of speed-freak French farce. But the true joy is Troop's champagne-giddy language and his besotted love for his houseful of bohemians. Armistead Maupin on laughing gas."
Kirkus Reviews

"[Burnett] skillfully handles multiple story lines, and he has a strong gift for wit—Troop's opening prologue, addressed to critics of his previous novel, is a thesaurus-fueled riot that could give a Bulwer-Lytton judge heartburn. . . . The novel is sweet and at times even wise, a celebration of la vie bohème."
Library Journal Review

"Hilariously repugnant . . . B.K. is exquisitely realized . . ."
Publishers Weekly

Writers Tribe Books

Copyright © 2011 by Allison Burnett

Book design by Amy Inouye, Future Studio LA
Cover art by DoubleMranch.com
Author photo by Chloe King

Published in the United States of America

ISBN 978-1-937746-00-1

www.writerstribebooks.com

Death by Sunshine

ALLISON BURNETT

ALSO BY ALLISON BURNETT

Christopher

The House Beautiful

Undiscovered Gyrl

For Bille Brown

"Where the heart is, there the muses,
there the gods sojourn,
and not in any geography of fame."
—RALPH WALDO EMERSON

"We say we have only two kinds of weather:
perfect and most unusual."
—KATHLEEN NORRIS, *My California*

Greeting

When, after a trial of long months, I had at last finished writing my second novel, *The House Beautiful*, I set down my ballpoint pen and lifted a flute of congratulatory champagne to the mantel mirror. Grinning back at me was a cruel conspiracy of folds, crannies, and flaps. I shuddered, but reminded myself that while such facial wear and tear is certainly the most obvious toll the artist pays on the road to immortality, it is hardly the most dear. An unknown galley slave once carved into his giant oar, "How often have I nearly perished, wrestling with thee!" I would like to have carved the same thing into the left breast of my muse, for she had all but wrecked me on this book. My body was weak, my spirit half-broken. Yet somehow I had prevailed.

"Well done, old feller," I whispered.

It was just then, as I raised the bubbles to my lips, that I was struck by a premonition that I would never write another word, for the simple reason that I would soon be dead. I lowered the crystal and saw myself sprawled on a filthy square of city pavement, clutching and wheezing, as the sky shrank to the size of a postage stamp. Concerned New Yorkers stepped over me as though I were a smear of dog dirt. Soon I would lie deep with Manhattan's nameless dead, gone forever, like a dream.

Quite frankly, it didn't take a psychic to predict my death by heart attack. Since boyhood, I had loved figs better than long life, which is just a fancy way of saying that I had feasted on fat things, huffed far too many cigarettes, and drunk deep the folly of cheap wine. As a result, I had in recent years suffered sporadic bouts of angina, my knees had begun to fail, and I was plagued by vertigo. And so, picturing my own death, I did not curse my fate. How could I? In almost seven decades on the planet, I had done nothing to earn longevity.

I sipped my champagne (it wore a golden crown with sensible shoes) and consoled myself with the reflection that maybe an end to my writing career was not such a bad thing, after all. Two superb novels were already two more superb novels than I had ever expected to write, and, as I had already mined my past of all its best ore, a third book would have to be drawn entirely from the present, which was unthinkable. What could be more tedious than the last days of a sick, lonely bachelor? Of course I might *invent* something, but this was well beyond the powers of my imagination. The book I had just finished writing, *The House Beautiful,* was, like my debut novel, *Christopher*, based entirely on fact. It told of a single summer in my Manhattan brownstone, which serves as a refuge for young, struggling artists. Although little more than reportage, the book glides by like a poem and is nearly impossible to put down. I could never make up anything even a tenth as good.

Reconciled as I was to my own death, imagine my surprise when, the very next day, just hours after mailing off my manuscript to the publisher, I was struck once again by The Itch, by which I mean, of course, that incurable itch for scribbling that Juvenal wrote about, the one that grows inveterate in the breasts of all born writers. It struck in the supermarket, as I was reaching for a jar of marmalade. Suddenly, I imagined the hero of my next novel. He was a pretty, young man, no older than twenty-five, with small gray eyes and a sunken chest. His hair was greasy. He chewed bubble gum. Who was he? Where had he come from? My memory? Or had I conjured him? Was I even capable of conjuring?

"You sure you want that kind?" someone croaked. I turned around and saw, just below my well-brimmed hat, the face of an ugly adolescent. His smile was chipped and his face bright with acne. He wore an apron. He pointed to a smaller jar. "Because that brand there's twenty percent off."

"Money is no object," I replied. "Anyway, I prefer my fruit *thick cut.*"

I tossed him a roguish eye.

He caught my drift and quickly swam away.

I pocketed the jam.

As I moseyed out of the store without a stop at the cash register, I noticed that my gum-chewing protagonist had vanished and that no amount of concentration could will him back.

Oh, well. Easy come, easy go.

At home I passed the long afternoon as one with his leg in a plaster cast: I was devoured by an itch that I could not scratch. When I awoke the next day, the itch was gone, and I resumed my daily routine of reading, gorging, huffing, voiding, and tippling, taking breaks only to serve as mentor to my ragtag band of lodgers, whose paltry rents, along with my psychiatric disability checks from Uncle Sam, allowed me to remain happily installed in The House Beautiful. And there in the coming weeks my heart would surely have sputtered to a stop had it not been for the fateful ring of the telephone.

It was a drizzly afternoon in early November when Hollywood called. The voice at the other end was raspy and avaricious. She asked me to hold. A moment later I was connected to her boss, a movie producer by the name of Mr. Harold Shipp[1]. In the brusque manner of his trade, he told me that he had just put down my novel *Christopher*, loved it, and were the film rights still available? I nearly wept with joy, not because I had any high regard for contemporary cinema—in fact, I did not—but because my novels had earned me less than the cost of my legal pads, and my lodgers had been paying me the same low rent for the past twenty years.

"As a matter of fact, they *are* available," I replied, "but I'm afraid you can't afford them."

I had read somewhere that Hollywood people, like cats and women, are irresistibly drawn to those who show them the most indifference. This insight proved itself to be true when, rather than taking offense at my rebuff, Mr. Shipp barked a skeptical laugh and asked me to name my price.

"Not so fast," I snapped. "Before we talk numbers, I must warn you that my narrative voice is absolutely impossible to imitate, so unless you're prepared to hire *me* to write the movie script, I'm afraid we have nothing more to discuss."

"Not a problem," he said.

Bouncing up and down in my chair, I decided to push my luck even farther.

"I'm sorry," I snitted, "but I can't bear telephones. Damnable contraptions. If you wish to continue this negotiation, you'll have to book me a first-class train ticket to California. If

---

1   The names of all people associated with Hollywood have been changed twice: first by the person in question to hide his religion, criminal record, or ordinariness, and then by me, to prevent litigation.

not, good afternoon, Mr. Shipp, and good luck."

I hung up in his face.

A bold gambit, yes, but I had not left Manhattan in years. I deserved a free vacation, and Mr. Shipp was just the man to give it to me. When thirty seconds had passed, my smile lost its cockiness. Fifteen more, and I was shaking like a leaf. I lunged at the phone. What had I done? I must track down Mr. Shipp at once! But when I lifted the receiver to my ear, the mogul was still in mid-harangue. He had not even heard me hang up!

"—and now you expect me to buy you a *train* ticket?" he shouted. "Who the hell takes the train, anyway? Who do you think you are? Kim Novak?"

"No, I'm Burt Lahr. A huge scaredy cat. The last time I flew, the approach to Idyllwild Airport was nothing short of kamikazean. I vowed if I made it back to earth alive, I would never fly again."

"Jesus Christ, you ever heard of Italy? People die in trains every god damn day."

"Yes, but they die of a bump to the head. In an airplane, you're dropped thousands of feet through space, trapped for what feels like an eternity in a tube of horrors. People moan and pray. Babies shriek. The cabin becomes a sauna of shameful, spontaneous defecation. And, worst of all, you have time to look back over your life."

Labored breathing gave way to complete surrender. Mr. Shipp told me that he would be happy to reimburse me for my train ticket, and then he screamed at his secretary to book me into the Palms Plaza for a week starting on Monday. She would get back to me with the details.

"See you soon," I thrummed.

"Just get here!" he shouted.

Click.

I danced a little jig.

Troop: 1 Dream Factory: 0

As I ran upstairs to announce my good news to my lodgers, what I did not know, could not have known, was that what awaited me in Los Angeles was no working holiday, no mere pay day in the sun, but the very story I had thought I would never live to write: my third and final novel, which you now hold in your hands, every blood-soaked word of which is true.

—B.K. Troop

An Opening Digression

To those who adore world travel but fear falling through space on fire, there is no feeling quite so snug as that of boarding a transcontinental train. My heart purred with contentment that damp November afternoon when I mounted the steel steps of the Three Rivers bound for Chicago. I was shown to my couchette by a dapper, little porter named Lewis, a fine old puss of a gentleman, all perfume, soap, and powder. His skin was rosy brown like a brand-new penny loafer and his manners were positively antebellum. Lewis, despite being in good old age, had no trouble managing my carry-on luggage: a leather suitcase filled with clothes, linen, toiletries, Los Angeles books, and plenty of cigarettes, and a canvas duffel loaded with clanking refreshments.

Although the narrow corridor of the train was not much warmer than the platform outside, I fancied I could feel already the rays of the Pacific sun, hotter than a bride's breath, toasting my freckled shoulders; over the whirring fans, I heard already the swoosh of palm fronds above my poolside hammock, where I scribbled every day, pausing only to bark out drink orders to my docile Mayan houseboy; and, despite my desperate poverty, I knew already the serenity of a man in the chips. Yes, I confess it: my unhatched chickens were not only being counted, but also breaded and fried. How naive I was that afternoon, how trusting of the Fates!

The first bad omen was my train compartment. It was nothing more than two seats facing each other next to a yard-wide window. A pygmy sink hung above a dollhouse toilet. Its mirror looked plucked from a lady's compact. When I asked where I was meant to sleep, Lewis yanked the bottoms of the seats together to form a cot barely big enough to hold one of my shoes. I exhaled my disapproval but left it at that. I could scarcely blame Lewis for the decline of Western civilization, especially when its progress had cost so many of his descendants their freedom and lives.

A half-hour later, the train jerked into motion, beginning my first trip west since 1958, when I had hitchhiked to San Francisco and taken it by storm. As we crawled free of Pennsylvania Station, I christened the enterprise with a glass of New Zealand Sauvignon Blanc (Maori pecs, kiwi rump). Gazing out at the bloodless urban landscape, my toes curling with delight, I inwardly sang the praises of this most enlightened form of travel.

Fumbling for a forbidden cigarette, I recalled the famous quotation of someone French, who said that travel was the most melancholy of exercises, because it means seeing a thousand objects for the first and last time; it is to be born and die every minute. I lowered the fag and felt a surge of panic. My heart raced and I was forced to gulp air to keep from vomiting. The reason was obvious: Nothing is more terrible to an old man than the thought of dying alone.

What if I were run over by a car in Los Angeles? Or murdered in my hotel room? Or my heart failed as I signed my contract? Who would come to the morgue to claim me? The poet Adrian was the only one of my lodgers who had made an appearance at the farewell breakfast that I had hosted for myself at the Parnassus diner. Where was everyone else? Was I really so odious? Would it have killed them to eat a lousy bagel with me? I lunged for the teeny toilet. I did not use it, however, because at that instant, as though God were nothing more than a third-rate melodramatist, the train rocked, my little door banged open, and there facing me was the backside of a strapping young man. His tight denims, cashmere sweater, and shiny designer boots told me that he was something special.

"Well, hello," I said.

Not even bothering to glance back, he disappeared into his couchette, slammed the door with tremendous volume, and let out a scream. A moment later, he uncorked a louder scream, followed by a burst of billingsgate so frank and foul that even today it makes me shiver.

Footsteps approached on the run.

Lewis appeared and pressed his little ear to the door. Listened. Nothing but a few whimpers. He looked at me and twirled a finger at his temple.

"Dude's crazy," he whispered.

"Crazy *sexy*," I whispered back.

Lewis frowned and fled.

Feeling right as rain suddenly, I propped my door open with my duffel. When the young man emerged, he would spot me and say hello. At the very worst, we would become pals; at the very best, we—I dared not even consider it. Falling in love on a train. Simply too wonderful. I reached into my bag for one of my Los Angeles books. I had packed two dozen of them, ranging in quality from literature to pap. I chose one of the latter group, an unauthorized biography of Ms. Cary Grant, which I hoped would offer me some insight into the early days of vaudeville and life inside Hollywood's pink satin closet.

Unfortunately, I was stricken with a case of the erotic jimjams and could not concentrate. I could think only of the young man across the way. Ah, youth, forever dear, forever kind! When would I outgrow the craving? I threw down the bio and fished for a meatier distraction—*The Day of the Locust*. Next to Raymond Chandler, Nathanael West was, for my money, the best friend Los Angeles had ever had. He made the place seem exciting, like the tenth circle of hell, when, in fact, it was merely bland and sunny. Or so I had heard. I had never visited Los Angeles and had never read a word of Mr. West.

"Hey, you! Wake up! What's in the bottle?"

I opened my crusty eyes—how long had I been asleep? — and there was my neighbor, softly focused, filling my threshold with his bulky frame. His skin was olive, his tendril hair Gypsy black. His upper lip wore a hint of Byronic scorn. His plum-colored silk shirt clung to his hard, sweaty, hairless chest. I thought of wise, old Democritus who deliberately blinded himself with sunlight so that he would never again behold beautiful, young things beyond his reach.

"Madeira," I replied with a smile, reaching for a clean glass. "Sit and taste." But the bottle was empty—this explained my deep slumber. I fell to my knees and unzipped my duffel. "I have every kind of wine in here. Monkey wine, lion wine, sheep wine, and swine wine. The monkey enlivens, the lion irritates, the sheep stupefies, and the swine brutalizes. Which do you prefer?"

"Red," he said.

"Excellent choice." I plucked out a new Chianti, unscrewed it in a flash, and poured. He stared into his glass for a long time. Then sniffed. It was a rough-and-tumble Southern vintage with the dry hands and big heart of the Neapolitan *scugnizzi*. He downed it in three mighty gulps, gave it back, and smiled at me strangely. His shoulders were broad. His legs a bit bowed. His black eyes were among the most disturbed and violent I had ever seen. He was at most twenty-seven and I suspected that he slept only with women.

"Tastes like piss," he said, then he jumped up and vanished.

I swapped my Oxfords for corduroy slippers, grabbed the bottle, and set off in hot pursuit. I bounced between the walls of the swaying car, but I never lost my footing. My heart was strong, my determination fierce.

For those of you who do not travel by rail, let me be the first to break the bad news: the glory days of the club car are over. Today, those who cleave to the hem of the Lady Nicotine are dragged into a cold, windowless room directly across from the handicapped shower. The indignity would be enough to make any sane man quit smoking, if any sane man smoked. It was here that I found my friend, barely visible through a bluish scrim of poison, slumped in the corner, sucking down a Marlboro. His hand visibly trembled; his eyes darted. A soul in torment. No stranger to suffering myself, I am, like Virgil, an expert at relieving the sufferings of others. I plopped down next to him.

"Curious," I said with a sympathetic smile, "we both travel first class, and yet we're both slaves to the vice of the proletariat."

He glared at me with contempt. Oh, he was a vicious one, capable of cold-blooded murder. Like a striking snake, he snatched the bottle from my hand. I watched in mute astonishment as his Adam's apple bobbed and bobbed until the entire vessel was drained. He swiped an arm across his mouth and asked if I had more. I sprinted back to my couchette and returned with two bottles of my cheeriest, chattiest rosé.

A half-hour passed as he guzzled, but nothing I said or did could engage his attention even for an instant, so, finally, I gave up and held my tongue. Every few minutes some home-grown passenger—dirty, ugly, and toothless—would enter the smoking car. After meeting the homicidal eyes of my blowtop companion, he'd take three fast puffs and run for his life. Yes, this brute was not to be trifled with, and so, when both bottles were empty, I stood up, half-mashed and fully famished, and bid him farewell.

"I'd invite you to join me for supper," I said, "but I get the distinct impression that you'd prefer to be left alone, that you have no desire to engage in even the most casual—"

Here, at last, the young man opened his mouth and did not just speak, but spoke without interruption for the next twelve hours. His outpouring was full of terrors and wonders. How I wish I had taken notes! Unfortunately, I was so deep into my cups that it was all I could do to inhabit the present, let alone cast an eye to the day when I might write another novel.

This is what I do remember: His name was James Paul D'Anunzio, no relation to the bald, fascist poet Mr. Gabriele D'Anunzio. He went by Jimmy. Although he spoke without a twang, he hailed from an affluent suburb of Dallas, Texas. His mother was a housewife. His father, an émigré from Coney Island, was a mobster, who traded in counterfeit computer chips. When I expressed surprise that the Cosa Nostra was active both in Texas and in the world of high tech, he frowned at me, as though he had suddenly noticed I was a mongoloid idiot.

"We're everywhere, old man."

As we rattled past the rough, rolling hills and the pale, runny-nosed Amish of the Keystone State, Jimmy spoke of his early childhood. His voice grew hushed as he recalled the nights he had spent slumped at his windowsill, watching his father play

bocce ball with his henchmen on the big back lawn. The loser
was forced to perform the night's hit. Later, Jimmy would lie
sleepless, wondering if the rat being murdered had a son of his
own, a boy who would have given anything to be invited to play
bocce with his father in the moonlight. As for his mother, he
told me only that she cooked the best Fettuccine Alfredo in
Texas (is that saying much?) and that when he was seven he
used to crawl under the table at her weekly pinochle games and,
using both little hands, massage the groins of her lady friends.
None of them let out so much as a peep. Even at such a tender
age, Jimmy knew that this reflected poorly on their husbands.

By the time we reached Youngstown, Ohio, two more bottles of rosé had been drained, and we were as full as a pair of
billy goats. Jimmy spoke even faster now, his mind sloppy and
dizzy, his foot jerking as though trying to start a dead motorcycle. He had moved on to his promiscuous adolescence. In high
school his specialty was blonde virgins, whom he plied with
pot and hallucinogens. By the time he graduated high school,
his sexual resume was most impressive: over a hundred and fifty conquests, resulting in numerous abortions and infections
and two suicides. He chuckled as he told me this. Everything
was a goof to this rogue.

Four years later, he graduated from the University of Con-
necticut at Storrs with a degree in math. Addicted to virtually
every illegal substance known to Man—with the exception
of steroids, which shrank the testes—he knew he could never
hold down a regular job, so he dropped out of society, and,
living off a small inheritance, devoted his life to traveling the
rails. (He was even more afraid of flying than I was, but only
because of the baggage inspectors.) Once or twice a month, he
would pull into a new city to party with friends. When they or
he grew bored, he would move on to the next town. For the last

seven years, his life had been nothing but a soulless montage of disco dancing, casual sex, and inebriation. His present destination was West Hollywood, where he would crash for the third time in the past year on the couch of a college friend named Rob Brandywine, whose livelihood was helping rich, fat ladies lift barbells.

I was wearing rosé-colored glasses when I said: "But you can't go on this way forever. Surely you must have some ambition, some greater vision for your future."

"Hell, yeah," he said, holding his stomach and rocking. "I've got a rich dad and two rich godfathers. Both are old as shit. When they die, I get everything."

Because these mobsters would have disinherited him at once had they known of his hedonism, Jimmy made sure that whenever he visited home he was relatively sober and that he bored them senseless with stories about his work as a financial analyst.

As the sun rose reluctantly over Fostoria, Ohio, Jimmy explained the source of his earlier screams and his present distress. They were not, as I had thought, the result of mental illness; it was that he had accidentally left his toilet bag, stuffed with various narcotics, in one of his six checked suitcases, and nothing could persuade Lewis and his courtly staff to fetch them from the baggage car. This meant that what I had just beheld was the first drug-free evening of Jimmy D'Anunzio's adult life, of which you, Lucky Reader, have been the beneficiary, because it triggered in him the acute logorrhea that made it possible for me to write this chapter—a digression that has made endurable for you the first leg of my long journey westward. It also meant that if I had any chance at all of bedding the creature, it would have to wait until tomorrow.

Windy City

Ravished by the grape and rocked by my couchette, I dozed like a sea lion with a belly full of squid. My snores were musical and my dreams gorgeous. A few times I actually burst out laughing, and twice I was so aroused that I was sure I had flopped over onto a roll of silver dollars. Yet I did not wake up. In fact, I had never slept so well in all my life, and, given the choice, I would never have opened my eyes again. But *why* was I so relaxed? Was it simply because I had left Manhattan behind? Was city life even more burdensome to my nervous system than I had imagined?

Suddenly, my reverie shifted, and I was floating in a sapphire swimming pool, talking on the telephone with a precocious screenwriter who wanted to come by with his latest script. He was desperate for my opinion and who could blame him? I was, after all, a master of the form. "But that's quite impossible," I said. "I'm not wearing any trunks." He replied, "So what?" I knew what this meant: in exchange for my cruel blue pen applied to his text, he would apply his ruby lips to—No, no, the boy was just fifteen. Such a swap was not just wrong, but also criminal. Yet I could not find the strength to refuse him. I told him to come over.

The moment I hung up, I paid for my sin: the deck chairs, the umbrellas, even my plastic life raft, burst into flames. I spun into the water and discovered to my horror that I had forgotten how to swim. I sank to the bottom. The water began to boil, and I knew that I would soon be dead. Abruptly, I burst to the surface, screaming for help. Ten feet away, a burly fireman clambered over a white picket fence. When I reached out a child's urgent hand, he cocked back a big red axe, held it high over his head, and brought it down between my eyes.

I awoke with a shriek.

Where was I?

My temples throbbed and my eyes were capable of everything but sight. The air stank of unshowered flesh. Weeping for no good reason, I groped until I found a curtain. I yanked it aside and discovered that we were coming to a stop in Union Station, Chicago. I was safe and sound. Thank heaven! Our baggage would soon be transferred to a mightier train, and after lunch we would be off again. Nothing between us and the Pacific Ocean but a measly two thousand miles. A big clock rolled into view and I saw that we were four hours behind schedule. This meant that our layover had been reduced to a mere three hours.

I flung myself into action. As neither I nor Jimmy had eaten a bite, I thought we might pass our time at a local restaurant. Squatting like Gulliver over the miniature plumbing, I washed as fast as I could, changed my duds, and flew across the aisle. I was shocked to find his couchette empty. Was he already prowling the platform, waiting for his stash to be tossed out of the baggage car? I hastily detrained, but saw no sign of him anywhere.

Feelings hurt, I toddled off alone in search of affordable

grub. I found it in a local greasy spoon filled with the sort of colorful lonely folk who populate downtowns everywhere, but who are fascinating only within the confines of an Edward Hopper painting. In real life, they make you want to shoot yourself.

After a Denver omelet, a side of hash browns, a side of kielbasa, and a double Bloody Mary, I felt almost human again. It was time to explore the City of Broad Shoulders and bad haircuts. I wanted to see for myself the vaunted architecture that makes Chicago the city Americans most regret never having visited.

A few minutes later, walking across a wide plaza, I was hit by an arctic gale that tore through my overcoat like a bear trap. I coughed so hard that my knees jellied. I reached out both hands and crashed to the sidewalk. My palms were scraped and my right kneecap exploded like a light bulb. The pain was so intense that I was tempted simply to close my eyes and die. But then I remembered with a jolt that I wasn't some homeless wretch forced to sleep on the pavement or an aging Inuit sent adrift on an iceberg because I had dropped a few teeth; I was a celebrated novelist on my way to the world capital of glamour, where, if a half-dozen of my ex-lodgers were to be believed, all of one's dreams might come true at any moment. They claimed that this endowed every Los Angeles business meeting, every ring of the telephone, every chance encounter, with a powerful, almost erotic charm. I had to see for myself.

Limping back to Union Station, I saw Jimmy drive by in a taxi cab. I waved a bloody hand and hollered, but he didn't see me. As if that weren't bad enough, my breakfast was now in full rebellion. Windy City, indeed!

I Met a Squaw

The Southwest Chief is a transcontinental train, so tall that it required two strong hands to hoist me aboard. The hands belonged to a porter named Lemuel, who bore such a striking resemblance to Lewis that I had no choice but to ask if they were cousins. Insulted, Lemuel let go of me, and I nearly tumbled. To day this day, I am not sure whether he was offended because I had implied that all African-Americans look alike, or because he and Lewis were, in fact, the same person, and I had confused the names.

Sadly, my new couchette was identical to the first, except that the wax cups above the sink were of a different color and the carpet was a bit less grimy. Eager to reconnect with Jimmy, I unpacked as quickly as I could, which, given my shredded palms, was not very fast. I tried to imagine what he would be like now that he was under the influence of narcotics. Gentler? Less impatient? More inclusive? In short, might he be open to a cuddle and a puddle?

The answer was an emphatic no.

Rattling into Missouri, dividing our time between the observation car and the smoking lounge, Jimmy and I did nothing but quarrel. No matter what I said, even when it was next to nothing, Jimmy attacked me. At one point, I referred to his red boots as "unique," and he lashed out as though I had called them vulgar and Woppish. When he asked whether I had read some silly book about a vampire, and I replied in as humble a way as I knew how that, being a novelist myself, I preferred literature to popular fiction, he called me a "fuckin' snob," and glared at my neck as though he wanted to bite it. One of his favorite subjects was the Dallas Cowboys. As I know absolutely nothing about football except that I am not interested in knowing more, I took the uncontroversial position that, when it came to this week's big game, I had my fingers crossed. Nope, too much. He accused me of having a "shit attitude" and said that if I didn't buy into the system, then why the hell should the players?

Certain now that I was in the presence of a bona fide lunatic, I crossed my arms and clammed up. He talked himself dizzy for the next few hours, pausing only to fill his nose or dump his bladder. The camel's back was irreparably broken outside Topeka when he staggered back from the john, patched with sweat, eyes bulging, tongue working the roof of his mouth, and asked what I wrote about in my books.

"Myself," I replied facetiously.

He laughed and jabbed at my belly. "Who cares about you?"

"Stop that!"

"No wonder I've never heard of you," he cackled. "Who wants to read a book about an old faggot?"

My mind went blank with hurt. I could not let him see it, of course. If he did, there would be no limit to his cruelty. I stared out the window, at the rows of dark crops flashing past. I blinked back tears and groped for something casual to say.

"You know I'm right," he laughed. "Nobody likes old fags. Not even fags like old fags. That's why so many young ones kill themselves, so they won't end up like you. Hey, hey, what's that on your cheek? Oh, shit! Is that *rouge?*" He roared, peppering me with spittle.

My patience snapped.

I stood to my full height.

"My friend, you have single-handedly accomplished what the cold-blooded slaughter of three hundred thousand innocent Ethiopians could not. You have turned me against Italians forever. Good-bye!"

I turned on my heels and limped away. As I exited the car, I could hear him behind me, roaring sadistically. Back in my room, I sat for a long time with my face in my hands. His words had been vicious, but instead of warding them off, I had let them *inhabit* me. Why? When had I learned to ignore my own high opinion of myself and defer to the scorn of others? I flashed on my adoptive father and his whispery midnight visits and knew that he was the start of it. But I was past seventy now. Shouldn't I have learned to love myself by now? Would I never be free of the past?

I yanked my seats together and fell asleep.

A few hours later, deep in the heart of America, Jimmy banged open my door, stumbled forward, and fell into my arms. He was stinking drunk and panting with desire. Discretion forbids me to describe what happened next. I will say this: Aristotle once famously noted, "One swallow maketh not a summer." True enough, but one certainly made my autumn. And, with that, I draw a veil.

No sooner had the act been achieved than Jimmy threw himself into my door, bounced off, flung it open, and escaped. For the next twenty minutes, I heard him down the hall, banging on the walls of his couchette, wailing his lungs out. It was quite a scene, and I was surprised it did not prompt a visit from Lemuel. Jimmy's regrets did not, however, spoil my pride in a job well done. I had struck a blow not only against same-sex bigotry, but also against bullies everywhere. On my watch, the civilized were still the fittest.

We did not speak another word to each other for the rest of the journey, which was just the way I wanted it. In fact, nothing at all occurred, except that I finished three Los Angeles novels and, somewhere in New Mexico, a Native American hopped aboard and, holding a little microphone, regaled us with the history of her hoodwinked, slaughtered, and degraded people. I might have felt a twinge of guilt, but while these crimes were taking place, the people of my adoptive father were in Scotland, gobbling sheep's guts and barking at the moon, and the people of my adoptive mother were attending the opera in Oslo. And I told the squaw so.

Unwelcome

I t is the great blessing of ignorance that it so often renders us unaware even of our own ignorance. Stepping off the Southwest Chief at Union Station, I brimmed with confidence, certain that I would take the town by storm, just as I had conquered San Francisco so many years before. This was not the 1950s, however, and this city was the farthest thing from the home of the Beats. L.A. is closer to an industrial mill town, where the lucky few are hired to weave our dreams, while the rest wait outside the fence, shuffling their feet and wringing their hands, desperate for a nod.

A few minutes later, waiting for my luggage in the shadows of the lovely old Spanish depot, I overheard a homely woman tell her homelier friend that the Santa Anas were blowing.

"What's that?" I asked, leaking forbidden smoke from both nostrils. "An all-boy Chicano marching band?"

They stared at me with bewilderment.

I had heard from many sources that the chief defect in the native Los Angeleno is humorlessness, but I had chosen to keep an open mind; now it had been slammed shut. The awkwardness of the moment was dispelled by the arrival of my steamer trunk.

"My good man, would you be so kind as to deposit it at the curb along with these?" I dropped my carry-on bags atop the trunk. He eyed me strangely. It was abundantly clear I was no local. I followed him outside. Having forgotten to pack sunglasses, I was blinded all the way to the livery stand. Once my eyes adjusted, I saw that the Santa Ana winds, which I had read about in the celebrated "hot-air issue" of *The New Yorker*, were indeed blowing, and that they had left the sky a sweet, cloudless blue. An auspicious start. But then I sneezed and my hat flew off and cartwheeled away. I chased after it, sneezing again and again. What *The New Yorker* article had failed to mention was that the Santa Anas do more than remove smog and set the stage for well-deserved wildfires; they also disperse a host of desert allergens. I yanked my hat down over my ears and returned to my luggage.

The porter was gone, so I could not tip him. Where on earth was my limo? Had the driver given up and gone home? I wouldn't have blamed him. My train had arrived five hours late.[2] I poked my head around a corner, but saw only a bunch of poor people shuffling aboard a city bus. Was this to be my fate, as well? I heard a squeak and turned around as a small white car pulled up to the curb. The driver's seat was filled by a behemoth of uncertain gender. It fought itself free of its seat belt, tumbled out, and landed with two loud slaps to the pavement. Its round, happy face resembled a toddler's drawing of the sun.

"Mr. Troop?"

"Yes?"

---

2 Ever since the terrorist attacks of 9/11, left-wing critics had claimed that the United States was sliding toward fascism. Apparently, no one had bothered to tell Amtrak.

It extended a paw. "I'm Sissy Winkle. Mr. Shipp sent me."

"That's not a name," I harrumphed, "that's baby talk. Where's my limo?"

"What limo?"

"The one your boss promised me."

She grinned and crinkled her nose in a way that might have been adorable in someone of normal dimensions. "Are you sure he didn't say *car?*"

Perhaps he had, but it was too late to back down now.

"He said limo! He doesn't actually expect me to be squired around in *that?* It was built for little Japanese people."

"Actually, it's Korean."

"The point is, I'm a large man and you're no sylph yourself. And look!" I stepped aside to reveal my steamer trunk. Her grin fell into her chins. "My point exactly. What are we supposed to do?"

She pointed to an aluminum rack atop her car. "I've got that. It's for surfboards, but—"

I was unable to hide my horror. "Good God, how long have you been surfing?"

"Not me," she chuckled. "My boyfriend."

"Good God, how long have you had a boyfriend?"

"Since June."

"Something tells me he's pimply, shy, and keenly intelligent. When he isn't surfing, he's hunched like a vulture over a chessboard or a computer screen."

"How did you know?"

"I'm a novelist—it's my job to know everything."

In less than five minutes, we had managed, with the help of a strapping Red Cap, to hoist the trunk onto the roof rack, where it landed with an audible crunch. I tipped the man a full two dollars. Sissy and I squeezed in, and we were off. The

Korean motor, as powerful as a sewing machine's, struggled to gain speed.

"Ever been to L.A.?" she asked, with the same dopey smile with which she had greeted me. I wondered if there was a correlation between morbid obesity and the need to make others believe that one is not miserable. It was worth looking into.

"Never," I replied.

"How do you like it so far?"

"Quaint train station."

"I think it's an awesome city. But I'm not objective. I was born here. I'm a Venice girl."

I tried to picture her in a gondola, but it would have taken a second Melville. She turned the wheel, and we glided onto Highway 10—my first Los Angeles freeway. I would like to report that the drive was fascinating, even from an anthropological standpoint, but it was sheer torture. My head was bowed beneath the caved-in roof, and I couldn't see past my duffel, which filled my lap. All I had were two narrow side views— one of the road's shoulder and the other of Sissy's sideburned profile. Even worse, the cabin was heating up with her smell— a blend of dime-store perfume, smoker's breath, and musky armpits. Then it struck me. The odor wasn't hers; it was mine. Mortified, I extended a finger and lowered the automatic window. Blinded by a dry blast of pollen, I sneezed again, banging my head on a wine bottle.

"Please . . . put on . . . the air conditioning."

"It *is* on," she chirped, as though this were good news.

The nearest vent was, indeed, blowing cold air, but directly into my kneecap. How wonderful for my kneecap. Before I could ask her to redirect it, I heard a tinkling lullaby. I looked everywhere, until I realized that it was coming from beneath me. I wormed three fingers into a dank crevice and pulled out Sissy's cellular telephone.

"It's for you," I said. "A collect call from my perineum."

She clicked on the speaker-phone and commenced loud chit-chat with her boyfriend, Ben Fuchs, who told her all about his morning's computer work on something called, if memory serves, a "transport interfacial prodigious cookie porthole." After they hung up, Sissy began to explain what it was, but I cut her off.

"I'm not even remotely interested, and if you cared about your health, you'd stay away from it. Cake and candy portholes, too, while you're at it."

It was cruel, yes, but my tailbone ached and my throat was dry as sand. Sissy settled into silence, which, as the Greeks knew, is the vestibule to the higher mysteries. She would profit from a little time there. Squinting out the window, I took in the sights—the shaggy foreskins of the palm trees, the grimy stucco of the apartment houses, the distant jumble of the crowded hillsides, and the solemn faces of a million solitary folks in slow-moving cars. So this was Los Angeles. The Big Facile. The City of Bottoms. Gomorrah West. Never for an instant did I suspect that I would one day make of it something timeless and beautiful.

I realized with a start that Sissy was speaking to me and that she had been for quite a while. She was praising my novel *Christopher*. Unlike most authors, I do not pretend to be uncomfortable with flattery, even at its most fulsome. Why should I, when it makes me feel so good? I was surprised to learn that it was Sissy who had first brought my novel to the attention of Mr. Shipp. She had spotted it by chance at work, in a studio recycling bin. A few hours later, while attending a lecture on the Kabbalah at a mansion in Beverly Hills, she had begun to flip through it. The speaker was saying that the mere fact that they were there was going to bring each and every one of them good luck, and even better luck if they signed up for a pricey twelve-week seminar. Sure enough, good luck did befall Sissy, because she grew so bored with the sales pitch that she read the first third of my book while still in her seat. The rest she vanquished that night in bed, while Ben Fuchs sat up late playing, I suspect, Dung-Eater III or some such other computer nonsense.

"It made me laugh and cry at the same time," she said. "I called my Uncle Harry and I was, like, 'You *gotta* buy this book. It's awesome!'"

I could not have been more astonished. "Mr. Shipp is your uncle?"

"Uh-huh."

"Yet you work as his driver?"

"I don't work for him," she laughed. "I volunteered to do it. I work at the studio. In the payroll department."

"But you called him your boss."

"No, I didn't, *you* did."

She was right.

Now that I knew who Sissy was, I regretted my earlier cruelty.

With two free fingers, I tickled her spongy arm. "So, you marvelous big thing, you gave your uncle my book, he read it, and then what?"

"Actually, he hasn't read it yet. He never reads. He can't. He gave it to Klevin Davies, his Director of Development."

"Do you mean to tell me that the stereotype is true? Your uncle is actually illiterate?"

She sputtered a laugh and assured me that he was perfectly *able* to read, but that he didn't have time. "Any producer who has time to read isn't very busy, which means he isn't very successful. That's why he hired Klevin. Klevin's a total genius. Klevin went to Harvard."

"And he likes the book as much as you do?"

"Klevin's a girl. She's only my age, twenty-six, but she's off-the-charts smart, and, yeah, she totally loves your book. If she didn't, no way would Uncle Harry want to acquire it."

She wrenched the wheel and pulled into the parking lot of the Palms Plaza. My face came apart at the seams.

"Why, it's nothing but a motel."

"What did you expect?"

"A proper hotel!"

"But it's called the Palms Plaza *Motel.*"

"No one called it that to *me.*"

"Well, don't worry, it's nice. Ben and me stayed here after a wrap party once when we were too drunk to drive home."

As Sissy's car crunched along the gravel, the wind blew harder, foliage swayed, and a plastic garbage can rolled past. She explained that the Palms Plaza got its name from the area, which was called "Palms." (Later, I learned that Palms is known neither for its beauty nor its low incidence of armed robbery, but rather for the diversity of its inhabitants, who hail from every corner of the globe between the Rio Grande and the Panama Canal.) As we pulled into a parking spot, a neon sign crackled dangerously overhead. I asked wryly if it doubled as an executioner of mosquitoes.

"L.A. doesn't have mosquitos,[3]" Sissy bragged.

No sooner had I ripped myself free of the clown car than two tip-hungry Mexican boys darted out. They set aside my carry-ons and lunged for my steamer trunk. As these boys were junior welterweights at best, I begged them to stop.

---

3 Killed off, no doubt, in the 1920s, by leaded smog and the blood of Joseph P. Kennedy.

When they ignored me, I fell back on my middle-school Spanish.

"*Il est trop molto grande!*" I warned. "*Tu es mucho petito!*"

Again, they ignored me. I could almost hear the herniation of their tiny vertebrae as they rolled the enormous vessel into their tiny, smooth arms.

After a quick check-in, Sissy led me to my quarters. Her pachyderm thighs, crammed into brand-new khakis, scraped as she walked, and her hooves powdered the defenseless gravel. She opened an iron gate. A bell tinkled. We walked carefully around a swimming pool and stopped at a pink door marked 6. At second glance, I realized that it was actually a 9 that had lost a nail.

What greeted me inside was not the suite I had expected, but a mere room, of the sort you might find in a Polynesian ghetto: bamboo chair, rattan couch, wicker blinds, jungle-print bedspread, paint-by-numbers Gauguin, and a rubber plant made of plastic.

"No slow-moving ceiling fan?" I snipped. But then I looked up and saw that, indeed, there was one. It wobbled as it turned. I was enraged, but far too exhausted to chuck a fit. Besides, none of it was Sissy's fault. I took it out on the bellboys instead. The way they stared you would have thought they had never seen a quarter.

"I'm real sorry you don't like your room, Mr. Troop," Sissy said. "But most producers wouldn't have paid for anything without a deal in place."

"I suppose so," I sighed with a hint of martyrdom. "You run along now, dear. What time will you be fetching me for dinner?"

"God, I wish. Tonight's my book club. We're discussing *The Bed of Crimson Joy.*"

"What on earth is that?"

"The new Traci Stevens. It's the fourth book in the Blithe-dale series. You should read it. It's awesome."

I flared indignantly. "You used the same word about *my* book!"

"What can I say? They're both awesome."

That nitwit grin again.

I peeked into the dingy bathroom. "Does that mean your Uncle Harry's actually going to drive me to dinner himself?"

"No, he's in Palm Springs. You're not having dinner to-gether. You're having lunch with him tomorrow at one o'clock. Here's the address."

She handed me a slip of paper.

"Won't you be driving me?"

"I'd love to, but I have to take my dog to the vet. He has worms in his poo."

She misunderstood my grimace.

"It's no big deal, Mr. Troop. Take a cab. Harry'll reimburse you." Although she was just two yards away, she began to wave. "Bye! Gotta get back to work now! Have fun! Bye!" On im-pulse, she lunged at my face. Startled, I knocked over a parrot lamp. She branded my cheek with a loud, wet kiss, then wad-dled out the door.

"Miserable pinch-penny," I grumbled to myself as I un-packed my trunk. If Mr. Shipp was too stingy to book me a decent room, how was he going to finance an entire motion picture? I limped into the shower stall and, under a tepid driz-zle, scrubbed myself free of three days of grime. The soap stung my raw palms. I emerged, popped a powerful allergy pill, and slipped naked between coarse polyester sheets. I asked the front desk to hold my calls. Too tired to fish around for a Los Angeles book, I grabbed a volume just inches from my nose. I read all about Yahweh and how busy he was those first few days. No sooner had he given Man dominion over the birds of the air than I fell into a sound slumber.

Katydid

When I awoke in the dark motel room, calling out the name of my favorite lodger, my voice must have sounded particularly shrill, because outside my door a man shouted "You okay, lady?"

"No!" I roared back.

The do-gooder ran away.

I switched on my bedside lamp and grabbed the telephone. I have found that the best way to dispel the fright of a nightmare is to call its star. Unfortunately, the poet Adrian was busy writing—he was in mid-sonnet, in fact—so our chat had to be brief. Still, it was a comfort to hear his voice, and he was much relieved that I had made it to Tinsel Town in one piece. He made me promise to call him the moment I had signed my contract. He said he would never forgive me if he read about it first in the *Arts & Leisure* section. This was mere applesauce—he rarely read the *Times*—but I agreed nevertheless. If his goal was to make an old man feel loved, he had succeeded.

After we hung up, I slipped on a dressing gown and poured myself a tumbler of fragrant Napa Valley Cabernet Sauvignon (spritz of diesel tour bus; whiff of retired investment banker).

I lighted a cigarette and lifted the wicker blind. What a sight! The winds were even stronger now. Scraps of litter and leaves cycloned past. The water of the swimming pool bobbed frantically and a giant palm frond drifted by like a dugout canoe. I noticed a strand of red and green Christmas lights swinging from an iron fence. Already? It was only mid-November! In the name of the almighty dollar, the holidays were threatening to devour the entire year. Soon, the last angel would be taken down in June and the first one put up two days later.

Abruptly, a scrawny, little girl swam past, performing a meticulous breaststroke. Her mangy mom sat on a deck chair at the far end of the pool, wrapped in a blanket, fumigating her brain and flipping through a wet copy of *Variety*. Oh, dear, a stage mother. With a mullet haircut. What could be worse? When she saw me staring, she flashed a chaos of jagged teeth. I knew I was supposed to smile back, but I was not in the market for a friend. I dropped the blind.

An hour later, desperately lonely but reluctant to dine alone, I remembered something. Three years earlier, a pretty young actress from Nebraska by the name of Willow Anne Stetz, had rented one of my basement rooms. One morning after I had gently rebuked her for being loud, vulgar, and three months behind on her rent, she lashed out at me, vowing to move to Hollywood, win an Oscar, and tell me, during her acceptance speech, to go fuck myself. True to her word, she moved out the very next morning. I never heard from her again. Was it was possible that she had followed through on her threat? Might she be a Los Angeleno now?

I called directory assistance and, sure enough, there was a W. Stetz living in Hollywood. A woman picked up on the third ring, and I immediately recognized Willow's loud voice. She was unfriendly, of course, but when I told her that I was

in town to sign a movie deal, she turned collegial and told me
how "awesome"[4] her acting career was going. I said I was glad
to hear it. And I was. In the arts, we lose so many of our most
talented young people to the twin scourges of madness and
substance abuse, and Willow was, indeed, talented. I knew
because I had seen her in a production of *Great Catherine*, an
obscure one-act written by that chatty old hen, Ms. George
Bernard Shaw. Willow's rendering of the eccentric empress
was more than a little convincing—a remarkable feat when
you consider that she was only twenty-one at the time and
had never ridden a horse.

A half-hour later I was standing at the gate near the parking lot, all duded up, puffing a cigarette, waiting for Willow to
whisk me to dinner. The wind tossed allergenic spores in my
face and threatened to steal my hat, but it could not spoil my
self-satisfaction. I had secured a dinner date on my very first
night in a new city. That made me rather a man of the world,
didn't it? A sharp whistle turned my head. The stage mother,
still serving as bored sentry to her daughter, was trying to get
my attention. I pretended not to see her.

Finally, she twanged: "Hey, ole man! How 'bout a smoke?"

I forced a smile and pantomimed that I was plumb out. As
I was holding a full pack in my hand, she had every reason to
doubt me. Insulted, she stripped off her blanket, revealing a
bony, tattooed torso in a stars-and-stripes bikini. She was on
her way over to confront me when I was saved by the arrival
of a big, black luxury car. It was not Willow behind the wheel,
but I pretended that it was. When I reached her open window,
I realized with a start that it was, indeed, Willow, but that her

---

4 When one of these young people is lucky enough to behold the Taj Mahal or
the Grand Canyon, what adjective will they use?

appearance had changed dramatically. Her lips were so plump that she looked freshly punched; her skin, once as clear as the summer sky over her native Omaha, was brown as toast now; her brown hair was dyed an unnatural shade of red; her nose boasted a new trajectory, and her breasts, once non-existent, were enormous, with nipples the size of escargot. My heart sank even farther when, climbing in, I saw that her sturdy farm-girl frame had wasted away to almost nothing.

"Dear God, don't tell me you have cancer."

"What do you mean?"

"Your legs are like arms, and your arms are like breadsticks."

"I spin," she explained, with a proud smile.

I still don't know what this meant.

I kissed her sunken brown cheek and handed her a copy of *Christopher*.

"For you," I said. "Soon to be a major motion picture."

"I can't wait!" She set it in the back seat, atop a pile of take-out food containers, dirty clothes, empty water bottles, and black-and-white photographs of her own face.

Driving to the restaurant, I was disappointed to discover that the only similarity between the old Willow and the new was her voice, which was just as offensive as ever. Why couldn't she have changed *that* while she was busy mucking with everything else? Willow explained that to make it in Hollywood, talent wasn't enough. An actress also had to be "super hot, go to the right parties, and drive the right car." I knew this was baloney—no one could convince me that Alexis Smith or Barbara Bel Geddes had gone to such lengths—but I pretended to believe her, all the while asking myself what defect of character could possibly have compelled this pretty Midwestern tomboy to transform herself, in so short a time, into such an awful, scary slut? I knew that if I wanted to understand

Hollywood I would have to understand Willow. Did I have the stomach for it?

The restaurant she chose was called Katydid, named after an appealing variety of locust. It was cozy and dark, with an exotic, vine-draped patio where, from the looks of things, smoking was mandatory. Willow and I flashed our packs and were led outside. I ordered a bowl of Moroccan gumbo, a double prosciutto and melon, braised lamb shank with garlic mashed, and a side of curried peas. Willow special-ordered a half-head of iceberg lettuce doused with lemon juice. In the meantime, we both acquired a hearty glow with big mint juleps.

It turned out that Willow was not doing quite as well as her automobile suggested. Her only acting work to date (under the *nom de cinema* "Willow Stetson") had been supporting roles in three C-movies. She didn't tell me they were C, of course. I inferred it from the characters she played: physicist, Chinese spy, and night nurse. As for her car, it was a gift from her current beau, an old man named Harry who owned an office supply distributorship in a place called Canooga Park. The man was generous to a fault and, thanks to a radioactive seed planted in his prostate gland, not particularly demanding between the sheets. Mostly, he liked to watch her touch herself, something she claimed she had been doing almost every day, anyway, since the age of four. Compulsive sexual behavior like this is not uncommon among those of us who were diddled as children.

Curiously, as Willow prattled about her acting career, she continually squeezed my hands and licked her fat, glossy lips. Was she *flirting* with me? It was a preposterous notion, but if she wasn't, then why were my hips tingling? Although I rarely spoke about my sex life to my lodgers, I assumed that my preference was fairly obvious. On the other hand, one must never underestimate the obtuseness of a starlet. Most wouldn't notice a fire in their underpants unless the smoke made their asses look fat. I ignored her caresses as best I could and wolfed down my chow. It was my first stationary sustenance since leaving Chicago, and I tasted every bite.

As our first juleps gave way to our second and third, my joints loosened and my heart swelled. Not only did Los Angeles look like a pretty swell place to me all of a sudden, but I even forgave Mr. Shipp his parsimony. Soon we would have a deal, and the minute the check cleared, I would rent a modest hillside home. My life would never be the same. While waiting for my coconut cake to arrive and for Willow to return from the little girl's room, I actually experienced a surge of joy from head to toe. Why not? The food was superb, my companion chatty, and my future bright.

"Yes," I thought, a la Papa Hemingway, "this is good."

A moment later, I was introduced to an essential truth about life in Hollywood: No sooner does one begin to vibrate with happiness than one pays for it with a cruel, corresponding misery. I was brought harshly back to earth when the reason for Willow's coquettishness suddenly became clear to me. After returning from the john, she fell in close to me, squeezed my biceps, and said, "So tell me about your movie! Which part do I get to play?"

How could I have been so blind? This was no dinner between old friends; this was an audition! She had always disliked me. Why would she stop now unless there was something in it for her? I was paralyzed with resentment. I despise opportunism in all its forms. What was I to do? Rise from my chair, denounce her, and find my own way back to the motel? Or force down my bile, offer her a role, and dig into my dessert? I remembered Lao Tso's Third Way. That was it. I would become an empty boat. Mirror the mirror. I would play push-hands with the shrew.

"Well, it's not a movie *yet,*" I said, coyly batting my eyes. "I'm merely in negotiations with a producer whose name I'm forbidden to divulge."

"Pleassse," she whined.

"Soon, my child, soon," I thrummed. "All you need to know is that his resume is as thick as the Yellow Pages. He has more Oscars than teeth and, let me assure you, he has plenty of teeth. His niece, a sweet-as-pie fatso by the name of—" I went blank. I had completely forgotten Sissy's name. "Anyway, she adores my book and so does his development person, a Radcliff gal by the name of Kevin something. They both think it's box-office dynamite. A blockbuster, if there ever was one. I must say, I agree."

"It sounds *awesome.*"

"Oh, it is. Totally." I lifted my empty glass, soggy with mint leaves, and nodded at the waiter for another.

"What's the biggest part? For a girl, I mean." Willow leaned in so close that I noticed red plastic braces behind her bottom teeth and a dusting of glitter stuck to her blue eyelid. Her breath smelled of fresh throw-up.

"Oh, there are quite a few female roles," I replied. "But I would say the ideal role for you would be that of Divina."

"I love that name! Is she white?"

"As a cracker."

"What's she like?"

"A young hooker."

This excited her tremendously. "But she hates it, right?"

"Hates what?"

"Hookering."

"Of course. She has a heart of gold."

"I bet she just does it because she needs the money because, like, her mother's really senile or something and has to be put in a home, or she has a little boy who needs an operation."

"Both. You understand her. But there *is* a catch." I leaned in so close that our noses almost touched. "The role requires full-frontal nudity."

"Really?"

"Mmm, yes."

She nibbled her lip. "Wow. Okay. I mean, as long as it's not, you know, like—"

"Gratuitous?"

"Yeah."

"Oh, no."

"Yay!"

She accepted the role on the spot without even reading the script. Good thing, too. Not only *was* there no script, but there was also no character named Divina. But it hardly mattered. Now that I knew what Willow was made of, I wouldn't have given her a role even if she were the last slutty ingénue on earth.

Dessert progressed swimmingly. Now that Willow had landed a role, she no longer felt compelled to pretend that she had interest in anything other than herself. She regaled me with more than I could ever want to know about her voice teacher, her psychic, her trainer, her masseuse, her spinning teacher, and her last six boyfriends. Not once did she ask me a question about myself. When the check arrived, I made a move for my wallet, ready to stand my corner, but she snapped down a credit card. This was not the Willow I knew, but then I saw that the name on the card was not hers. When I saw whose it was, I nearly fainted.

"Is that your boyfriend's card?" I gasped.

She flashed a smile of connivance. "It was till he gave it to me."

It was a coincidence of both Dickensian improbability and Kafkan portent.

The name on the card was Harold W. Shipp!

If this was *my* Harold Shipp, it meant that my producer was not a producer at all, but a ridiculous old man with a faulty prostate selling legal pads and pencils to support a self-serving slut. It also meant that Willow Anne Stetz was a shoo-in for any part she wanted. Why hadn't I researched Mr. Shipp before boarding the train? I felt like a fool, and a fool at my age was a fool indeed. Willow noticed my frown and asked what was wrong.

"Does your boyfriend produce movies and, if so, does he have a gargantuan niece named Christy Winkler?"

"What?" she laughed. "No, Harry hates movies. He says he can't hear what anyone's saying 'cause the black people won't shut up. And his only family's a daughter in Scottsdale he cut off 'cause she's a druggie. He calls her the Crystal Methodist."

She barked another laugh.

I breathed a sigh of relief.

Los Angeles was not Dickens, after all, nor was it Kafka. Coincidences occurred here, yes, of course, but they neither advanced the story nor lent it meaning.

Driving me back to my motel, Willow told me the sad tale of Esmerelda, her favorite bikini-waxer from Colombia, whose recent death from mad cow disease had left an empty chair at the Thanksgiving dinner that she and her Harry were hosting. If I wasn't too busy with my movie, I should come. I told her I'd think about it.

Lunching with Lucifer

For as long as I could remember, I had thrilled at the prospect of being tempted by Lucifer, of being offered cold, hard cash in exchange for my eternal soul. "Buddy, you've got yourself a deal!" I would cry as I shook his scaly hand. And, yet, now that the moment was upon me, I was scared to death, and I knew why: there's nobility in poverty, and in nobility safety. I was about to dismount the high horse of my poverty and enter the dirty, dangerous marketplace. My wares were not wheat or eggs or olives, but a single book. What if Shipp's offer was insultingly low and he refused to budge? What would I do? Swallow my pride and make a deal, or slink home empty-handed like so many New Yorkers before me, with nothing to show for my trip but a mad-eyed recital of everything wrong with Hollywood? My fear, then, was not that Mr. Shipp's offer would be stingy, but that it would be stingy and I would be stupid enough to refuse it.

Even as a boy, it upset me terribly when a hard-up character in a movie is offered much-needed cash to betray the person or thing he cherishes most, and, in a fit of high dudgeon, he rips up the check and storms out of the room. How many times had I seen this scene? I vowed that when I grew up, I would be different. No matter how sweet the melody of my idealism, I would never let it distract me from the clang of the dinner bell. When Satan held out his bribe, I would snatch it, deposit it in the bank, wait ten business days for it to clear, and only then would I denounce him. In other words, even as a lad I knew that self-righteousness is a luxury of the financially secure.

Waiting at the iron fence for my taxi to arrive, I saw the little girl again, but she was no longer swimming. She stood on the cement patio, shivering under a sopping-wet towel, gawping at me. I couldn't say that I blamed her. I was sharped up in a sky-blue zibeline blazer, yellow linen trousers, a white short-sleeve shirt, a burgundy silk scarf, and, as a sort of visual anchor, a simple black tie. It struck just the right balance. It told Mr. Shipp that I was an artist, yes, but not so eccentric that I would embarrass him at the press junket.

The urchin shuffled closer, teeth chattering. I could see blue veins in her white neck. Her mouth was caked with chocolate. Or was it dried blood? Her calves bore black-and-blue marks the size of quarters. Her knobby knees showed the first signs of rickets. A real Appalachian, this one. No wonder she stared at me—I was probably the first adult male she had ever seen who wasn't trying to lure her up the steps of his trailer with a piece of beef jerky. I flashed a sweet smile. She stuck out her tongue at me. I did not find this adorable in the least. I flicked my cigarette, and, to avoid it, she skipped and almost fell into the pool. I heard a gravel-crunch, turned around, and there was my taxi. It bore a patriotic bumper sticker. The driver, believe it or not, was a Caucasian male. My God, L.A. *was* provincial. Like the 1950s all over again.

Within minutes we were speeding either east or west along Venice Avenue—or was it Boulevard?[5]—a broad thoroughfare without a single memorable feature, and then the man turned the wheel a few times, and now we were speeding along Robinson Drive, which was just as unmemorable, but a bit narrower. Soon everything became prettier, and then, after a few more turns of the wheel, we were gliding into a district that looked very posh, indeed—like Park Avenue, without the fur coats and Jamaican nannies.

"What's this area called?" I asked.

"Beverly Hills," he replied.

"Ah, yes, I've heard of it."

I sat back, torched a fag, and studied the inhabitants. The young men, dressed in dark suits, held cellular telephones to their ears and laughed as they walked, exuding more confidence than smarts. The older men wore short-sleeve shirts, linen trousers, and no socks. Their wrists and hands were heavy with diamonds and eighteen-karat gold. As for the young women, the homely ones looked like career secretaries and the pretty ones like Midwestern catalogue models. Both had dreadful taste—white high heels, garish blouses, and too-short skirts. The mature women were hidden in scarves and sunglasses and walked very quickly, as though they were fleeing a herd of pesky reporters, when, in fact, the only thing chasing them was Father Time, and he was gaining. The only locals who lived up to the area's reputation for glamour were the dogs. From their rhinestone collars to their sporty plaid vests, they were indeed impressive.

The hackie yanked the wheel this way and that and this way again (all the while grumbling about my smoking and pretending to have asthma), and suddenly we were outside a ritzy restaurant whose name I forget. The parking lot was lined with

5 I am no geographer and did not take notes.

expensive cars, all of them black, white, or silver, except for the
sole Rolls Royce, which was hunter green. Was it Mr. Shipp's?
I hoped not; no one splits a check down the middle faster than
the fabulously rich. As I emerged from the taxi, I checked my
watch. I was a half-hour late. Excellent. Mr. Shipp would know
who was boss.

I opened the door, but before stepping inside, I paused
to savor the moment. My first power lunch. I was beginning a
whole new life. At long last, B.K. Troop was in the game.

"Well done, old feller," I whispered to myself.

And then I plunged in. The tiny old man I knocked over
was surprisingly agile and almost funny about my rude mistake. I wondered if he had had some experience in this arena.
Might he have been a Keystone Kop? Before I could ask him,
his caretaker snatched up his fallen walker and led him away. I
spun around and resumed the fairy tale, taking in every detail.
It was like a cafe in the French Riviera: green-and-white striped
banquettes, chintz curtains, big potted plants, numerous sky-
lights, and sitting at every table a variety of glamorous old people. The women's delicate shoulders were draped in the most
glorious silks, and their tiny necks and wrists were strung with
diamonds, pearls, and platinum. The men were not thin—in
fact, most of them were pot-bellied and bull-necked—but they
were just as superbly attired as the women, with their double-
breasted navy blazers, white hankies, and spotted ties. This was
the inner sanctum of Old Hollywood. These were the ruling
elite whose liver-spotted hands pulled the strings that made
the movie stars dance, and these fluty voiced women were
their wives. (Their mistresses were at home sleeping off last
night's tussle.) This was *true* power, born of unlimited access
to Wall Street capital and Capitol Hill clout. I doffed my beret,
and stepped to the maitre d'. He was a suave, little mummy who

looked as though he might once have given dance lessons to Fred Astaire.

I breathed into his hearing aid: "Mr. Shipp, please. He's expecting me."

He grinned as though we were old friends and had shared many filthy secrets. As he whisked me through the room, a hundred eyes devoured me. I was like a young zebra parading his juicy flanks past a den of hungry, old lions. Never in all my life had I felt so desired, so in the thick of things. The maitre d' stopped in front of a banquette where a handsome gent with a deep tan and coal-black hair sat talking on a cellular telephone. He wore a brown velour leisure suit and a paisley ascot. Despite the tightness of his facial skin and blackness of his hair, he couldn't have been a day younger than I was. In a flash I wondered if I, too, like Willow and Mr. Shipp, would one day succumb to the knife. I pictured my face without its flaps and folds. I would not be me. Perhaps that was not such a bad thing.

When I plopped down in the booth, Satan covered the phone and greeted me. His handshake was boneless. His jewelry rattled. I noticed that his shoulders bore twin sprinklings of dandruff. As one who had suffered from the same curse for most of my life, I made a mental note that, when the deal closed, I would send him not the usual scone hamper or brie wheel, but a six-pack of tar shampoo.

"Hey, kid, you want the truth?" he growled into the phone, with an accent that fairly shrieked of a borough that was not Manhattan. "You don't buy this picture, someone else will. And when they open the envelope and your name's not on it, don't come cryin' to me, 'cause there's no way—"

A telephone rang. Not *a* telephone, but *the* telephone. The one he was holding. For a moment, he looked surprised, then he panicked and shook it.

"God damn piece of shit! Fuckin' Japs! We save their asses in 1945 and this is how they repay us?"

I was tempted to remind him that it was Western Europe we saved, not Japan. The Japanese we radiated. And even if we had saved Japan, his ire was misplaced. I was fairly certain that his telephone had been manufactured in Finland. Shaking his head with disgust, Mr. Shipp dropped the contraption in his pocket.

"What'll it be, Troop? Tell Ricardo."

A swarthy waiter stood by—the spitting image of a young Caesar Romero, but darker and better looking. Another mental note: after the deal closed, I would return with a lavish tip.

"A Fitzwilly, please," I said. "With a slice of banana."

Despite his tropical skin tone, Ricardo managed a blush. "I'm sorry, sir, I'm not familiar with that particular drink, but if you tell me how to make it, I'd be happy—"

"A gin gimlet will be fine," I sighed, lamenting his lack of worldliness.

In fact, there is no such thing as a Fitzwilly. I just wanted Mr. Shipp to feel that he was my social inferior. Before the ruse could take hold, however, he was pointing a crooked finger at me and barking himself red.

"Don't you ever be late for a meetin' with me again! You got that, Troop? Who do you think you are? You think I got nothin' better to do than sit around here for half an hour with my thumb up my ass?"

His rage was so ferocious and abrupt, and the spit forming at the corners of his mouth so foamy white, that I thought he would strike me. I shrank away and stammered an apology, but he swatted the air.

"Forget it. I said my piece." And, just as fast, the fury was gone. Had it been sincere or had he trumped it up to gain advantage? Had the negotiation already begun? If so, I was in way over my head.

"I'll order for you," he murmured. "They got a helluva chopped salad."

He ordered us both chopped salads and an order of garlic French fries to split, and then he got down to business:

"Here's the story, Troop. My girlfriend digs your book. So does my niece."

"And Kevin, too." I sang cutely, lifting a finger. "Don't forget Kevin!"

He grimaced. "You mean *Klevin*. My girlfriend."

"I thought she worked for you."

"She does. Harvard grad. An incredible piece of ass." He chuckled grimly. "For a white girl."

I was doubly offended. First, by the thought of him in bed with a young girl, and, second, by his crude remark. What was I meant to do with it? Join him in his praise of black derrières? Never. It doesn't take much to incite a bigot to throw on his white hood. If Mr. Shipp proved to be a racist with whom I could not in good conscience do business, I preferred to find out *after* his check had cleared. Ignoring his remark, I opened the wine list. My eyes bugged at the prices. I had come a long way from the Parnassus diner where the most expensive carafe was twelve dollars.

I heard a rustle. Mr. Shipp pulled from his leather valise a document with Klevin's name typed across the top. I angled my eye and saw that it was a two-page plot summary of *Christopher*. I read along with Mr. Shipp. In the first paragraph, I spotted a nasty typo; in the second, a war between a subject and its verb; in the third, "burlesque" was spelled with a "k." Harvard, like every other college in America, was graduating nincompoops.

As Mr. Shipp read, eyes fierce, he muttered, "We're gonna make movie magic together."

"I certainly hope so."

"You're gonna write me a winner, I can feel it. But you gotta promise me one thing."

"Anything, H.S."

He set aside the notes. "No *fagela* stuff."

Like the shying of a dozen clams, every valve in my body eased shut. "I . . . I beg your pardon?"

"The guy who tells the story—what's his name?"

"The narrator?"

"Yeah."

"B.K. Troop."

"That's your name."

"I know."

"I want you to keep him just the way he is, but make him female, okay? Call her whatever you want. How 'bout Betty? Always liked the name Betty. She's forty-seven years old, but still hot as hell. Great bod. Never had kids. Into yoga. After a messy divorce, she moves in next door to Chris and falls hard, even though he's young enough to be her son. The rest stays the same. Except she seduces him. Just once. The night before the kid moves out forever. Next morning, she pretends she's okay, but her heart's broken. The ladies'll love it. There'll be snot runnin' down the aisles."

My drink arrived. I gulped at it so lustily that I splashed my shirt.

"You're upset," he noted. "How come?"

I knew that if I told him even a particle of the truth, I would lose my composure and, a few minutes later, find myself walking back to the motel with my ideals intact and my pockets empty.

"I . . . I simply don't understand why you would want to make me into a woman."

He startled me with his volume. "'Cause I want the picture to open on three thousand screens, not in one god damn art house in Pasadena!"

"Please don't spit on me."

He wiped a velour sleeve across his lipless mouth. "Look, you wrote a love story. Love is love, right? Doesn't matter if it's between a guy and a girl, a guy and another guy, or a guy and his god damn chihuahua. Am I right?"

"A fine argument for keeping my character male."

"Except this country's fulla people who don't agree, who think love between two guys is wrong![6] It turns their stomach. You add to the mix that one of the guys is old and fat, and they're gonna wanna burn down the theatre. This can't be news to you, Troop. Where you been living? In a shoebox?"

Unable to control myself, I rose indignantly from the booth, my back ramrod straight. "Mr. Shipp, I wrote this book from the heart, about one of the most important attachments of my life, and while I need money as much as the next fellow, I simply cannot, *will* not, compromise my integrity in exchange for a few—" From deep inside me a wave of pragmatism crested and broke. I lowered my voice. "How much *are* you offering me?"

"Depends on the buyer."

I blinked three times slowly. "But *you're* the buyer."

"The studio is."

---

6 This argument took place even after a certain Hollywood film had proved that a fortune could be made selling a love story between men, as long as those men were cowboys, profoundly unhappy, and did not kiss each other with tongues. As most of the story took place post-Stonewall, I could not fathom why the two did not simply run away to Key West and open a saddle shop.

He saw my confusion.

"This is how it works, Troop." He patted the vinyl like a patient tutor. I plopped back down. "I send your book to the studios, right?"

"Right."

"I tell 'em not to worry, we're gonna cut the homo shit. If a studio likes your book and is okay with you writing the script, they make an offer, and we can take it or leave it. If two or more studios want it, then we got a bidding war. That's how you get rich."

It took only a moment for me to arrive at the most obvious question. "Why do I need you then?"

"Excuse me?"

"I spent months and months writing the book. What have *you* invested? You haven't even read it, for heaven's sake."

"You lost me."

"Why couldn't I bring the book to the studios myself?"

Now that he understood, he began to spit again. "Who the fuck're you? I got fifty-seven years of relationships in this town, you ungrateful son of a bitch!"

Remaining calm, I asked a question that I should have asked during our first, fateful phone call.

"Mr. Shipp, just what movies *have* you produced?"

He smiled strangely. It was the first time I had seen his teeth. They were discolored, as though he had recently gargled with sepia ink.

"What, you want me to read you my résumé? How much time you got?"

"Days."

I don't remember the exact moment that I knew Mr. Shipp was a fraud. Maybe at the first glimpse of his teeth, or maybe it was an instant later when I was throttled by his cheap cologne, or maybe it was the way his hands trembled as he recited his professional credits, but even if I had missed these clues, I knew enough about American movies to know that none of Mr. Shipp's films—a few of which were pretty good—had been released in the past twenty-five years. Suddenly, across from me sat a broken-down old man, blown out on cocaine or alcohol or hired sex or all three, trying to ride my novel to a comeback. For the first time, I noticed his battered briefcase, the scratched crystal of his watch, and how the monogram on his frayed shirt pocket did not match his own initials. And why had he pushed the chopped salad? Because it was tasty or because it was the cheapest thing on the menu? I glanced around and more shingles fell from my eyes. This was no cloister of the high and mighty. It was a house of horrors. With their bobbed noses, stiff hair, shiny skin, crooked mouths, unblinking eyes, and marble-smooth foreheads, these ghouls were relics of the Selznick era.

"Before we take this negotiation any further," I said, my voice quavering, "why don't we settle up?"

I pulled from my pocket an invoice, a tally of all my travel expenses thus far. I found my taxi receipt and added it to the stack.

"What's wrong with you?" Mr. Shipp cried. "Don't bother me with this bullshit! The studio'll cover it!"

I stared him down. His drawn, haunted look told me that he was as poor as I was and that I would never be reimbursed for my expenses. There would never be a deal for my book, because even if the studio loved the story, they would never make a movie with this pitiful vulture.

I flung down my napkin and stood.

"Liar!" I shrieked. *"Thief! Vampire!"* Every head turned, but I did not care. "You lured me across the country for nothing!

You call yourself a film producer? You're incapable of producing anything but a foul odor and the contempt of genuine artists everywhere! I despise you, Mr. Shipp! Good day!"

I headed for the door, striding past a gallery of dull, rheumy stares, leaving Mr. Shipp not only with my words ringing in his ears, but with one of my most prized possessions lying at his side.

"Hey, crazy person!" he screamed. "Your scarf!"

I did not turn around and spoil my exit.

It was spoiled *for* me, however, when, unable to hail a taxi, I was forced to walk home. My humiliation grew even more acute when Mr. Shipp whizzed past me in a rattling old convertible, wearing my scarf and laughing into his cellular telephone.

Greenness Recovered

It is one thing to suffer a nervous breakdown in your youth, when even the most intense anguish is tinged with romance; then, even as you weep, crawling across the shag, you imagine yourself the hero of a novel, the unfolding epic that is your life, and sometimes you even crave, deep down, perversely, more pain (longing for the death of a grandparent or even of a close friend), so that your narrative will be rendered all the more tragic. It's an indulgence you can afford, because you know that other, much happier chapters lie ahead.

It is quite another thing to suffer a complete neural collapse when your cheek is loose, beard white, hair gone, chin triple, memory failing, wind short, and heart nearly kaput. Your life is coming to a close, and a story that began as a hopeful idyll has devolved into an intolerable bore with far too many endings and no surviving readers. Your pain is mere pain and its progress is unspeakable.

In the days following the fiasco with Mr. Shipp, during which I did not once leave my motel room, I mostly whimpered and sobbed. A blind veterinarian passing by would certainly have broken down the door and jammed a merciful needle in my neck. On night two, I cried out until I lost my voice. The next morning, I spent an hour on my hands and knees in the shower stall, hand-washing my sheets and bedspread. My mind returned again and again to the lament of Mr. Phineas Fletcher, an all-but-forgotten Elizabethan poet who wrote: *"Discouraged, scorned, his writings vilified/, Poorly—poor man—he lived; poorly—poor man—he died."* From this threnody, written as though for me, my brain turned to thoughts of suicide and murder, but mostly of murder, because I knew that were I to take the Way of the Red Bath, my lodger Adrian would be wrecked forever, whereas if I killed Mr. Shipp no one on earth would care. When his friend, family, and colleagues heard the news, they would break into spontaneous applause. So would Klevin. It was obvious to me that she only dated the old fake to fulfill some twisted need to be penetrated by her grandfather. It is common knowledge that when you act on dark urges like these you come to hate your unwitting accomplice as much as you do yourself. Within minutes of his death, Klevin would feel like a girl again.

All suffering must have a limit—not only Jesus Christ, but Don Quixote as well, figured this out after just three days in the cave—so, on the fourth morning, I willed myself to my feet and rolled back the rock, as it were. I stepped into the bright, clean sun, blinking like a freshly hatched lizard. The water in the swimming pool bobbed a merry blue. I would swim. Yes, that's what I would do. A second baptism to mark my second birth. But then I heard a splash and saw that the urchin was bobbing in the pool, clutching some sort of flotation device and gawping at me, this time so blatantly that I thought she would swallow water. A cool breeze blew, and I realized why she was staring. I looked down and confirmed that I had forgotten to dress. I spun around, fanned a hand across my bare bottom, and cantered inside. A minute later, I strode out in my Madras swimming trunks as though nothing had happened. I barreled into the pool with a splash. It must have startled her, because in an instant she was sitting on a deck chair, squeezing her knees to her chest, with a look on her face that I would describe as "astonished to be alive."

The water was glorious. I side-stroked the full length of the pool, letting the grime of my confinement slither away. It no doubt challenged the filter. After a few laps, I had reclaimed my smile, and, soon after, I began to contemplate my future with something better than dread.

It was time to return home, I decided. Although I was Manhattan's sternest critic, I missed her terribly: the bustle of the streets, the sharp aromas of the ethnic food and of those who cooked it, the ineffable charm of the approaching winter holidays. But most of all I missed my lodgers, those young barbarians at work and at play who made my life in the House Beautiful so meaningful. Thanksgiving was only a week off. If I left tomorrow, I would have time to surprise them with a turkey feast. I had nothing to be ashamed of. I was merely the latest in a long line of American novelists who had ventured to Hollywood in search of wool only to be shorn themselves. Feeling the full pride of my failure, I climbed the swimming pool's aluminum ladder. I would go inside and book my train ticket at once, then I would pop out and celebrate with a first-rate meal. I looked everywhere for a towel. The management did not supply them. I flitted toward my room, but then a hideous sight stopped me in my tracks. Next to a set of rusty dumbbells some young swell had installed a full-length mirror, and my reflection filled it.

Dear God! My tired, old face was saggy and sunburnt. My hair looked like a dab of wet cobweb. My freckled arms and legs were a stomach-churning combination of scrawny and flabby. My belly was third-trimester and my scrotum drooped like melted taffy down my leg. I heard a peep, like that of a newborn chick. I spun around and there was the tiny girl again. In her wide stare, I read pity and terror.

I will spare you the gory details of my second breakdown. Suffice it to say that my despair was floodgate. I felt like the oldest, ugliest man ever to breathe the exhaust of trees. So profound was my self-loathing that I did not bathe, brush my teeth, or budge my bowels. Never before had it seemed so rich to die. My imminent demise was as real to me as my own sour smell. I spent the morning of my birthday in bed, spooning the telephone, but unable to dial for food. Instead I guzzled wine, gnawed cigarettes, and begged the stucco ceiling to tell me how, how, how, after so many years on earth I had ended up all alone in a tropical-themed motel room on the far, drear edge of the charted world without a hope in sight.

This second trial lasted six days.

The end came during a moment of crepuscular calm, when, bathed in the pinkish, magical light slanting in from the edges of the rattan blind, The Itch was back. That's right, the incurable itch for scribbling that Juvenal wrote about. Suddenly I was thinking about what to write next. As I was a physical and emotional wreck, my ideas were hare-brained and prosaic[7], but that didn't matter. What mattered was that I was casting nets toward the future. I was rolling back the rock once more, ready to embrace life. My timing could not have been better, because tomorrow was Thanksgiving. I lifted the telephone and punched out the number of Willow Stetz

---

7   *Organ Recital* (erotica), *Almost Dead* (authorized autobiography), *Sodom by the Sea* (Hollywood tell-all), *Enough about You* (self-help), *Tipped Uterus* (feminist critique), *A Long History of the Literary Carte-de-Visite* (reference).

dash actress exclamation point. Why? you ask. Why did I call that horrible girl? Simple: the drowning man questions not the soundness of the branch.

"Hello?" she answered, with a hint of that titillated paranoia found in the voices of all beautiful women when they receive an unexpected late-night call.

"B.K. Troop here," I said, with crisp confidence. The last thing she needed to know was that I had just spent a week on my belly.

"You sound like shit," she replied.

Too exhausted to keep up the act, I told her all about my lunch with Mr. Shipp. I concluded colorfully: "And then I walked home. That's right, dear, you heard me. *Walked! Miles!* Past hideous apartment complexes and strip malls. The sun roasted my dome. My feet throbbed. I larded the lean earth as I trudged. A thousand cars, each containing a single unhappy person, roared past me. I had never been so degraded in all my life, and that's saying a lot. I only just now found the will to call you. It's been over a week since I've eaten a proper meal. I'm desperately in need of tender loving care."

The silence that followed would have made Helen Keller squirm. Silly me, I had thought Willow might at least pretend to be concerned. It was, after all, her art to pretend. But now that I had no movie in the offing, her dislike of me had returned, and she could not muster a single civil word.

"So what do you want?" she finally asked.

"I . . . I was just wondering if your offer was still good. You know, Thanksgiving at your boyfriend's house." Willow said nothing for five long seconds. As far as I could tell, she was not even breathing.

"I understand perfectly," I whispered.

I hung up and called Amtrak.

As depressing as it would be to spend the holiday alone in Los Angeles, I knew it would be even lonelier to spend it on a train, so I booked myself on the Southwest Chief for the day after the holiday.

Late the next morning, freshly showered and shaved, I emerged into the pool area. I knew exactly how to begin my Thanksgiving. I strode bravely to the mirror. The old man standing there was no Apollo, but neither was he the running eyesore of the previous week. (Nothing sheds pounds like a wine-and-mucus diet.) His best features were his height, his bearing, and his eyes, which were wise and most kind. I tipped my hat to him and trotted off.

At a local Mexican restaurant, I broke my fast with a gigantic breakfast crepe filled with spicy, healthy, Hispanic things, and an ice-cold pitcher of Sangria (a silent vintage, but pious and eager to work). To amuse myself, I had brought along a volume of George Herbert. "Who would have thought my shriveled heart/Could have recovered greenness?" the great man wrote. This line had always inspired me, reminding me that one is never so close to death that one cannot make a new start, but now I found myself silently retorting, "I wish my *wallet* could recover a little greenness." This pointless trip had cost me an arm and a leg.

After lunch, I stopped at a convenience store to load up for the holiday night. I purchased several chocolate bars, a family bag of corn chips, some fizzy water, a cheap pair of sunglasses, three naughty magazines, a tube of water-based lube, eight wine coolers, a roll of antacid tablets, and a carton of name-brand cigarettes. Flip-flopping home, hugging my bag to my chest, my eye landed on a give-away newspaper, marked triple-X, lying open on the hood of a car. I broke into a Cheshire grin. Why had I not thought of this before? Inside I found a veritable buffet of aspiring actors willing to trade their bodies for cash. I had sworn off sporting boys years ago, but this was a special occasion. I needed something to be thankful for!

When I got back to the motel, I plopped down poolside with the publication. The sun violated my new sunglasses, so I grabbed a fuzzy yellow visor off a nearby deck chair, and, ignoring the *Hey, old man!* and *yoo-hoo!* and *Yo, that's my visor!* of the stage mom, I went to work. It was crucial that I choose wisely. (I have always had bad luck in this area; I act on impulse and more often than not end up with a Chatty Cathy or a Lazy Susan or, worst of all, a Fast Freddy.) I carefully studied each listing, comparing pecs and specs. I devised a sort of scoring system, giving extra points for the literacy of their copy and deducting points for cockiness of grin and Naziness of haircut.

Finally I chose a raspberry-nippled, cocoa-eyed, high-chested hombre named Miguel. From his million-peso smile it was obvious that he was given to moments of fierce cruelty mitigated by outbursts of sloppy passion. Already hot in the zipper, I lunged for the phone, accidentally dropping the newspaper. As I reached down for it, I saw, staring up from its pages, a photo of a pale boy with tiny eyes and a sunken chest. He was identical to the lad I had conjured back in New York City! The hero of my next novel! A chill ran down my spine. How was it possible? What did it mean? His ad said that his name was Calvin W. and that he preferred older men. His hourly rate was marvelously low. As I pecked out his telephone number at lightning speed, I wondered if he was the reason I had been lured westward. Did my trip have a purpose, after all?

A Lovesome He

Through my open window, a cool breeze carried the mouth-watering aroma of roasted pig. Laughter also staggered in, blind drunk, along with a roar of mariachi music. Everyone but me, it seemed, had been invited to the bellboys' Thanksgiving fiesta. Why had I been excluded? Was it merely because I was old and ugly, or was it also because I had tipped them so poorly? If I had known they were going to hold a grudge, I would have tipped them much less.

I opened another wine cooler and soothed my wounded pride with thoughts of Calvin W. and the hour of manly stage-craft about to ensue. I would not make the same old mistakes. No pleasantries, no coy badinage. In fact, I might remain entirely mute. I would be as cold as I knew how, all business, as I forced on the lad a round of deft abominations that would leave us both weeping with holiday thankfulness. I checked the time. The scamp was twenty-seven minutes late.

"No work ethic!" I inwardly cried.

As though the Gods had overheard me, footsteps crunched the gravel. I leapt from my bamboo. The gate tinkled. More footsteps. As I flung open the door, the wind tossed aside my robe, revealing, for just an instant, my indecencies. Truth be told, I didn't care. I was paying the lad, for heaven's sake, and was so old I might never pay another lad again, so why bother with modesty? I untied my robe, threw it wide open, and laid a fist on my hip. I felt masterful and, for, perhaps the first time in my life, entirely unashamed. Any minute Calvin would emerge from the shadows, and if he looked even half as good as he did in his photo, I would be the happiest man in the motel, and that was saying a lot when you consider that it was hopping with drunk Mexicans.

When Calvin appeared in the shimmying light of the swimming pool, my face unhinged. He bore so little resemblance to his photograph that I burst out laughing.

"Why you're black as pitch!" I crowed.

He did not understand what I meant. He averted his eyes from my nakedness and checked a slip of paper.

"Mista Tloop, yes?" His dialect was distinctly Sub-Saharan.

A bolt of fear ran through me. On the phone, Calvin's speech had been as American as mine, and how did he know my name? I had given him a fake one. I turned sideways, lifting a defensive hand and leg, ready to be punched, kicked, or knifed. He frowned and held out a white bag. The smell of pork reminded me that an hour before, resenting my exclusion from the fiesta, I had ordered a double rack of St. Louis short ribs from a local soul-food joint. I laughed at my mistake and tipped the delivery boy a full dollar. As he was swallowed up by the night, I sighed with wistful regret. Why was he not my hired boy? There is nothing quite so yummy as the narrow hips and high, sharp buttocks of the Kenyan marathoner.

Ten minutes later, licking my fingers clean of barbecue sauce, the gravel crunched again, followed by the tinkle of the gate. I burped into my hand and flung open the door. When the real Calvin W. stepped into the light, my face, once again, unhinged, this time with naked wonder at my psychic powers. The boy's gray eyes were identical to the ones I had imagined back in New York. Even more remarkable, like my figment, this boy was chewing bubble gum. The only detail I had not foreseen was his height and build. He was at least six-foot-three, all legs, and could not have weighed more than a hundred and thirty pounds. He resembled an upright grasshopper.

"My God, you're divine," I said. "Enter."

In his advertisement, he had claimed to be twenty years old, but, as he brushed past me, I noticed a faint reticulum of wrinkles at the corner of his eye, which told me that he was at least twenty-seven. His hair was thick and dirty blond. His nostrils were passionate, his lips ascetic and sensitive. His cheeks were stippled with the scars of old acne, which added a rugged patina to what might otherwise have been a too-birdlike face. He wore a red T-shirt, faded to pink, bearing the logo of a lumberyard, big dungarees worn much too low off his bony hips, and ragged tennis shoes. Although he was the farthest thing from my type (from *any* type, in fact, except the type that plays center on a high school basketball team in rural Canada) I adored him in a way that was absolutely unsupportable. He cast a confused glance at the convenience-store booty scattered on the bed.

"Forgive the mess," I said, grabbing the pile of magazines and hurling it across the room like a pesky cat. A Hawaiian-idol lamp crashed to the floor.

"Wine cooler?" I asked, hurrying over to rescue the deity before it brought me eternal bad luck.

"Sure, Eddie, what flavors do you have?"

"Sour Cherry."

He removed the bubble gum from his mouth, rolled it between his fingers, and smiled sweetly: "That's it?"

I have found that the smiles of most youngsters these days reveal teeth, gums, and little else. Calvin's brimmed with heart and soul. Unfortunately, both were deeply damaged. I suspected already that he had been raised in foster care, which meant that he was a survivor of the worst sorts of emotional and sexual abuse. Touched, I walked over, laid a hand on his shoulder, and gently kissed his hair. It shifted a few inches.

"Oh, dear," I said.

He crimsoned to his eartips and straightened his toupee. "I started losing my hair in high school. It sucks."

"Tell me about it. My hair's thinning, too."

"What hair?" he teased good-naturedly.

"Oh, that's right," I laughed. "I'm as bald as an old coot. I feel so young inside that I forget how ancient and ugly I am."

I grinned, waiting for him to contradict me. I heard, instead, a distant mockery of accordions.

"Just you wait," I said, fetching his drink. "You have no idea what it's like to grow old. You think we old-timers are a different category of human, but we aren't. We're just like you. Only one morning we woke up, and there, staring back at us in the glass, were our naked grandfathers. That's what aging is like. An abrupt humiliation with no advantages. In the words of the wildly underappreciated Mr. Henry Wadsworth Longfellow, 'Whatever poet, orator, or sage may say of it, old age is still old age.'"

Calvin frowned at me as though he had never heard of Longfellow, or even of old age. I wondered if he had graduated from high school. I sat down onto the bed and patted the jungle-leaf comforter. He sank down next to me. He was obedient, yes. I inhaled his neck. He smelled of puppies, clove cigarettes, and sweaty feet. He was an original. I handed him his cooler.

"Down the hatch," I said.

He gulped and gulped.

"Calvin," I said, "before the games begin, there's something you need to know. My name is not Edward Lytton. It's Bryce Kenneth Troop. Call me B.K."

"Okay."

"Try it."

"B.J."

"B.*K*."

"B.K."

"Excellent." I handed him a fold of tens. He lifted the leg of his denims and tucked the cash into a lime-green sock.

"Why don't you dress better?" I blurted. "I realize your hourly rate is low, but you could certainly afford a decent pair of socks. And a shirt with buttons."

"Not really," he said, striking a plaintive note. "My expenses are high. I have to drive a lot. And I don't get *that* many calls. I'm not exactly—"

"Nonsense, you're a great beauty. Far more interesting than those California clones with their white T-shirts, faded jeans, blonde hair, and bobbed noses. They look like chorus boys from *Wehrmacht: the Musical.* You're something special. Yours is the sort of lanky, homegrown beauty that would have inspired Andre Gide to move to Iowa and Walt Whitman to become a top."

He had no idea what I was talking about, but I could tell that he wished he did. Without warning, he set aside his drink and laid his head on my chest. A gesture of infinite vulnerability.

"You dear thing," I whispered, stroking his long back. "Everything's going to be all right."

I would like to have stayed in this position until the end of recorded time, but it was impossible. His neck was bent awkwardly and his platypus feet hung off the bed.

"Please, make yourself comfortable," I said.

He kicked off his sneakers. One of his crazy, green socks had a hole in it. A big toe stuck out. Had any young man ever needed my mentorship so desperately? Give me six months and I could turn this work-a-day clay into gleaming porcelain. We repositioned ourselves so that I was propped up against the headboard and his head was tucked into the folds of my flabby chest. Rather than speak, we lay in complete silence. Because I had known for quite some time that the odds of my ever fathering a child were less than nil, I had long-contented myself with rearing my lodgers (artistically, that is), and that had always been enough. Yet, as the gentle minutes passed, I discovered with a gradual shock that I had been lying to myself. Tending to the needs of my lodgers no more satisfied my paternal yearnings than breastfeeding a plastic doll would the maternal urges of a chimp or a spinster. I swooned with a feeling of boundless love and protectiveness toward Calvin. He might as well have been my son or, more accurately, my grandson. I could not make love to him, not tonight, not ever. It would be worse than wrong. It would be criminal. It would be incest. I tied shut my robe.

When I informed Calvin of my decision, he sat up with alarm.

"Don't worry," I said, "you can keep the money."

Relieved, he sank back down, and we resumed our cuddling. He laid a hand across my beach-ball tummy and began, softly, to tell me all about himself.

A Distinctly American Tale

C alvin Otto Klausen grew up in a small town in Alaska, the son of a registered nurse and a long-distance trucker. When he was seven years old, Calvin's father, the victim of a workplace needle-stick, died of a staph infection. His mother, forced to stay closer to home, quit her trucking job and signed on at the local fishery, where she promptly began sleeping with her co-workers. Among the batch of fishermen she brought home, four were violent drunks and two were child molesters.

"How did you learn this?" I asked. "The hard way?"

He nodded painfully.

So, I was right. As usual. I wished I had not been.

Lucky for Calvin, his mother's promiscuity ended soon thereafter when she fell in love with an Irish immigrant named William Wirt, who was more than happy to marry her and adopt her still-grieving son.

Despite Fisherman Bill's generosity, Calvin hated his guts, not only because he had supplanted his father, but also because the walls in Bill's lake house were paper-thin and, at least two nights a week, Calvin was kept awake by his mother's orgasmic cries, which, until he was ten years old, he thought were caused by some sort of barbaric torture. When he came to understand their true nature, he hated Fisherman Bill even more.

Growing up, Calvin dreamt of a career as a major league shortstop. When, in his freshman year of high school, he sprouted past six feet tall, he switched to pitcher, and he was happy for a while, until a tactless coach casually noted that he couldn't "bust a wet paper bag with a fastball from three feet way." Crushed, Calvin made a second switch, to something more practical— maritime welding. Years later, the day after Calvin had graduated first in his class from an industrial training school, his mother and Fisherman Bill were found guilty of conspiracy to distribute marijuana and were sentenced to sixty-three months in state prison. With nothing to keep him at home but his love of snowmobiling, Calvin migrated to sunny California.

Almost at once, Calvin was hired as a carpenter's assistant on a condominium site in a town called Chapsworth. Émile Tonkin, the contractor who hired him, was a jovial, fifty-something bodybuilder with a teardrop tattoo and a big, handlebar mustache.[8] After only one day on the job, Calvin was invited over to Émile's house for a fried chicken dinner. Despite the fact that Émile lived in a suburb with the unfortunate name of Seamy Valley, his ranch house was a slice of heaven: white picket fence, tidy green lawn, rose bushes, and a collie named Laddie. It didn't matter to Calvin that he was not really attracted to older men. Or even to men his own age. After so much painful upheaval in his life, Calvin longed for stability. And so, minutes after gobbling down half a chicken and three biscuits, Calvin dove into Émile's king-sized bed, surrendered his prune, and never left. Moving in was a breeze,

---

8 I pictured a modern-day John L. Sullivan, with an even bigger chest and a dainty nipple ring.

since all of Calvin's worldly possessions fit into a Seattle Mariners gym bag.

Two years passed before tragedy struck again. Émile was overseeing the reconstruction of a strip club that had mysteriously burned to the ground. One night, Émile found, amid the still-sopping embers and rubble, a metal file cabinet that had somehow eluded the worst of the heat and the hose. He dragged into an alleyway and busted open the lock. Inside he discovered the damp but still legible files of an elaborate criminal conspiracy. For the past twelve years the Russian owners of the club had been scooping runaway girls off the street, then raping them into lives of stripping, whoring, and porno.

Émile brought home the damning evidence and spent a terrible sleepless night wrestling with his dilemma. If he handed the files over to the authorities, he risked deadly reprisal; if he did not, how could he live with himself? As the sun rose over a valley that had never felt seamier, Émile made up his mind. He would tell all. Calvin combed out Émile's mustache, applied sun block to his teardrop, helped him choose a white T-shirt, and kissed him good-bye. Émile climbed into his red pick-up truck with Laddie at his side, gave a big wave, and drove off. Calvin never saw Émile or the dog again.

Émile's disappearance, triggering memories of his father's sudden death, plunged Calvin into a profound depression. The police had promised him that they would call as soon as they knew something, but they never did. Calvin rarely budged from his bed, while bills stacked up, utilities were cut off, and the yogurt in the fridge grew a beard. When it seemed that his life could get no worse, a freaky, skinny Filipina showed up on a scooter claiming to be Émile's lawfully wedded green-card wife. When Calvin did not believe her, she returned the next morning with two deputy sheriffs and an eviction order.

"It was weird," Calvin whispered to the tropical shadows of my motel room. "After Ivy-Mae kicked me out, all I wanted to do was save up money as fast as I could, get my own place, crawl back in bed, and go back to missing Émile."

"Is that when you became a candy cane?" I asked.

"A what?"

"Gay-dirt."

"What's that?"

"When you took to the stroll?"

"Huh?"

"Started whoring!"

"Oh, yeah, yeah."

Calvin said that because of his unusual body (endless legs, small thorax), he had trouble attracting customers, so he lowered his prices and strove for quantity over quality, but he found that even that was easier said than done. Now, eighteen months into his stroll, he had earned only enough money to rent a tiny room in a place called Sun Land and drive a twenty-year-old Volkswagen. There was, however, a silver lining. In his new line of work, he had been lucky enough to meet some Hollywood "big shots," a few of whom were supporting him in his latest ambition, which was to become a movie star.

I tried to hide my disappointment. After a long life serving as mentor if not muse to young artists, I had come to the conclusion that actors were among the most unhappy beings on the planet. And they spread their unhappiness, too, because there is nothing an actor loves to do more than discuss his hopeless dreams with others. Sure enough, for the next hour, Calvin did just that. I remember little of what he said. Truth be told, I was not listening. To hold him in my arms was enough. My fancy roamed far and wide. The ceiling was the infinite sky, the mattress a spring meadow, and there was nowhere else on earth I wanted to be. A proper Thanksgiving, after all. When Calvin at last fell silent, I offered him some much-needed counsel.

"Dear boy," I said, "you don't *really* want to be an actor. It's a miserable existence. That's why so many actors turn to drugs and plastic surgery. They're nothing but hired jesters, really. We build them up, stick our noses into every nook and cranny of their personal lives, and then, when we grow tired of them, and we almost always do, we toss them into the trash like used Johnny sacks."

When he did not reply, I looked down, expecting to see him gazing up at me with wonder, but he was fast asleep, sucking his thumb. I chuckled at my arrogance and squeezed him closer. My affection for him was grandpaternal and pure. I fell asleep without effort, murmuring to myself old lines whose origins I did not remember: "Age, I do abhor thee; youth I do adore thee."

When the alarm clock rang the next morning, I was in the middle of baking an angel food cake. When I leaned over to slide it out of the oven, I realized that I was, in fact, sound asleep and just inches from falling out of bed. I grabbed the end table for support but found a handle instead, and together the drawer and I crashed to the floor. Wide awake now, I saw with horror that I was alone. I jumped to my feet and looked around. Had I dreamt Calvin, as well? My eyes fell to the top of the TV set where there sat a dusty wad of bubble gum. He was real, after all.

"Calvin?" I called to the bathroom.

Nothing. The lad had fled. I fell back on the bed, feelings wounded. Sickly morning light sifted through the shade, as it always does after a debauch, but this had not been a debauch; it was a pagan sacrament, a twining of two lonely male hearts. I had nothing to show for it now but a fond memory. Was this the best an old man could hope for? Before my waterworks could get going, I noticed something remarkable. Calvin had left his cash behind! There it was on my end table, the full forty dollars. I felt like a new bride. I jumped up and that's when I realized that it was not my alarm clock ringing. I didn't even own one. It was the telephone! I leapt for it.

"Hello?"

"Hi, Eddie."

"Calvin?"

"Uh-huh."

"My darling boy, where are you?"

"Home. I promised to feed my landlady's dogs. She's visiting her sister in Escondito."

"I thought I'd never hear from you again. I thought you'd fled me in horror."

"Why would I do that?"

"Because I am old and ugly."

A long silence.

If the boy was serious about acting, he *must* learn to pick up his cues.

"I saw that you left behind the money I gave you."

"Yeah, that was stupid. It was itching my ankle, so I took it out of my sock, and I forgot it. I'm such an idiot. I was gonna drive back and get it, but then I thought maybe I didn't really deserve it. It's not like anything happened."

"Anything sexual."

"Yeah."

The silence lingered.

"Anyway," he said, "I was wondering if you want to come to my birthday party."

"I'd be delighted. When is it?"

"Tomorrow night. At six o'clock."

"Oh, dear, I forgot. I'm leaving for New York this afternoon."

"The Big Apple?" he asked with wonder.

"The biggest."

"You live there?"

"I own an entire building. It's called The House Beautiful and it's full of young artists. You should come visit me. Or move in, if you'd like. I have a room opening up on January first. The rent is modest and I'll treat you like a grandson."

"For real?"

His voice trembled. He was on the verge of grateful tears.

"All I ask in return is that you give up acting. I think your gangliness would make it very hard for you to find work. Is there another art that interests you?"

"Is welding an art?"

"It can be, in the right hands. Often those of a strapping lesbian. But there are no hard-and-fast rules."

"You think I could do it?"

"Absolutely." Then, with the abruptness of one who puts his heart before his head, I blurted: "I can't miss your birthday party! What sort of friend would I be? I'll change my reservation."

"Wow, thanks. That's so cool of you."

"By the way, how old *are* you? Honestly."

"Twenty-two?"

"What a coincidence," I chortled, "I was twenty-two once. In fact, just like you, *more* than once."

He laughed. I demand that all my lodgers appreciate my wit, or at least pretend to. I grabbed a pen and wrote down the complicated directions to his home in Sun Land.

Killing Time

As chance would have it, Amtrak was in the middle of its slow season, which runs each year from New Year's Day all the way until the week before Christmas, so they were more than happy to change my ticket. Equally accommodating were the fine folks at the Palms Plaza Motel, who gladly extended my stay in Room 6/9. The only penalty for my decision to attend Calvin's birthday party, other than the small financial one, was that I had thirty hours to kill. I slaughtered two of them at breakfast, lingering over Eggs Benedict and the last wonderful chapters of *Ask the Dust*. The rest I decided to butcher like a native—poolside. I wriggled into my Madras swimming trunks and discovered that they were already snug again. How was it possible that the results of ten days of starvation had been reversed so quickly? It defied science.

I emerged into the cruel sun, wearing sunglasses and a raffish straw hat, and toting a large, ragged, pink towel that I'd found, two nights before, draped over the ice machine. The urchin was in her usual place, bobbing in the middle of the pool, clutching an inflatable toy, staring at me with wide, spooky

eyes. Mr. Victor Hugo or Mr. George Eliot once asserted the
goodness of a mother is writ large in the gaiety of the child. If
true, this child's mother was clearly rotten.

"Stop staring at me like that!" I scolded. "Why are you
always here? Why aren't you in school? Where's your awful
mother?"

"Lewkeeen," she murmured softly.

"Speak up!"

"Lookin'," she said louder, with a rural twang.

"For what?"

"A job."

"For *you*, I'll bet." I set a tube of sun block and two drip-
ping wine coolers onto a lounge chair, along with a paperback copy of *After Many a Summer Dies the Swan*. I unfurled
my towel with a snap. "You're a little actress, aren't you? Don't
deny it, I can tell. Your mama moved you here from a holler
in Tennessee. Or maybe Georgia. Someplace where the Klan
still prospers. And now she's hawking your photo to the local
flesh peddlers, hoping one of them will take you on, agree to
shuttle you from producer to producer until one of them bites.
It's despicable! She ought to be strung up by her thumbs! No,
no, then she'd have no way of getting you home after your spirit
is broken. You hitchhiked here, didn't you? Admit it." I threw
her a stern look. She and her toy rose and fell on the miniscule
swell caused by her kicking. She did not show any sign that she
had heard me. Was she autistic, retarded, or merely shy?

"Am I right or not?!" I barked.

"Fightville," she said.

"You mean Fayetteville, Arkansas?"

She nodded.

"So I was right. And you *are* an actress, aren't you?"

Looking vaguely anguished, she nodded again.

"How old are you?"

"Seven and a half," she whispered.

"Well, you look five. You're malnourished. If you spend one more minute in there you're going to perish. Chlorine causes cancer, you know. Of the gonads. In alligators. Come along, get out."

She mustered the last of her of strength to hoist herself over the cement rim. The child was nothing but sharp edges. Sopping wet, her golden hair looked as thin as an old feminist's.

"Where's your towel?" I demanded.

She looked around, then her eyes narrowed and she pointed to mine. I gestured for her to come closer. She obeyed without hesitation. Her limbs shivered and her teeth chattered as I spun her around, drying her off. I dried her head gently, lest her hair fall out and I be blamed.

"Are you hungry?" I asked.

She nodded enthusiastically. I sprinted inside and returned with the last of my Thanksgiving treats. Her eyes popped with glee when I handed her a candy bar and the bag of chips. While she munched, I smoked a cigarette and lounged. She looked better already.

"What's your name?" I asked.

"Molly Elizabeth Patmore," she managed, through a mouthful of nutty, chocolate goodness.

"Any relation to Coventry Patmore?"

She did not respond.

"Well, someday when you're all grown up, you must investigate the matter. He was a minor Victorian poet, all but forgotten now, but he wrote some quaint things." I fell back on the plastic chaise and recited from memory:

Love wakes men, once a lifetime each;
They lift their heavy lids and look;

And, lo, what one bright page can teach
They read with joy, then shut the book.

I had recited with more difficulty than I care to admit. I wasn't sure if I had all the words right, but it hardly mattered— she was just a child.

"I, myself, have loved more than once," I shared. "Twice, in fact, but rather than shut the book on love, I had it shut for me. Right in my face. By the Fates. At least that's how it felt. I could be wrong, of course. It could be a rationalization. Maybe it was all my fault that neither love was reciprocated."

I glanced over. She was smiling at me. Her teeth were as tiny and sharp as a kitty cat's. Her pale cheek was smeared with chocolate and corn dust. She was a darling creature. I patted the spot next to me.

"Come, little one, sit here. Let's talk about *you*."

She sat in the exact spot I had patted and crunched down another chip. I laid a paw on the nape of her wee neck. "When was the last time you saw a doctor? Have you ever been checked for something called 'ringworm?' It's not half as bad as it sounds. Nothing to be ashamed of, really. It's actually quite common among the perpetually barefoot and those who—"

The bell tinkled and the gate banged. We both looked over. Molly's mother was there, wearing a beastly grimace, rigid with envy that her daughter had found food.

"Relax," I said, "there's plenty to go around."

She stomped over, grabbed Molly by the hand, and bellowed at me in a hillbilly accent, "Yer not a nice person!"

Before I could shove her into the swimming pool, she stormed away and disappeared with Molly into Room 13. A moment later, I heard a loud slap, and then a tiny anguished whine, as though someone had touched a burning cigarette to the nose of a rabbit. It took all of my self-control not to break down the door and give the selfish hick the drubbing of her life.

Abruptly, my concern was cut short by Helios, who parked his flaming chariot behind a mighty cumulus, turning the sky dark. Suddenly, I smelled autumn in the air. A chilly breeze made me shiver. Giving up on my tan, I returned to my room, where I showered and changed into my only fall ensemble—a Harris tweed blazer, wide-whale corduroys, and a sturdy pair of Hebridean walking shoes.

If I was ever going to be able to deliver a convincing cock-tail-party diatribe on the horrors of life in Los Angeles, it was crucial that it be chock full of supporting detail, of which I was, at present, in woefully short supply. After all, what had I seen so far of the great metropolis? Union Station, Highway 10, the Palms Plaza, Venice Avenue, Robinson Road, and a few restaurants. It was time to explore! At the very least, how could I leave without a glimpse of the sea and a whiff of its great salt tonic?

An hour into my westward walk, Helios was back in the driver's seat, galloping past every cloud. Because I had show-ered away my sun block, my neck and face baked, and, because I was dressed for a November tea in Mayfair, my back and belly dripped with sweat. And still no sign of the sea! I longed more than ever to see it, to stand at the open back door of America and to enjoy, if only for a moment, that sweet dilation of lung and spirit that the ocean induces in all but the most hardened souls.

Suddenly, I was struck by a terrible thought. On my way out of the motel, I had stopped at the front desk and spoken to the East Indian clerk, Tupta Parween. He was a tiny man with an accipitral nose and eyes of burning coal.[9] I asked him how far it was to the ocean and he had replied: "Not far. Twenty

---

9 To this day, I suspect that he was a Muslim posing as a Hindu. As though torch-bearing patriots knew or cared about the difference!

minutes." What if he had assumed I would be *driving there?* This was, after all, a motel located in a city where, according to one of my lodgers, no one walks but homeless veterans, poor immigrants, and pairs of gorgeous men in tight white T-shirts. Well, "not far" meant one thing to the driver of a car and quite another to an ancient, fat pedestrian. I grabbed the arm of a scowling Japanese man emerging from a bank. He looked to be at least eighty.

"How far is the Pacific Ocean?"

His scowl deepened. "Two miles!"

He yanked his arm away and hurried off. Clearly he had been impounded during World War Two and never recovered.

Oh, no. I looked up at the sky. The sun, which a minute ago had been melting me like butter, was suddenly gone, and the blue sky was chalky white. What a strange city this was. On the one hand it never changed and on the other that's all it did. I looked ahead: nothing but a collage of capitalistic ugliness as far as the eye could see. If I made the walk, what would be my reward? The Bay of Santa Monica was said to be nothing more than a giant toilet with a broken flusher. Did I really need to behold it?

Giving up, I crossed the avenue to a dingy market, where I picked up a new batch of supplies. I trudged back to my room, and for the next twenty-six hours, I tippled, munched, read, snoozed, dreamed, self-adored, and watched movie after movie. It was my first immersion in American cinema since boyhood, and I was deeply dismayed. The films were pitched at the intellectual level of a first grader. Perhaps I was lucky that Mr. Shipp had turned out to be a vulture and a fraud. Even for a million dollars, I could never have written nonsense like this, because, as everyone knows, a true artist can fake anything but sensibility.

Down in the Valley

As the taxi cab inched north along Highway 450, carrying me lower and lower into the San Fernando Valley, I pressed a hankie into one of my weeping armpits. The air conditioning system was surely broken, because what leaked from its vents was no more refreshing than the breath of a German shepherd. If only Calvin had told me that Sun Land was miles and miles away and that the road leading there was as congested as any in the Western World, I would have packed a flask of cold Chardonnay, my Huxley, and a pair of earplugs; because he had not, I was forced to endure, without comfort or distraction, the vile chit-chat of Mookie, the driver.

"I paid for her private school," he groused, easing us to a stop two inches from the back of a horse trailer. "I spoiled the kid rotten and how does she thank me? She marries a god damn Mexican."

"What sort of Mexican?" I asked.

As these were the first words I had spoken in the past fifteen minutes, he was surprised. The wretch turned around in his seat, pawing at his sweaty bangs. His face was square and underbitten.

"What d'ya mean?" His forearm was tattooed with a woman's torso, complete with bushy crotch.

"Eyes on the road," I said, snapping my fingers.

He turned around and saw that an immense four-foot gap had opened up between us and the horse's swishing tail.

"Is your son-in-law a *mariachi?*" I asked. "A *caballero?* A *campesino?* Each canton of Mexico is unique, you see, and each has its own signature type."

"What's the worst type?"

"They're different, Mookie," I tarted, snapping flame to leaf, "not better or worse. My personal favorite is the *pescadoriti* of Mazatlan—ginger-skinned lads, smelling of surf, marlin, lime, and petroleum jelly. But I know a retired choreographer, whose taste I respect enormously, who swears by the *Zapatisti*, the fiery rebel lads of Chiapas. He claims their manual calluses, born of rifle and plow, create a unique scrotal frisson."

I twitched a smile.

I blew smoke.

I really was *too much.*

Mookie was astounded by my vast knowledge of his son-in-law's homeland. He would have been even more astounded had he known that I had never been to Mexico and had never actually known a single Mexican. My improvisation had been based solely on the works of Diego Rivera and a 1957 wank-skim of a restroom paperback called *The Confessions of Ricardo Duro.* But it did the trick. His bigotry was derailed and he was forced to search for another train of thought. As he did, his eyeballs grew almost sapient.

I took advantage of the silence to admire my wrapping job of Calvin's birthday present. Have you ever wrapped an antique snow globe with toilet paper and toothpaste? It's even more difficult than it sounds. I had picked up the treasure early that morning at a local flea market—which the natives call a "swap meet." I had been all set to pay for it, when I had a funny thought and secretly "swapped" it for a cigarette which I laid discreetly on the edge of the vendor's table. I had chosen the globe because it reminded me of my spindrift childhood back in Fargo, North Dakota. When I told Calvin this, he would appreciate the gift even more.

Abruptly I realized that Mookie was speaking again, singing the praises of retirement in Las Vegas (dirt-cheap food; dirty, cheap women). He was a foul creature, the sort of character one encounters only west of the Mississippi—the hybrid descendant, no doubt, of the hard-luck prospector and the rapacious buffalo killer. Not listening to a word he said, I lowered the window. I fancied I could smell in the hot gust of air that smashed me in the face, a hint of recent brushfires. Far away, the late-afternoon sun shone feebly behind a scrim of ochre smog. Beneath it, the scrubby hills were dotted with stucco houses lying in circles behind high walls. These homes were of identical bland design, each painted a single color from a palette that ran the gamut from mushroom to beige. Inside, there were no doubt ornate ceiling fans, frosted-glass saloon doors, plaid sofa beds, polyester carpeting, state-of-the-art electronics, and miles of bookless bookshelves. The residents were typical American suburbanites: nitwits with ever-ready smiles that barely concealed their desire to dash into the desert, fall to their knees, and blow their brains out or, more selfishly, stay at home and crush the spirits of their children. Why did they live behind such high walls when they had so little worth stealing?

A honking of horns jarred me back to reality. Never in all my life had I seen traffic like this. How was it possible? Down below us, a sturdy brown peasant in a straw hat was selling strawberries roadside. I wondered if I had time to leap from the taxi, lope down the ramp, buy a pint of berries, bake them into a pie, eat it, digest it, grab a quick siesta, pass the pie, and make it back to my seat before the cab had advanced another ten feet. I gnawed at the filter of my fag, suppressing the desire to scream. It was a Saturday afternoon, for heaven's sake and we were heading *away* from the metropolis not toward it! Surely this was the greatest urban exodus since the epic flight of the Jews from Brooklyn to Long Island. Could it be that this was a daily occurrence?

A moment later, I got my answer. The congestion was, in fact, a mere anomaly, caused by a spectacle so freakish that even the world-weariest driver had no choice but to stop and gape. While mere words are inadequate to spell its wonders, I'll give it a try: A motorcycle cop had pulled over an elderly motorist and was *writing him a ticket.*

I am not making this up.

When we reached the scene, Mookie, like every other driver, came to a complete stop. I was so disgusted with my own species that I shouted a profanity and flicked my cigarette out the window, hoping to spark another brushfire. Instead, it hit the old scofflaw in the neck. His hoary head turned on a stiff swivel. The cop's head turned, too, but much, much faster. Frightened, I ducked fast, cracking my nose on my kneecap.

"Drive! Drive!" I shrieked.

Mookie gave it the gas, and within seconds we were flying along at a healthy clip. The hot wind danced among my last few sad hairs, but I could not celebrate our new velocity. I was too busy staring at the roof of the cab, trying to redirect the tide of nasal blood. By the time we arrived at Calvin's, I had swallowed a quart of it and the meter read $104.60. I slapped the fare into Mookie's hand and scootched out. Only then, pressing hankie to schnozzle, did I see that I had been delivered fully nowhere.

It was the sort of block one sees only on the nightly news after it has been liberated to rubble by the United States Air Force. The houses were flimsy, their yards mere patches of scorched grass and weeds. Ugly laundry hung from flaccid lines. Cars without wheels rusted in driveways. The air was an oven-blast of baked feces. Only one house was attractive and well tended. I prayed it was Calvin's. I checked the address again. It was not Calvin's. It was his neighbor's. Calvin's ugly house was distinguished from the others only by a miserable Volkswagen in the driveway and a brand-new chain-link fence, from which fluttered a shiny balloon reading, "Bon Voyage!" It grieved me to think of the dear boy celebrating his birthday with a mismarked balloon, purchased, no doubt, at a deep dis-count. I resolved then and there to follow through on my offer and spirit him away to The House Beautiful.

I pocketed my stained hankie, opened the gate, and was stopped by a blast of far fresher feces. My shoe squished into its source. Before I even had time to curse my luck, a mad chorus of barks tore the air, and out of a flap on the front porch sprang a flood of snow-white puppies, wearing black saddles and buff chapeaux, yelping a single, mad hello. I have always adored ter-riers (for the simple reason that, unlike the British who bred them, they are passionate and loyal) but given the minefield of filth across which they ran, I questioned their cleanliness and did not dare pet them even as they frolicked at my ankles.

"Don't be scared! They won't bite!" A hag shuffled onto the front porch. "Come on in! Hurry up! We been waitin' for ya!"

I tiptoed slowly, carefully avoiding both the puppies and their piles of dirt.

"I'm usually prompt to a fault," I said, sniffing back blood, "but the traffic was murder."

"Tell me about it," she rasped.

I stopped at the porch and attempted a smile, but it was impossible. Her face was late-Auden. Her throat bore, among its many hairs, a substantial mole. Her housedress was stained with mustard. Was she serving cheeseburgers? I certainly hoped so. I was famished.

"Gin Reinheimer," she said. "I own the place."

"I'm—"

"Eddie Bullard. I know. You're all the kid's been talkin' about. He was afraid you weren't comin'.'" She held out a mannish hand. "Put 'er there."

I did as I was told.

"Hope you aren't allergic to Jacks."

"To what?"

She pointed a broken finger at her brood. "Jack Russells."

"No, not in the slightest. Only to dust mites, mugwort, pollen, halibut, and cats."

"Good for you," she said, opening the torn screen door. "Come on in. I got the AC cranked."

Before entering, I scraped the smelly sole of my shoe on a welcome mat that showed a frowning face and the words, "Good Riddance!"

The Birthday Boy

The room was as dim and chilly as a crypt. As my eyes adjusted, details emerged: thrift-store gewgaws and gimcracks crowded every dusty surface; a Santa Claus candle burned on the TV; the illusion of a hearth was created by a revolving plastic log bearing a single red light bulb, and the coffee table was made out of a wagon wheel. In short, a living hell. Where was Calvin? I must rescue him at once. I looked everywhere, then almost screamed when I saw his little face staring down at me from the ceiling. He appeared to have grown at least a foot since our night together and his toupee was bushier.

"Hey, Ed," he said sweetly, his little gray eyes blinking. "Cool tie!"

"It's not a tie," I replied with a playful smile. "It's an ascot. And my name is *not*—"

"I'm so glad you came."

He hugged me, pressing my injured nose into his sternum. I hugged back—his ribs were like piano keys—then I wiggled my face to the side and managed to steal a breath beneath his armpit. He smelled of pine. I heard a chorus of yips and saw Gin leading her excited pups toward a dark bedroom, luring them with a single potato chip.

"Let me introduce you," Calvin said, stepping away and taking me by the hand. "Eddie meet Eddie."

A dapper black man of perhaps thirty grinned at me in a happy, white-toothed way, which I found offensively stereotypical.

"Eduardo Wiggins," the man said. "*Such* a pleasure. Calvin's been banging on about you for the past fifteen minutes."

Although Eduardo hailed, I later learned, from Muncie, Indiana, his speech was high Oxford, the sort of English accent that African-American opera singers affect ten minutes after landing in London. I gave him my hand, but instead of shaking it, he kissed it. He was the type of homosexualist I liked least—the Beau Brian. He wore a pink button-down shirt with a stiff white collar, golden cuff links, silky black trousers, and shiny tuxedo shoes. He reeked of lavender and self-adoration. He was not just dull, but the cause of dullness in others. In bed, he was no doubt an avid spelunker.

"The pleasure's all mine," I countered with cooing insincerity.

"And this," said Calvin, bursting with excitement, "is the one, the only . . . *Rowdy Diamond!*"

There was a silent crash of cymbals as Calvin flung his hand toward a skinny blind man of about sixty sitting on the sofa, holding a can of domestic beer. All that's worst of ranch and trailer park met in the man's aspect and eyelessness. His hair was matted down with grease. He wore stonewashed denims, dirty high-top sneakers, and, of course, black sunglasses. He held no white cane, but he was flanked by two ancient Jack Russells, who, marking time until the arrival of the taxidermist, eyed me with grim indifference.

"Rowdy lives across the street," Calvin explained.

"But don't tell anybody," the man smirked, holding out a gloved hand.

Given that he was blind, he aimed very well.

"Rowdy's a famous stuntman," Calvin explained.

"Not anymore, kid."

That, I'm afraid, was the entire guest list.

"Soup's on!" Gin barked, as she emerged through a swinging door, carrying a bag of corn chips and a bowl of guacamole. She set them down on the wagon wheel and everyone but me dug in. I loathe avocado. It has the texture of clay and loses its freshness far too quickly. I would fast until dinner.

The conversation flowed easily, thank God. Everyone was enthralled that I hailed from New York City. Gin began to reel off the names of the actors on her favorite TV situation comedy, which took place in Greenwich Village.

"Ever met any of 'em?" she asked me.

I told her that I had not, but, then again, it would be far more likely that *she* would have met them, as the show in question, like virtually every other TV show, was filmed not in New York but here in Los Angeles.

Eduardo smirked at my mistake.

"It's New York," Gin patiently explained. "You can see it outside the windows. It even snows sometimes."

I bugged my eyes at Calvin, expecting him to be as astonished by her stupidity as I was.

"Gin's right, Eddie," he said with a touch of pity. "It hardly ever snows here."

I leapt at the perfect segue: "Never snows? Oh, really? Well, then how do you explain this?"

Like a magician revealing his bunny, I plucked Calvin's gift from my pocket.

"Happy birthday!"

With a look of rapture, Calvin tore off the toilet tissue. Everyone ooh'ed and ah'ed, including Rowdy, which, given his blindness, bewildered me.

"What is it?" Calvin asked when he saw the globe.

I turned it upside down, then righted it. The young man marveled as the snow drifted down onto the shivering girl inside.

"Whoa," he murmured. Did he see his own tortured childhood in the suffering of the child?

"It's an antique," I explained.

"It reminds me of Alaska."

"Yes, except this little match girl, hallucinating as she dies, hails from Denmark."

"That's far away, huh?"

"Only if you don't live there."

He carefully set down the heirloom, then leaned over and kissed my cheek.

"You rock," he whispered.

I vibrated with happiness.

The chitchat resumed, but within a minute or two I could not even pretend to enjoy it—my stomach had turned volcanic. I was so hungry, in fact, that I would have gladly filled myself with guacamole, except that it had already turned brown, and a tumor had appeared in the center of it, which, as people scraped closer and closer to it, seemed to swell and grow hair.

"Hate to be a bother," I gasped finally, "but do you supposed I could have something to drink?"

"Shit, Ed!" our hostess cried. "Why didn't you say so? What'll it be?"

"What do you have?"

"Beer . . . ."

I waited patiently for her to finish the beverage list, but she simply stared.

"Well, you want one or not?" she snapped.

"Oh, no!" Calvin exclaimed. "Eddie drinks wine. I forgot. I'll get you some."

He jumped up, almost bumping his head on the pebbly ceiling, and made for the front door.

"Don't be ridiculous," I protested.

"Hey, no problem. You're the guest of honor!" He grabbed his keys. "It'll only take a sec."

He flew out the door so quickly that he did not hear me beg to be taken along. In his wake, there was only silence. We eyed each other as though trying to detect the source of an unpleasant odor. Was it possible that dear, inarticulate Calvin had been the sole engine of our conviviality? Faint with hunger, I set aside good manners and asked Gin if there was anything to eat besides guacamole.

"You betcha!" She waddled out of the room and returned thirty seconds later with a platter of deviled eggs. I had popped two in my mouth before I realized that instead of paprika she had dusted them with cayenne pepper. My throat closed and my injured nose burned as though with phosphorus. I lunged for my drink, but then remembered that I did not have one. I swallowed hard and dry, blinking back tears. This was one of the worst parties I had ever attended.

After my sight and breathing had returned, I decided to kill time questioning the other guests. Rude interrogation is permitted the serious novelist. Gin Reinheimer, it turned out, was a widow. Her only child, a giant named Chip, had died in Vietnam of a black-tar heroin overdose while serving with the 50th Infantry. Her husband R.J., the love of her life, had died nine years ago, of a massive heart attack while driving eighty miles an hour on the freeway. Today she survived on Social Security checks, R.J.'s small pension, and whatever pennies she picked up breeding Jacks and renting out her spare room. Gin was currently in remission from "ovrarian" cancer and hope to fall in love one last time before she died.

"Aw, bullshit on that," Rowdy muttered, crushing his beer can in one hand. "You'll bury us all."

"You and me, certainly," I replied. "Perhaps even Miss Thing here." I threw a cold glance at Eduardo. "If he doesn't start taking precautions. But not Calvin. He's just a boy."

They all smiled at each other.

"What did the rascal tell you?" Eduardo purred. "Twenty? Twenty-one?"

"Twenty-two."

"He's twenty-nine," Rowdy said.

"Impossible!" I cried.

"If you'd ever seen him without his toupee, you wouldn't say that."

"Ever since he took up the acting," Gin growled, "he's turned into such a god-damn liar."

I judged Calvin for an instant, but then I reminded myself that I was hardly beyond reproach in this regard. When I had answered Calvin's ad, I'd said my name was Edward Bullwer-Lytton and that I was fifty-two years old, 180 pounds, and ten inches cut. I supposed we were even now. The next time I got Calvin alone, I would propose we make a fresh start.

Eduardo Wiggins, by coincidence, worked as a night security guard at the studio where fat Christy Winkler worked in payroll. He and Calvin had met a few months before in an acting class. At the moment, Eddie was in dress rehearsals for a production of *Desire Under the Elms,* which was to open in a fifty-seat theatre in a place called Augura Hills.

"Who do you play?" I asked, startled that a black sissy could find a toehold in O'Neill.

"Well, old boy, you'll just have to pop 'round and find out." He handed me a flyer, flashing that bright minstrel smile of his—an insult to Dr. King and all the Hebrew idealists who sacrificed so much so that he might publicly kiss white boys.

Next came a big surprise: Rowdy Diamond was not, in fact, blind. He only wore sunglasses, he explained, to hide the scars of third-degree burns suffered on the set of a war movie, shot in Bulgaria.

"Flashed me good," he said. "Cooked me like a French fry. Last job I ever did."

"That explains the gloves," I said.

"What do you mean?" he asked.

I dropped it.

Living on disability checks and a settlement from the insurance company, Rowdy divided his time between the racetrack and an independent living center, where Anson, his mentally retarded son, was warehoused. As Rowdy told us all about the center's new jungle gym, I grew bored. I glanced at a cuckoo clock and saw that Calvin had been gone a full forty-five minutes. Interrupting, I asked Gin where the liquor store was.

"In the mini-mall. Few blocks away."

Everyone fell silent again, as we all had the same thought: *What on earth was keeping Calvin?*

Hypotheses were offered: a flat tire, an empty gas tank, a fender bender, a chance meeting with a pal. All reasonable enough. Gin called him on his cellular telephone.

"He never leaves home without it," she said.

Five seconds later, the wagon wheel buzzed. We found Calvin's toothpaste-smudged telephone buried under a mound of toilet paper. The mood grew anxious. Rowdy took off his shades to rub his tired eyes and, seeing his scars, I was flooded with compassion for anyone who had ever seen him this way. I fled into the kitchen and resorted to a beer.

After Calvin had been gone a full two hours, during which I drank four more beers and suffered through more abysmal small talk, Gin rang the police. They told her that, despite appearances, Calvin was not a missing person, and would not become one for another twenty-two hours.

At midnight, Rowdy, exhausted from his play day with Anson, trudged home. Eddie begged off, too, as he needed his beauty sleep. He had an audition early Monday morning to play a bumblebee in a honey commercial.

"Do let me drive you back to your motel," he said, with a licentious flash of teeth.

"Oh, no, I couldn't possibly leave until I know that Calvin's all right."

I asked Gin if I might sleep on her couch.

"Sure, knock yourself out," she said.

Eddie handed me his business card, kissed Gin's cheek, and flounced into the night.

Mine was a shallow sleep, plagued by nightmares. I fully expected that at any moment I would be awakened by the creak of the front door. Calvin would find me, lay his small head on my chest, and I would rub his back as he told me all about his impulsive, boyish rove. Naturally, he would apologize for his selfishness, and, just as naturally, I would forgive him.

When I awoke, however (not with the lark, but to the whimpers of a dozen starving, full-bladdered pups), Calvin was still not back. A moment later, a loud knocking shook the walls. I stumbled off the sofa and nearly collided with Gin as she emerged from the bathroom, wearing a see-through nightie. I closed my eyes, threw an afghan at her, and flung open the door. A fat cop stood there. Reading his grim expression, I knew at once that the birthday boy was dead.

Dante, Petrarch, and Troop

The fat cop was not a fat cop at all—merely a fat security guard named Freddy, who patrolled the local strip mall on weekends. In high school, he had been the best friend and locker partner of Gin's son, Chip. At Chip's funeral, Gin had wept to Freddy, "Don't be a stranger," and he had sniffled back, "I won't, Mrs. Reinheimer." He had been a fixture in her home ever since.

Walking to work this Sunday morning (his driver's license had been revoked after a drunken car accident involving a crafty light pole), Freddy had decided to pop in for a quick visit. Gin greeted him like a long-lost son, and he repaid her affection with a Sabbath surprise: a marijuana cigarette the size of a hog's nipple. They fell together on the couch, torched the joint, and started to suck. Eventually Gin offered me a hit, but I waved it away. I deplore drugs in broad daylight.

"Oh, that's some good shit," Gin croaked. "Now I'm gonna be horny all day."

I was appalled on many levels. I left without a word and helped myself to a shower, letting the scalding water sluice away yesterday's aches, grime, and blood. I barely minded that her tub was foul and that her big underwears hung from the towel rack. When I emerged, much improved, I found the two roach-benders giggling like Catholic schoolgirls after lights-out. I looked around for the source of their mirth, but saw nothing. The drug is bad enough when it renders intelligent people stupid, but when it's smoked by those who are stupid to begin with, its effects are nothing short of catastrophic. Is this how she expressed her concern for Calvin's well-being? What good would she be to the police in this condition? Furious, I shed my towel and began to dress. Normally, I am modest to the extreme, but Gin and Freddy had been reduced to such a level of stupefied giddiness that I could have slapped on rhinestone pasties and danced the Highland Fling and they wouldn't have noticed.

As I tied my ascot, I heard barking outside. I peeked between aluminum blinds and beheld a puppyscape of frolic and roughhouse that made me smile. At least *someone* was glad to be alive. Then, behind me, I heard Freddy mutter something that sounded like "flaming fat-gut." Gin splattered a laugh. I spun around, eyes flashing. Before I could attack, Rowdy Diamond entered from the kitchen, carrying a supermarket birthday cake and a gallon of *vino rosso*. The cake he had plucked from Gin's refrigerator, but the wine he had picked up at the nearby Liquor Barn, where he had gone to investigate Calvin's disappearance. He said that Calvin's Volkswagen was not parked in the lot and that the owner did not remember seeing him at all last night. Trailing Rowdy was his retarded son Anson, who looked to be about forty, but was, I later learned, just seventeen.

"The sun is hot!" Anson moaned with glee.

"You can say that again," I replied. He took me literally and said it again every thirty seconds for the next fifteen minutes.

Rowdy explained that once Anson got a thought in his head, he held on for dear life.

We all settled onto the sofa. Rowdy and I dug into the cake and the wine, while Anson ate just one tiny sliver of cake, pinching it apart with the meticulous care of a child dismembering an insect. Later, Rowdy used a paper napkin to dab crumbs from the boy's face and lap. It was touching, in a way.

"My butt hurts," Anson muttered irrelevantly.

Now that my stomach was full, I was ready to take control of the situation. I announced a rash decision: I would stay in Los Angeles until Calvin reappeared. To demonstrate my resolve, I picked up the phone and canceled my train reservation. Then I called Tupta Parween and extended my stay at the Palms Plaza. Gin and Rowdy were more than a little impressed, and they told me so. They had assumed I would simply wash my hands of Calvin. After all, I hardly knew him. What had he done to merit such generosity?

I offered up a few reasons, but not the true one, which was that my loyalty to the boy was inspired not so much by Calvin's virtue, but, rather, by their *lack* of it. Gin had greeted the day with ganja, completely shirking her duty as the boy's de facto guardian. Rowdy was not a bad guy, but he was far too busy doting over his square-headed son to be of any help in finding Calvin. Eduardo Wiggins was a poor excuse for a friend, indeed. He had not even telephoned to find out if Calvin had returned. No, he was too consumed with his career, standing in front of his bedroom mirror, deciding which yellow vest to wear with which black blazer. In fact, there was only one person in Calvin Wirt's life who cared whether he lived or died and that was his lover and protector, Émile Tonkin, and he had gone missing himself. (Were the two events related? Already I was thinking like a detective.) And so, despite the fact that

Calvin and I were near-strangers, I would stay until the mystery of his disappearance was solved. Was it really such an extraordinary thing to do? Yes, of course it was, but not entirely unheard of. Man's noblest devotions are often those that defy logic. Dante only saw Beatrice twice; Petrarch hardly knew the married Laura. With fidelity as my sword and tenacity my steed, I would unriddle Calvin's fate or die in the attempt.

The Case
of the Missing Calvin

Heaped with dozing pups, I passed the day alone in Gin's living room, sipping wine, eating cake, smoking my throat raw, and watching professional football, the rules of which I only dimly recalled from my years in the high school marching band. I found the physiques of the players most impressive, especially those of the ball-catchers, whose fast-twitch muscles were just my cup of tea. The team with the prettiest uniforms won the contest, but I was unable to cheer, because the slightest movement awoke the pups, and it took many minutes to settle them down.

The reason I was all alone was that my stoned hostess had left the house, treating herself to a lady day that included a perm, a mani-pedi, and a thorough waxing. Not long after the second game had ended, Gin barged in, toting a bag of fast food. All twelve puppies jumped up from the couch to greet her. She kick-herded them into front yard, slammed the door, and closed the doggie flap. Working our way through a feast of cheeseburgers and fries, she launched into a racist diatribe on the Korean waxer who had gone "way overboard" and nearly killed her, which led to a blanket denunciation of everyone who lived from Calcutta to Pyongyang. It seemed that she blamed all Asia for the death of her son. As though it were not the boy himself, but a giant land mass and a population of billions, who had made the decision to stick a needle of supercharged heroin into his neck.

At precisely 7:46, our twenty-four-hour wait was over. Gin and I packed into Rowdy's old van and drove to the police station, where Calvin Wirt finally, officially, joined the ranks of America's missing. After filing a complete report, we were told to go home and wait for a visit.

Sure enough, the very next morning, bright and early, two policemen, both tall, well-muscled mouth-breathers, arrived and peppered us with every obvious question, most of which I could not possibly have answered, and all of which Gin ought to have been able to answer, but could not. She had lived with the boy for months, but knew almost nothing about him—not his social security number, middle name, date of birth, or even his profession.

"Some sorta delivery boy," she shrugged.

I'll say!

The officers promised a thorough investigation and left. A moment later, Gin burst into tears.

"He's dead!" she wailed.

She was not such a cold creature, after all. Just as I was about to hold my breath and give her a hug, I learned that she was sobbing not for Calvin but for her long-lost Chip.

"They murdered my boy!" she moaned. "Little yellow bastards!"

"You said he died of a drug overdose."

"They hooked 'em on it!" she shouted.

Even though he had been dead for three decades, she sobbed as though it were yesterday. I ignored her selfish histrionics and got down to business.

"I am writing down the telephone number of the Palms Plaza," I said. "Have you heard of it?"

"Uhhh, yeah," she sniffled. "Fancy place in Beverly Hills."

"That's right, I have a suite there. Should Calvin return or should you hear from him, ring me at once. If I'm not in, call Calvin's cellular phone, because I'm taking it with me. I'll need it for my investigation."

"You mean, like a detective?"

"Precisely. If I'm going to tarry here, I might as well make myself useful. I'll be devoting myself day and night to the case."

"What do you know about detecting?"

"At least as much as those bull-necks do. Plus, I have a huge advantage. I'm profoundly intelligent and have absolutely no scruples. A winning combination. I'd like to forage in the boy's bedroom, if you don't mind."

"Why you wanna do that?"

"For clues, woman!"

I strode down the hallway.

"Clues," I explained, "are the threads that lead us from the dark corners of the labyrinth into the clear light of day."

"It's a pig sty," she said, as she hurried ahead and flung open the door.

I thanked her, entered, and, requiring peace and quiet, shut the door in her face.

Were an anthropologist, a thousand years hence, to stumble upon the fossilized remains of Calvin's room as it stood that day, he would hypothesize that the dwellers of the San Fernando Valley in the early third millennium were only one rung above their apish ancestors. Clothes were strewn everywhere, as well as banana peels, orange rinds, peanut shells, take-out food containers, beer cans, a dirty toupee, dozens of black-and-white photographs of Calvin's face, and a slew of battered teen magazines. I found a clean bandana and tied it around my face like a grave robber.

While it is true that in my lifetime I have applied myself to few physical activities (preferring the life of the mind), when I do, I am a sight to behold. I dug into the trash with the fierce determination of a Normandy pig in search of truffles. Within minutes, my ardor was rewarded: I found Calvin's little black book, which contained twelve first names followed by last initials, and, below each, a home address. Surely these were his regular customers, whose anonymity he protected with the initials. (But only twelve? He had said business was bad. He wasn't kidding!) Next I spotted what looked to be the re-charger for Calvin's cellular telephone plugged into a corner socket. I would need it. Third, jammed between his mattress and box spring, I found 3800 dollars in small bills. Words can-not express, even now, my happiness and relief. My chief wor-ry was that my decision to behave honorably would bankrupt me. Well, not anymore. As I stuffed the bills into my pockets, I lifted my eyes to the pebbly ceiling and pledged to whichever goddess it is who oversees all things household, that I would not abuse my bounty. I would use Calvin's money only to pay my expenses, salary, and nothing else.

Last, under a pair of Calvin's boxer-briefs (whose perineal strip bore a faint reddish skid), I found a spiral notebook, of which only the first page had been used. Calvin had scrawled a love poem there, entitled "You." As it was clearly not writ-ten about me (the first line read: "Soft and silky, young and pink/Would you like to have a drink?") I ripped it out and on the next page wrote "The Case of the Missing Calvin." Then I scribbled: *Sunday, November 30. Calvin Wirt has disappeared into thin air. I gained entrance to his pigpen. Should I find the boy alive, I will teach him what lies next to godliness. Foraging, I found a few items of value to my investigation. At dawn, I will flee this terrible valley.*

My Squire

I awoke on Gin's sofa to an aching back and the monstrous growl of a garbage truck. Afraid of rousing the Jacks, I dressed in the dark and ordered my taxi in a whisper. Even though the dispatcher warned me of a thirty-minute wait, I was so eager to be free of Gin's hovel that I tiptoed outside, closing the door silently behind me. The lock made a definitive click, which was a shame, because it was much colder outside than I had expected. What I did not know, but soon learned, is that before the sun rises, the desert is like the far side of the moon. I walked through a minefield of nearly frozen dog-dirt to the curb where, hugging myself against the cruel wind, I settled in for my wait.

An hour later, I was racked with sniffles and shivers and could not feel my hands or feet. Where was my taxi? How could a company stay in business that treated its customers so shabbily? Then I remembered something a lodger had once told me: "In L.A., service people are friendly, but do a lousy job. In New York, it's the opposite." Watching the sun reluctantly crawl to its feet at the end of the block, I heard a splashing sound, spun around, and saw a man standing in the bright, open garage of the pretty house next door. He was about forty, with curly hair, a thin mustache, and broad chest. He was rinsing out a bucket of blood with a garden hose.

"How ya doin'?" he said. His accent was Hispanic, his voice gentle and pleasing.

"Not well," I said, feigning calm, but scared out of my wits. It is one thing to slaughter your neighbor, but quite another to hose out his blood without so much as a tremor. I walked closer, but stopped far enough away that should he turn on me I would have time to run. "Do you mind if I ask you where all that blood came from?"

"It's not blood," he chuckled. "It's paint. See?" He pointed. Ten feet away stood a doll's house, its roof painted red.

"Awfully early for hobbying, isn't it?" I asked.

"I always wake up real early."

"Is that for your little girl?"

"I don't have girls. I got three boys. It's for my church."

"I see. Well, that's very nice. My name is B.K. Troop. Who are you?"

He smiled strangely. "Gin says your name's Eddie."

"Well, Gin, bless her soul, is as thick as mud. My name, I assure you, is Bryce Kenneth Troop. Of the Fargo Troops. If my fingers weren't frostbitten, I'd show you my library card."

The man stood up. For a Mexican, he was towering. Nearly five-foot-seven. He wore faded denims, a flannel shirt, and a thick fleece-lined jacket. His face was quite beautiful, particularly around the eyes and lips. Born into a different caste, he might very well have been a movie star.

"What's *your* name?" I asked.

"Jesus Cabrera," he replied, extending a horny hand of toil. "A pleasure."

"You're very cold," he said as we shook.

"I've been waiting for my taxi for over an hour."

"Where you goin'?"

"Los Angeles. The Palms area. To my hotel."

"That's gonna cost you a lotta money."

"I know. It cost me a over a hundred dollars to get here."

"That's too much."

"Tell me about it. And for what? To attend a party where there were almost no refreshments and the birthday boy vanished into thin air."

"Calvin still not come home yet?"

I considered correcting his English, but decided against it.

"No, and he hasn't called either. I've made it my mission to determine his whereabouts. I won't return home to New York until I do."

"You're a good person."

"Yes, I am, but how do you know that?"

"I'll take you."

"What do you mean? Take me where? You know where he is?"

"No, no," he laughed, showing white teeth. "To your hotel. I'll drive you." He stepped back and clattered the garage door to the ground.

"You're serious?"

He wiped his hands on his denims, and then beckoned me to follow him to his bright red pick-up truck. It was not new, but well maintained. Delighted, I hopped in and buckled up. When he turned the key, a blast of air hit me.

"Oh, I gotta tell Maria where I'm going." He jumped out and hurried inside. In the blink of an eye the cabin turned toasty. I was so grateful that I felt like crying, or laying my head on the driver's seat and purring like a big, fat kitten. Abruptly, Jesus was back. The engine roared, and, as we pulled away, the

Jack Russells spilled from their little flap, begging to be taken along. Surely they would have preferred to live anywhere else. Even the gas chamber at the Humane Society would have been an improvement. At the end of the block, we passed a taxi, making the turn. I scowled and gave the driver my middle finger. She was visibly shaken to have lost such a hefty fare.

The trip back was much faster than the one out, not due merely to the hour but also to the driver's far more engaging personality. Jesus Cabrera seemed to enjoy my interrogation. He was by trade a landscaper, but, months before, his career had been cut short by a fall from a carob tree. The operation to repair the chipped bone in his neck was only partly covered by his insurance, so he was forced to skip it and live in pain instead. He performed odd jobs now, while his wife Maria worked for nickels, emptying bedpans at a local senior center.

What touched me most about Jesus, besides his obvious grace and intelligence, was his acceptance of me. As one who is considered flamboyant or worse by most working-class men, I am used to inspiring suspicion, sometimes even hatred, in them. But Jesus, like his famous namesake, seemed entirely oblivious of everything that set me apart from the ruck of men. He saw only my great humanity. I liked him very much, and by the time we had pulled up to my motel, I felt that I had made my second real friend in Los Angeles.

I insisted that Jesus take fifty dollars for his trouble. He fought me hard, and, in the end, took thirty. I was so impressed by his lack of avarice that I offered him four hundred dollars a week to be my driver and guide. (I could hardly be expected to conduct a thorough investigation on foot!) He was overjoyed, of course, as it was a far better gig than handyman. I brought him down to earth by adding that the job required him to be at my beck and call twenty-four hours a day, seven days a week.

He swallowed hard but did not back out. I could tell it was more than money that was motivating him; already he sensed that a close association with a man of my breeding could not help but improve his grammar, manners, and overall chances for societal advancement. I had never mentored a grown man before, and certainly not one who owed more to Hephaestus than to Apollo, but, as the great Mel Tormé once said, "It's never too late to add an octave."

After giving Jesus the rest of the day off, I tippled, showered, self-adored, showered again, tippled some more, ordered a pepperoni pizza, and snoozed. Only then, at dusk, did I sit down with Calvin's cellular telephone. I had no idea who or what I was looking for, but the courage to proceed, even flourish, while squarely in the dark is something every creative spirit, including a detective, must possess. Negative Capability, Mr. Keats called it. But *was* I a creative spirit or a mere recorder of facts? My novels suggested the latter. Luckily, my doubts were allayed by a bottle of Chablis. When I swirled it, a faint aroma of burnt matches told me that it was well cured.

My First Lead

My first task was to match each of the twelve first names and initials in Calvin's little black book to a phone number stored in his cellular telephone. No easy task, because the phone numbers were listed by initials only. I am a hopeless dunce when it comes to modern-day technology, so it took me more than an hour to accomplish it. While I was in no way convinced that one of Calvin's regular customers had killed or kidnapped him, I hoped that one of them might be able, at the very least, to send me in the right direction. Fed up with Calvin's gadget, I picked up the house phone by the bed instead. As I dialed, the room shifted suddenly, and it occurred to me that I might be drunk. No wonder, I had already drained the bottle.

I told each man the same thing: that my name was Dave Mitten, a landlord in Sun Land, and that a tenant of mine, a young man named Calvin Wirt, had skipped town without paying his rent, and that among his possessions I had found a scrap of paper with their name and number on it. "Any idea where he might have run off to?" I asked, preposition flapping.

A few of the johns responded with panic—none more

pronounced than that of the man whose children I heard laughing in the background—but most seemed either annoyed or indifferent. When I hung up, this is what I had scribbled in my crime journal:

Jim A.—Grouchy hang-up.
Cliff C.—"Haven't seen Calvin in months."
Mark E.—Rude and arrogant.
Ron D.—"Sorry, doesn't ring a bell."
Paul P.—No help at all. High voice. Born a woman?
Julian L.—"Don't know any Calvins."
Giles K.—Ancient and alone. Asked me to tea.
Lee N.—Defensive; married; kids.
Alan W.—I left a message with his wife.
Ted S.—Nice guy, no idea who Calvin is.
Jason B.—"Never call me again, do you understand?"
Dan L.—"Scrawny and bald. Not my type."

I sat motionless, staring at the list. I had read somewhere that the life of a detective consists mostly of cold coffee and brick walls, but I had not expected to be stymied so quickly. I had also read that in the investigation of crime, as in the creation of art, it is more important to be dogged than inspired. I walked to my open door and lit a cigarette. Truth be told, my resolve was already wavering. I wanted to give up. I might very well have done it, too, had something not buzzed at my groin. Terrified, I did a crazy jig, unfastened my trousers and jammed them, along with my underwear, all the way to the floor. I was barefoot, so I easily skipped out of them. I spun around, crouched and wide-eyed, expecting to see a hungry cicada crawl out of my boxers. Instead I heard another buzz. It was then that I remembered that I had pocketed Calvin's phone and that, when a call came in, instead of ringing, it merely vibrated. If I had not been alone, I would have died of embarrassment. My only excuse was that I was plastered to the hairline. Crouching to retrieve the phone and my cigarette, I saw Molly's mother staring at me from across the swimming pool.

"What the hell's the matter with you?" she hollered. "I oughta call the cops!"

"I *am* the cops!" I hollered back.

I slammed the door. On the face of Calvin's phone glowed the initials T.S. and a number that looked oddly familiar. Was it possible? I hurried to my crime journal and ran a finger down the list. The number belonged to Ted S., the friendliest of all the men I had called, and the only one who had been absolutely convincing when he said that he didn't know Calvin. Yet here he had phoned the boy just a few minutes later! I doubted that Ted had anything to do with Calvin's disappearance—if he had, he would know where Calvin was and would have had no need to call him—but one thing was certain: Ted S. was a spectacular liar.

I selected the listing in Calvin's phone marked Voice Mail and, acting on a hunch, pressed the green button[10]. A moment later a recorded voice came on, interrupted by a bunch of fast beeps, then a snatch of the same voice, then another beep, then a bit more voice, then more fast beeps, then the voice said, "You have one unheard message." This is what I heard next:

"Calvin? What the hell? It's—It's me. Some weirdo just called from a motel, claiming to be your landlord and that you skipped town on the rent, but you don't have a landlord, right? Just the hag. So who was it and how did he get my number? Anyway, give me a call. Hey, did you ever hook up with Joe? If you did, I hope he

10 At my farewell brunch, Adrian had teased me that I better not "go Hollywood" on him. "Never!" I had replied, and yet here I was, mastering the cellular telephone!

*wasn't too rough on you. Did you freak out? Anyway, just call me.
I hope you're okay."*

Unless this was a ruse to throw me off his trail, Ted knew
nothing about Calvin's disappearance, but perhaps this Joe
fellow did. Had Calvin, in fact, "hooked up" with him and, if
so, *had* Joe been "too rough?" I consulted the address book
and matched Ted to T.S., living on Fern Road in a place called
Brentwood. Beneath it, scrawled in pencil, were driving
directions.

Minutes later, lying in bed, my brain all a doo-dah, watching the ceiling shimmy and swim, I decided that before knocking on Ted's door, it might be a good idea to know something
about him. His last name, for instance. While I did not own a
computer or even know how to use one, I suspected that one
would be invaluable right about now. I thought immediately
of Christy Van Winkler, the chubby girl who had picked me
up at the train station. If I remembered correctly, her boyfriend Bob Fox was some sort of computer genius. I called
Directory Assistance, but Christy was not listed. I tried the
studio where she worked. Again, no luck. It wasn't until the
wee hours of the morning, after downing another bottle of
sulfurous Chablis, that I remembered Eduardo Wiggins, the
black dandy. He guarded the gate at Christy's studio, and his
calling card was on my dresser. I spilled out of bed. The card
was embossed with gold and adorned with the masks of tragedy and comedy.

Eduardo answered on the first ring. Having been schooled
by Willow Stetz in the psychology of the Hollywood actor, I
applied sugar before plunging in.

"Eddie number two here. Hope I didn't wake you."

"Certainly not, old boy! Delightful to hear from you!"

"Did your audition go well?"

"It did not, I'm afraid. The director was absolutely beastly. I felt like knocking her spots off."

Oh, how his affectations rankled me. It was hard not to laugh in his face.

"I'm so sorry," I said.

"Alas, what *can* one do, but soldier on?"

"Better luck next time, I suppose. You're clearly a genuine talent. A force to be reckoned with."

"Thank you so much for saying that."

"Nonsense," I thrummed, "I enjoyed it. Now, down to business. I need your help. I don't know if you've heard the news, but I'm staying in town to investigate Calvin's disappearance."

"Well, I'm glad someone is. I rang that beastly Gin last night to see if he'd appeared, and she seemed to have given up on him entirely. She said if he wasn't back by week's end, she was going to throw all his belongings in the street."

"She's loathsome."

"Beastly. I fear something terrible has befallen him."

"So do I. That's why I need your help. I need to speak to an employee at your studio. I called the switchboard and they have no listing for her. Maybe you know her? Christy Van Winkler."

"Hmmm, can't say that I do, and I know everyone on the lot. Are you certain she doesn't work for one of the other studios?"

"No, no, it's yours."

"What does she look like?"

"Quite fat. Never stops smiling."

"Well, that hardly narrows the field."

"I'm sure if I could get past the front gate," I hinted, "I'd have no trouble tracking her down. She's hard to miss. What time do you go on duty?"

"Oh, crikey, old boy, I work nights this week! I'm at the studio now. My shift ends in an hour."

"Damn!"

"Don't fret, I'll sort you out."

Behind Studio Gates

There, directly across the street, stood the open mouth of the studio. Three guards manned the gate, all of them hulking African-Americans dressed like cops. Jesus must have sensed my apprehension, because before I got out of the truck, he patted me on the shoulder and wished me luck. Putting on a brave face, I told him that I did not need it. Who knows? Maybe I didn't. I had followed Eduardo's instructions to the letter: I was wearing linen pants, a loose blouse, and no socks. I held a thick manila folder in one hand and a cellular telephone in the other.

"You look good," Jesus said.

"Thank you," I replied, slipping on dark sunglasses.

As I crossed the street, I lifted the phone to my ear. Absolute precision was necessary, Eduardo had warned, because in recent years studio security had tightened to an almost paranoid degree. I strode at a brisk clip along the cement walkway that ran parallel to the car lanes. One of the hulking guards, a female with six-inch fingernails, was checking under a visitor's car with a mirror on a stick. She looked at me as I approached.

"Listen to me, you dunderhead!" I shouted, remembering the words of Mr. Shipp. "You don't buy this feature film, I assure you that someone else will. And when they open the envelope and your name's not on it, don't come blubbering to me, because—"

As I was about to pass her, a telephone rang. Not a telephone, *the* telephone. The one I was holding. All three guards looked at me. I felt a stabbing pain in my chest. Flop-sweat blossomed across my back. I was short of breath. Was this to be the site of my heart attack? Echoing Shipp again, I pressed the red button and violently shook the phone. "Piece of shit! God damn Japs! We save their asses in 1945 and this is how they repay us?"

The male guards smirked and nodded their heads.

"You got *that* right," the female muttered.

With a show of exasperation, I slapped the phone shut. Not a peep from anyone, as I strode past. Thirty seconds later, I exhaled. I had done it. I had breached the citadel, entered the holy of holies.

I suppose every American whose formative years were spent in the dark, staring up at the silver screen, thinks he has some idea of what the back lot of a movie studio is like, but I can assure you he is wrong. A more banal patch of concrete has never existed. Imagine a hundred beige airplane hangars set amid ramshackle bungalows and rundown villas. As for the mythology of the golden past, occasionally you spot a tiny plaque bolted to the side of a bungalow with the name of a dead movie star on it, but so what?

I wandered the lot for over an hour, stopping to make inquiries, but no one had heard of Christy. I was amazed at how corporate everyone looked. There were fast-walking young suits laughing in packs, thick-calved secretaries eating muffins on the run, and bloated money-people whizzing by on golf carts. The only exceptions were the rude mechanicals, the beer-bellied union men, squatting on oil drums, sucking down cigarettes. No wonder I attracted so much attention. I doubted that anyone present had ever beheld an actual artist. With my russet beard flaked with snow and my well-brimmed hat strung with plastic laurel, I perambulated past them with enormous pride in my position. I was no hack, but an authentic man of letters.

Finally, I plopped down in the commissary, near the doughnut display, where I knew Christy was sure to make an appearance. Another hour passed without event. Profoundly discouraged, I was ready for a swim, a tug, and a long nap. Was I too old to be a detective? Part of me wished I had never heard the name Calvin Wirt. As I hoisted my guts out of my chair, the universe rewarded me. There she was: Christy Van Winkler in all her massive glory, smiling ear to ear for no reason, filling a quart-sized plastic cup with cola. I scampered up behind her.

"Christy Van Winkler?" I purred, poking her in the back.

She spun around.

"Oh, my God! B.K! Hi! You scared me. What are you doing here?"

"It's a long story. A friend has mysteriously gone missing and might very well be dead."

"No way!"

"I need your help to find him. I tried to call you, but are you aware that your number is unlisted in both the city and studio directories?"

"It's in both," she chirped. "You just forgot my name is all. It's Sissy Winkle. Not Christy Van Winkler."

"Oh, dear. I *am* getting old."

"Good thing you found me. Today's my last day. I got fired. My boss was super pissed off when I got back so late from driving you to your motel. He says I'm way too distracted. By the way, I'm really sorry you and Harry couldn't make a deal."

"So am I," I sighed, casting my sad eyes to the window like a martyr.

"But if you don't mind me saying, Mr. Troop, I really think you shouldn't have walked away from the table. There's no way my uncle or anyone else is gonna let you direct the movie at your age. I'm just being honest."

I nearly choked. So that's how the old vulture had explained our parting of the ways? Indignation rose like lava in my throat, but, in a rare moment of prudence, I did not blow my top. I would let the child have her illusions about her uncle.

"Anyway, as I said I need your help. In the area of computering. I must speak to Bob."

"Who?"

"Bob Fox. Your boyfriend. He's a computer genius, isn't he?"

"Yeah, but his name is Ben Fuchs." She tittered. "You really suck at names. He'll help you. Do you have a pen?"

"I'm a professional writer. Of course not."

Sissy found one in her purse and wrote down his number. We took a short walk across the lot and stopped outside her building. I think it was obvious to both of us that we would never meet again. I detected a tear in her eye and felt a twinge of regret. If only she, instead of her wretched uncle, were a producer. On my way back to the truck, I phoned Ben Fuchs and he answered on the first ring. He said that he'd be more than happy to help me. How soon could I get to Pasadena?

Pasadena

"Those are the San Gabriel Mountains. When the sky is clear, they're beautiful, Mr. Troop. Very beautiful."

"I don't see any mountains," I said, listening to the fourth worried voice message from Ted to Calvin. "All I see are a jumble of ugly homes."

"No, *that* way," Jesus corrected.

I looked in the other direction and saw mountains barely outlined behind a grimy scrim. "Oh, dear, don't tell me that's smog."

"Yeah, it's smog," Jesus sighed. "But when the wind blows, the sky turns blue, and you see that this is one of the most beautiful places in the world. So many mountains. Some have snow, even in summer."

"You must be referring to the Santa Ana winds. They were blowing the day I arrived, but I never got a chance to admire their cleansing effects. I was too busy sneezing up my cilia."

"What's that?"

"The little hairs in my lungs."

"You got allergies?"

"And how."

"Me, too. Cats and dogs."

"Lucky for you it never rains here."

"What do you mean?"

"Never mind."

Ben Fuch's computer company was housed in a black office tower in a section of Pasadena known as Old Town. Regrettably, the only thing old about it was the architecture; everything else was as new as can be. With its chain restaurants and national retail outlets, this could have been downtown anywhere.

"I sure hope this guy can help you," Jesus said as he parked.

"Yes, it's an awful long way to drive for nothing."

"I'll be in there." He pointed to a toy store. "I need Christmas presents for my kids."

I was so preoccupied with the case that I had completely forgotten about the holiday, which was now just three weeks away. I silently prayed that by the time the blessed day arrived, Calvin would have turned up safe and sound, and I would be happily restored to The House Beautiful.

"Very well," I said, "have fun. Don't blow your wad."

Ben Fuch's company was a five-floor maze of oddly placed desks and carrels, staffed by workers whose average age I reckoned to be no more than twenty-six, but who behaved as though they were much younger. Everywhere I turned I saw them joshing, giggling, and roughhousing. More than a few received neck and hand massages at their desks. Each floor had a kitchenette, well stocked with candies, cakes, chips, and pastries. When I popped in for a nibble, I saw a trashcan stuffed with pizza boxes and beer bottles. Was it possible that a fraternity-house environment like this was actually conducive to serious work? I supposed it must be, or else they would not be in business.

I found Ben Fuchs sitting at a carrel in a far corner, typing at blazing speed and gazing with fierce intensity into a data screen. From the look on his face, one would have thought he was aligning the trajectory of nuclear missiles. Imagine my surprise when I saw that, in fact, he was cutting Taliban fighters in two with well-aimed spurts of cartoon gunfire.

"Ben?" I said.

"Yeah?" he answered, not even bothering to pause in the slaughter.

"B.K. Troop."

"Hey, hang on a sec."

For two minutes, I watched him lay waste to wave after wave of dusky assailants, sending them to a paradise of hot virgins and cold lemonade. Finally, when his proxy exploded into a well-deserved fireball of wriggling arms and legs, he spun around in his chair and reached out a hand. I half-expected to see powder burns.

"Nice to meet you," he said, pointing to an office chair. "Go ahead, sit down."

I obeyed. The chair was tiny and wheeled. I laid my hat on my lap. I was forced to remain very still, so as not to roll away. Ben was surprisingly trim and fetching, considering that he was dating Sissy. He was about twenty-eight years old, with twinkly blue eyes, a receding hairline, and a sneaky little mouth.

"You had no trouble finding me?" he asked.

"A little, but as every artist knows, the journey is more rewarding than the arrival."

"I don't get it."

"Neither do I," I said. "Let's get down to business."

He smiled and handed me a tissue. When he saw my confusion, he pointed to my shirtfront, which was flaked with chocolate shavings.

"I guess you found the doughnuts."

"Yes, I did," I answered, dabbing myself clean.

"Awesome place to work, huh?"

"The awesomest. It happens to be my first exposure to the world of high-technology. If you don't mind my asking, what on earth do you do here?"

"I'm part of a team that's developing a transport protocol cookie port."

I blinked slowly, trying to conceal the vacuum to which my mighty brain had been reduced.

"And what do they do in *there?*" I asked, pointing to a gigantic control room, whose walls bore huge, hectic, electronic displays.

"That's our Network Operations Center. We have five people running it full-time, with six main plasmas, each showing one of our serving clusters. There are thousands of individual machines and, with a click of a button, one of those guys can launch new software, reboot a machine, or kill one anywhere in the world. It also allows them to re-distribute traffic, as hackers attack, machines fail, or software that we launched is debugged."

Once again, had a cannonball and a feather been dropped through my consciousness, they would have fallen at the exact same speed.

"So what can I do for you?" he asked.

"I need forensic computer help. I'm investigating the disappearance of a friend. I suspect foul play. "

"You mean like murder?"

"Or murder itself. My only lead is a man by the name of Ted S. I have his address." I pulled my crime journal from its manila envelope. "I'm hoping that you can trace the address and tell me Ted's last name."

"You tried a google search, I assume."

I stifled a laugh: "Pardon me? A *what?*"

I imagined myself digging an index finger into my nose.

Ben swung over to his keyboard and unleashed a blaze of typing and smacked buttons. Not five seconds later, he said, "Ted Sommers, 1210 Fern Drive, Brentwood. Born in 1951. Graduated from Duke with a degree in History. The second youngest man ever to run a film studio."

I was gobsmacked. "Good Lord, you're a genius."

"Maybe, but a seven year old could have done what I just did. Let's see, what else? He's the founder and president of Durham Entertainment. He's got a bunch of stuff in development."

I started to scribble in my journal, but Ben stopped me. He hit a key on the computer and, moments later, a one-page biography of Ted Sommers slid out of a machine, piping hot. A few more struck keys and out came a color photo of Ted walking the red carpet. He was tanned, tall, handsome, and looked appallingly smug.

"Don't tell me a seven year old could have done *that.*"

"Afraid so."

"You're being modest."

"No, I'm not. You didn't even need to drive all the way out here. If I'd known what you wanted was so easy, we could have done the whole thing over the phone."

Ben was kind enough to walk me to the elevator, with a quick stop at the kitchenette.

Crunching down a handful of chips, he said: "I only eat junk food at work. I don't wanna set a bad example for Sissy. She's got diabetes, you know. Her doctor says if she doesn't stop with the sweets, she'll lose her legs someday."

Having been robbed of my appetite, I pocketed the rest of my jelly beans. Riding down in the elevator, I cursed myself.

I had always thought that the only penalty for my resistance to all things technical was the acorn-sized callus I bore on my writing finger, but now I knew better. I had wasted half the afternoon in search of data that I could have obtained without ever leaving the bamboo. Oh, well, we live and learn, I supposed. If we're lucky.

After a tiresome walk around many identical blocks, I at last found Jesus's truck. It was empty, so I crossed the street and found him at the toy-store cash register, buying a tiny plastic demon wielding an assortment of weaponry, an illustrated book of the Arabian Nights, and a zany girlish doll with spiked red hair, a mini-skirt, and whorish heels.

"I thought you had three *sons*," I said.

"Yeah," Jesus said matter-of-factly, "but my middle one, Domingo, he likes to play with dolls."

I nodded as though this were nothing out of the ordinary, but inwardly I was knocked for six.

Walking to his truck, I confessed: "Jesus, I must say I'm astonished. Not that your boy likes to play with dolls, but that you're so accepting of it."

"What can I do, Mr. Troop? My boy, Jesse, he likes *Star Wars*. The little one, Omar, he likes to read. He reads all the time. But Domingo, he likes dolls. Make-up, too. And Mommy's shoes. All day sometimes, he go through magazines, looking at the pretty clothes. If I tell him to stop, he'll just keep doin' it. Or maybe he'll stop, but feel very bad about who he is inside. Keep it secret. That's no good."

A divine man.

We crawled home during the six hours known in L.A. as rush hour. We were but one vehicle amid tens of thousands. The thought that so many people endured this insult every day of their working lives filled me with bottomless pity. What sort of an existence was this? My disquiet bled into the long hours of the night. Lying in my bed, listening to the distant ocean-sound of traffic whizzing by on Venice Avenue, I was overwhelmed by what the Germans call World-pain. My soul was suddenly as wide as the universe, and all I saw around me were lonely, anguished humans trapped in a meaningless dream, making the best of a terrible thing. One fleeting chance at life, yet most of them knew no joy at all except for an occasional pause from labor, a good meal or bowel movement, a particularly violent orgasm. I saw the city as an endless tract of winding roads, clogged with motorized coffins, leading nowhere. My malaise grew white hot, until not just this city, but all the earth was reduced to a cruel limbo, a waiting room before death struck home, ineluctable and absurd.

A Brief Torpor

Now that I had secured some insight into the identity of Ted Sommers, what exactly did I intend to do with it? Under what pretext would I ring his door bell? Would I tell him the truth or assume a false identity? I ventured out quite early, hoping to walk my way to an answer. For hours I trod the sunny autumn streets, exploring block after block of homes as mundane and depressing as any to be found in, say, suburban Florida. (Or so I imagined; I had never been south of Baltimore.) Cheap Christmas lights and plastic reindeer mocked me from windows and rooftop.

How on earth had it happened? I wondered. How had I, a man of more than seventy summers, ended up in this foul Eden, embroiled in a mystery that not a single living human being but me was working to solve? Was I a hero or a fool? I knew from my vast knowledge of Greek mythology that this was a question that every hero asks of himself when faced with insurmountable odds, but I also knew from Shakespeare that plenty of fools ask it, too.

Just before noon, I emerged from a block of Soviet-style apartment towers onto a roaring thoroughfare, and there, facing me, was a diner called American Hamburger. It looked like the syphilitic little sister of my beloved Parnassus Diner—there was no flashy chrome, no fiery neon, no ten-foot cake carousel in the window—but it was a good, old-fashioned hash house all the same, and I fairly galloped toward it. Before I had even entered, I knew that this was to be my home away from home.

Inside, I found not a crew of convivial Greeks, but a dead-pan trio of mustachioed Persians—father, son, and daughter—and even though the place had an ancient fishlike smell, the vinyl was spotless and the grill well scraped. As it was still a bit early for lunch, I fell into the booth of my choice and ordered a piping-hot *olla podrida*, curly fries, fruit salad, and half-caraf of Colombian Red (rooster greeting, bloody send-off).

I snatched a newspaper off a vacated booth and skimmed it: Snow expected in the East; the sloppy aftermath of a Turkish bombing; more heroes had perished in the sands of the Middle East, plus some of our own troops, too. All very dispiriting. I tossed the rag aside and, keen for another distraction, I engaged the daughter, a homely girl with fuzzy dundrearies, a criminal nose job, and a fat diamond ring on her finger. Her nametag said "Nedia." Unlike my favorite waitress back home (the retired Cassandra), this girl proved to be a real stick-in-the-mud. She did not approve of a man drinking alcohol before lunch and told me so in the bluntest way. I changed the subject to the approaching Christmas holidays, but she was half-Jewish and half-Muslim, and that was the end of that.

Later, lying on my back as the sinking sun robbed my room of its last light, I reflected back on my wasted day. At the core of my paralysis, I felt, was an irrational hope that this was not, in fact, reality, but a cheap paperback crime novel, and that at any moment the phone would ring, as it always did in such fictions, and the voice on the other end would provide me with a sign as to how best to proceed. A moment later, the phone rang. Overjoyed that the universe was falling into line with my hopes, I tumbled out of bed.

"Hello?" I said.

I heard only a dial tone. Odd. Then it rang again. I remembered with a curse that the night before I had fiddled with Calvin's phone, instructing it to ring instead of vibrate. It rang again. I raced over to the recharger. The phone glowed with the single word, "Bitch."

"Hello?"

"Eddie?" It was Gin, stoned off her tits.

"Yes, what is it?" I snapped.

"Buttermilk."

"What about it?"

"For his room. Paint. Buttermilk."

"Oh, I see. If Calvin doesn't turn up soon, you're going to paint his room buttermilk."

"Yeah."

I considered hanging up in her odious face, but then I decided to have some fun with her instead.

"A shade of yellow, isn't it?" I asked.

"Yeah ... pretty ... pretty ... yellow."

"The color of your son's murderers."

A long silence. She began to weep. Her moans were more than masculine, they were those of a tortured steer. I hung up, leaving her to her grief. Still incensed by her indifference to Calvin's fate, I dove into the swimming pool in the hopes of sharpening my senses and reviving my determination. I breast-stroked for many minutes, distracted only occasionally by the stage mother who glared at me from between her blinds. By the time I crawled out of the pool, gasping like a dying Poseidon, I had formed an ingenious plan.

Guns Kill People

When Jesus stopped the truck, I was certain that we must be in the wrong place. I had imagined a stone mansion lying in deep shadows behind impenetrable gates. Instead, Ted's home was a happy, white hacienda fronted by a cactus garden and ablaze with warm light. In the windows, a hundred guests were visible, milling and chatting. The street was jammed with luxury cars, being parked by eager, red-vested valets.

"Big party," Jesus said.

Seeing that there was no one checking names at the door, I changed my plan in the blink of an eye and asked Jesus to come with me. I could tell from the boyish smile on his beautiful face that he was more than a little flattered. Luckily, Jesus was a good dresser (white shirt, khakis, bomber jacket, clean boots), so we would not need to waste time with wardrobe. After handing over the truck, we strolled up the lighted walkway to the house, as though we had been there a hundred times before. I wore a gray tweed suit, a fedora, black Oxfords, and a classic detective's trench coat, all of which I had picked up at a local thrift store. The coat was stained and had lost its belt, but it had cost only twelve dollars, so I could hardly quibble. Pinned to the inside of its breast pocket was an essential prop delivered to me in a rare moment of selflessness by Eduardo Wiggins.

In the tiled foyer, I was surprised to see a heavy Spanish table stacked with pamphlets. A quick look at them told me that this was not a party, after all, but a fundraiser. Excellent—we would·not be shown the door; our money was as good as the next guy's. We descended three steps to the sunken living room. The ceiling was vaulted, its dark beams painted with a geometric design. Yards of shelves were filled with Pre-Colombian statuary.

Among the guests, most of whom were elderly married couples thick in waist and wallet, I noticed a number of mismatched pairs—debonair old men with poofy, silver hair and bright gold watches, holding onto the knotty biceps of gorgeous young women. It was only when I took a closer look at these females that I noticed their greasy skin, multiple healed piercings, rock-hard breasts, and tattoos at ankle and shoulder. These were not trophies to be paraded. They were strippers, porn stars, and call girls[11].

I led Jesus to the refreshment table, where I chose a lazy Santa Ynez Champagne and he a hard-working sangria. After a short stop at a big tray loaded with crab cakes and coconut shrimp, we stationed ourselves in a corner to observe. I spotted Ted Sommers at once, making his way through the crowd, doling out fifteen seconds of quality-time to each guest. He cut a dashing figure: well-built and well-tailored, with the immobile hair, dark tan, and chiseled features of a United States senator

---

11 During my sojourn in Hollywood I learned that there is a vast difference between an actress and a prostitute (whores are happier and have business sense), just as there is a vast difference between an actress and a porn actress (there are certain things to get ahead in her career that a porn actress will not do).

or a jewel thief. But I sensed at once what he was hiding underneath: the flat feet, spindly legs, swayed back, and barrel chest of the sociopath. I suspected, also, that in his undies lay nestled a mere acorn.

Suddenly Ted's eyes landed on me and consternation puckered his brow. He knew something was amiss. He walked straight over, smiling queasily, but just as he was about to speak, a male voice rang out: "Everyone? Folks? Hi, I'd like to say a few words!"

The room quietened and the guests turned around to face the speaker, a pretty boy with a Roman nose, longish black hair, and bedroom eyes drooping half way down his cheeks. Ted Sommers was the only person who did not turn around. He was too busy inspecting me from heels to hair.

"I'm sorry," he whispered. "I don't believe we've met."

"Don't be an imbecile, Ted. We met through Calvin Wirt."

For a fraction of a second, he looked scared, then he showed his most practiced smile.

"Calvin who?" he said. "I don't know any Calvin."

"Shhh!" I pointed to the speaker. Ted had no choice but to redirect his attention.

"Hi, I'm Paul Parisi, the president and founder of NMHV. No More Handgun Violence is a non-profit, tax-exempt organization founded in 1999 by a group of concerned citizens, moved by the increasing number of gun deaths in this country. We work to prevent firearm violence through a program of public education and prudent legislation. We're not working to ban handguns—we know that's a losing battle for now—we're just working to teach the public about their dangers. Up in San Francisco and Sacramento, we've made real progress. Now we're bringing the NMHV to Southern California and we need your help."

What followed was a lengthy testimonial about what had inspired Mr. Parisi's efforts. I don't remember the details, but they involved the violent murder of his sainted mama outside a Marin County cash machine. As he rabbited on, I watched Ted. It was clear that he could not concentrate on the tragic tale. He was far too preoccupied with me. The mention of Calvin's name had, in the idiom of my youth, knocked his socks off. When he was brave enough to meet my gaze, I stared back with a look as menacing as any I had ever mustered. Finally, when he was well marinated in his own sweat, I leaned into his ear.

"What do you say we park ourselves someplace quiet, *faggot?*"

He nearly jumped out of his turtleneck.

"What are you talking about?" he exclaimed.

I knew right then that he kept his sexual preferences secret even from his own psychiatrist.

"The ugliest living face is better than a mask," I snarled back. He had never read Schopenhauer, so he took the aphorism for my own. I gestured for Jesus to follow me. We marched away and ducked into the first room we found. Just my luck. A tiny powder room.

"Uh-oh," Jesus said, eloquently summing up the situation.

We had no choice but to stay and wait.

Moments later, Ted entered.

"You want to talk in *here?*" he asked.

"Yeah, I do," I said. "You got a problem with that, honey?"

He shrugged his broad shoulders. "I guess not."

He closed the door behind him.

"Cop a squat," I said, pointing to the turquoise toilet. Everything was turquoise. Part of a Santa Fe theme. He stared at me blankly, then obeyed.

"I'm Detective Inspector Edmund Reid of the LAPD Missing Person's Unit," I said, whipping open my trench coat and flashing my cookie cutter—which was nothing more than the studio security badge of Eduardo Wiggins.

"Can I see that again?" he asked, frowning.

"You had your chance. This is my associate, Lieutenant Jorge Vasquez."

"Good evenin', sir," Jesus murmured, playing along quite smoothly. "Sorry to interrupt your party."

Without planning it, we had fallen into good cop/bad cop.

"We're investigating the disappearance of a male prostitute by the name of Calvin Wirt. As you were one of his regular customers, I find it hard to believe you don't know him."

Silence.

"You called me before, didn't you?" he asked. "Using a different name?"

"No," I lied, blushing through my beard.

He stared for a long time, then exhaled heavily. "So he still hasn't turned up?"

"No, he hasn't, but his phone has, and there are seven messages from you on his recording service."

"Voice mail," Jesus murmured.

"Okay," Ted said, "I'm worried about him. So what?"

"I suggest you start talkin' right now. Come on, Abigail, blow the works."[12]

"Or you'll be in trouble!" Jesus exclaimed.

Suddenly, it was two bad cops. I threw Jesus a stern glance, and he instinctively exhaled and backed off.

"I was alone one night," Ted began. "Two or three months ago. I was lonely. I found Calvin's ad in one of those underground

---

12 I am a beautiful reader of the *New York Post*. I do the Police in different voices.

newspapers. I hired him. He didn't come as advertised. He was skinny. Bald. Homely. I felt sorry for him. He was sweet. I liked him. After a while, it wasn't business anymore. We became friends."

"You getting this, amigo?" I said to Jesus.

As he did not have a pen and paper, he looked at me bewildered.

"Go on, Sommers," I urged, leaning back on the sink and opening my trench coat. The garment released a foul odor worse than anything even my old carcass was capable of producing. At best, it had been worn by a vagrant; at worst, a dead one.

Ted continued: "One day, out of nowhere, Calvin said he wanted to be an actor. So I gave him a couple of contacts. An acting teacher. And a TV producer pal of mine, who gave him a job as a production assistant. Unfortunately, it only lasted a few days. Calvin hit on one of the actors. A minor, I guess. He was lucky they didn't press charges."

I wasn't sure I believed him. Then I thought back to the love poem he had scrawled in his notebook. Young and pink, indeed.

"Who's this Joe?" I asked. "The one you were afraid might have been too rough on him. Might have freaked him out."

Ted stared at me gravely. I had done my homework. I was a formidable foe.

"Joe Kenny," he sighed. "He's the acting coach. He has a theatre in Venice. I have a feeling Calvin isn't very talented, so as a gift I gave him a free hour with Joe. Joe's pretty tough. I figured he'd set Cal straight. Maybe convince him to give up acting altogether. When I never heard back from either one of them after their hour together, I was afraid maybe Joe had gone overboard. Cal's fragile, you know. He's attempted suicide a couple of times."

"Four times," I snapped back. This was a bluff, of course—I had had no idea Calvin was suicidal—but I needed to keep the upper hand.

"You got Joe Kenny's number?" I asked.

"It's in the book. In Venice."

I looked at Jesus. "You know where Venice is?"

He nodded.

"Is that it?" Ted asked, swallowing a smile. "Because I really should be getting back."

I studied his face. I noticed for the first time that his chin was weak. It was his only facial flaw, and he no doubt hated it, but his lack of testosterone made it impossible for him to grow a beard.

"Yeah, that's it," I growled.

Ted turned a saucy smile to Jesus and said, "So what's *your* story?"

No fool, Jesus read his meaning. "I got a wife and three kids," he declared stoically.

Ted winked. "Me, too."

I thought Jesus might throw up.

Then, right on cue, a knock. Ted opened the door. Outside stood a woman of thirty-five, as warm and wholesome as a blonde can be.

"There you are!" she sang. "What's going on? Paul's about to show us the new PSA."

"Honey, this is Ed Reid and Mr. Vasquez. They're starting the Glendale branch of the NMHV. Ed lost his boyfriend to handgun violence. Vasquez lost his father."

My Lord, he was an expert liar; it explained his success as both an adulterer and film producer.

"Hi, I'm Louise Sommers. We lost our boy Toby last year. He was playing with his grandfather's hunting rifle."

I felt as though I had been smacked in the chest with a medicine ball. I could not find words.

"I'm sorry, ma'am," I whispered.

She laughed and waved a hand in front of her face so that we wouldn't see her cry. "No, *I'm* sorry. These events always bring it back."

We all left the powder room.

"Let's scram," I whispered to Jesus. When he did not understand the word, I grabbed him by the elbow and led him toward the door.

On our way through, we stopped and watched, along with the other guests, a public service announcement that showed a toddler blowing into the barrel of a pistol as though it were a toy trumpet. It was so scary that before I knew it I was donating two hundred dollars. Ordinarily, I would have regretted it, as I am wasteful only within the compass of a dollar, but the money was Calvin's, so why not dig deep?

Impresario to Impresario

had booked a two o'clock appointment with the great man himself over at The Kenny Academy of Acting, but, having been forced by Eduardo to return his badge and having tossed my smelly trench coat, there was no possible way I could repeat my performance as Detective Reid. Lying in bed, braining it around, looking for a new identity, I heard a shriek and a splash. I jumped up and made it to the window just in time to see the stage mother screaming at poor little Molly, whom she had just tossed into the swimming pool. Pointing an evil finger at her, she screamed, "And I'll do it again, you give me anymore of that lip!"

"I'm sorry, Mama!" Molly whined, dog-paddling to the edge.

"You better be, you little brat!"

My new identity came to me like a thunderbolt. Five minutes later, I was standing at the woman's door, knocking loudly. I wore a Hawaiian shirt, khakis, and sunglasses—my new costume. Shivering on a deck chair, watching me timidly from inside the cape of her towel, was little Molly, clearly excited that the kind man from across the way was about to confront her tormentor.

"Yer time-out ain't over!" the mother barked.

"It's not Molly. It's your neighbor from across the way. I need a word."

The door flung open. "About what? Mind yer own business!"

"I have a financial proposition."

Her face changed shape, revealing long yellow teeth. Certain that I was about to offer her cash in return for sexual favors, she opened the door wider and stepped back. I flip-flopped in. The room was identical to mine, except that the base of her lamp was a toucan not a parrot and their bed was a queen not a king. The thought of that poor child being spooned all night by her mother was nothing short of tragic. I banished the image and hit the bamboo. She plopped onto the rattan across from me. Her cut-off denims were tiny. A tuft of pubic hair clawed out from one side like the hand of a buried miner. On her exposed midriff, I noticed a Caesarean scar and the edge of a jingoistic tattoo. How I would loved to have dismissed her as a rural freak, a mere suspicious mole on the body politic, but I knew she was more representative of America than I was, and it made me want to swim for New Zealand.

"Here's the deal," I said. "I would like to buy Molly an hour with a top-notch acting coach."

She took a moment to overcome her disappointment that she was not about to be rooted for beer money.

"She *is* an actress, isn't she?" I continued impatiently. "That *is* why you're here in Los Angeles, isn't it? To secure her acting work?"

"How'd you know that?"

"I'm highly intuitive. Has she ever taken an acting class?"

"She don't need to. She's what they call a natural."

"You're no judge of that. You can't possibly be objective.

Only a professional can make that determination, and Joe Kenny is just the man for the job. You *have* heard of Joe Kenny?"

Her eyes filled with panic. "What? Oh, yeah. You betcha. He's a good one, all right."

"Damn straight," I said, speaking her language.

"You say you wanna pay fer it? How much is that gonna cost you?"

"A small fortune."

"How come you wanna do it then? What do *you* get out of it?"

"The knowledge that I have contributed to Molly's welfare. I like her. I believe she has star potential."

"I don't gotta pay you back?"

"Nope."

"When you wanna do it?"

"Right now."

"Well, okay then, but I'm taggin' along. Gotta make sure there ain't no monkey business."

"You will *not* tag along, but I assure you my business is show, not monkey. I'm not sexually attracted to little girls. Or even big ones."

"I kinda figgered that."

"I salute your perspicacity."

"My what?"

"Your horse sense. I'll be back to pick her up at 1:15 sharp. Doll her up, please. I've never seen her in anything but a ratty bathing suit and a jacket of goose pimples. I have a hunch she cleans up nicely."

"Oh, yeah, pretty as all outdoors."

"Very well."

The next thing I knew, Molly and I were belted into the back seat of the pick-up, streaking down Highway 10. I hated

for Jesus to sit up front alone like a chauffeur, but I could not
have the frightened girl alone in back. When I explained the
situation, Jesus was more than happy to oblige. Another tes-
tament to his outstanding character. He was secure in his
self-worth.

Molly did, indeed, look as pretty as all outdoors, if the outdoors happened to be a garbage dump on the outskirts of Little
Rock. She wore baggy, faded blue jeans equipped with a dozen
zippered pockets, battered black sneakers, and a low-plunging
silk blouse that bared, where cleavage belonged, her bony, little
sternum. Her straggly golden hair, still reeking of chlorine, was
tied with green yarn. Poor neglected creature. I curled an arm
around her as a precursor to a great-grandfatherly hug. Her
little hand flopped right onto my crotch. She did not have to
think about it. It was a reflex.

"No, no, no!" I said, removing it at once. "We'll have none
of that."

She was bewildered, maybe even a little bit hurt.

"I am your friend and benefactor, Molly. I want to do nice
things for you, but I ask for nothing in return. Nothing, do you
understand? And certainly not that. Never, ever that."

She stared at me moon-eyed, as though I had just fallen
down her chimney, carrying a giant teddy bear. She smiled
vaguely and pulled my ear down to her cold lips.

"I love you," she whispered.

I snorted and coughed, but, in fact, I was stifling tears
that had sprung from nowhere. No, no, they were *not* from
nowhere—they sprang from my own dandled childhood,
from memories of midnight whispers, strange rashes, painful bruises, waking from nightmares to something far worse.
When I was just a boy, a concerned neighbor had dropped by
and found me holding a hammer and a screw, trying to install a

padlock on my bedroom door. I hugged Molly to my big belly and marveled at how we survivors find each other every time, and at how vital it is that we never reenact on others the cruelties inflicted on us, but instead give love, unselfish love, the only kind there is. We sat in silence for a long time, Molly and I. I watched the city streak past us beneath an unabashed blue sky. At one point, I met the eyes of Jesus in the rearview mirror, and I knew that he somehow understood everything.

Eventually, I explained to Molly that an hour of expert instruction lay ahead, whose sole purpose was to determine if acting is what she really wanted to do, or if it was merely what her mother really wanted her to do. If it was the latter, then she must tell me so, and I would see to it that she was returned at once to Fightville.

The Kenny Academy of Acting was located in a neighborhood that, according to Jesus, enjoyed its fair share of gangland activity. Looking at the benign blocks with their blooming gardens and trim lawns, I found the notion that criminals thrived there absolutely unimaginable. If a resident of the South Bronx fell asleep and woke up on these lawns, he would think he had died and gone to heaven, or, at the very least, suburban New Jersey. I supposed it was the illusion of safety that made life in Los Angeles so uncommonly dangerous.

A case in point came at the next stoplight, in the form of a mouthwatering young black man, well-scrubbed with a porcelain smile, wearing a powder-blue jogging suit. As he glided up, I whispered to myself, "O, pretty boy, trust not too much to your rosy looks," and gave him a kittenish wave. He scowled back as though we had some long-standing feud. Jesus urgently explained that the fellow was a gangster and that if I didn't stop waving at him, he might very well shoot me in the head. How he knew this, I have no idea. What a topsy-turvy place, I thought as I turned away, where the thugs are as good-looking as the actors, and the actors as ruthless as the thugs.

The Academy stood between a junk shop and a liquor store. Sliding four quarters into the meter, I informed Jesus that we shouldn't be more than an hour and that he should keep himself occupied in any way that he could. In front of the humble storefront, I gussied Molly up a bit, fluffing her lank hair and wiping the rouge off her cheeks with two spitty thumbs.

"Just be yourself," I told the child.

She nodded emphatically.

Someday she would understand that there is nothing more difficult.

When we entered the Academy, a little bell rang and, a moment later, a toilet flushed. Joe Kenny emerged from the restroom, wiping his hands with a coarse paper towel. He was a slim-hipped fellow of medium height and build. He was about forty, I guessed, and wore black lizard-skin cowboy boots, black denims, and a Western-style shirt with mother-of-pearl snaps. His small, black eyes, prominent nose, and olive skin, told me that Kenny was not his birth name. No, Joe was an East-coast Jewish boy, who, rebelling against his bourgeois up-bringing, had, like so many before him, escaped his mother's vampiric embrace and father's brow-beaten silence, by heading west and embracing all things cowboy.

"How ya'll doin'?" he said.

"Splendidly. How are *you* all?"

"Fine and dandy. Guess you're Mr. Reinhardt."

"Please, just call me Max."

"And who's this little beauty?"

I realized in a flash that I did not know the child's surname, so I made one up.

"My latest discovery. Molly Maguire."

Joe knelt and studied the girl. I seized the opportunity to look around. It was a makeshift theatre lobby, hung with dozens of black-and-white stills from various dramatic productions. Smack dab in the center of each was the great Joe himself, wearing a sleeveless, white T-shirt, in the throes of some intense, and no doubt sincere, anguish. On a peg above the plywood refreshment counter hung a tasseled buckskin jacket and a five-gallon cowboy hat. He was a regular Zebulon Pike, this one, but with a bald spot and small potbelly, and on a leather cord between his pectoral muscles (I had a hunch) an 18-karat Star of David.

"Whatcha wanna be when you grow up?" he asked Molly.

"A movie star," she replied.

"Say it louder."

She said it softer instead: "A movie star."

"Louder!" he commanded.

"Movie star," she mouthed silently, a tear rolling down her cheek.

"She's shy," he diagnosed, glancing at me.

The great man did not disappoint.

"Yes, she is," I said, "but not on stage. Last year, she played Helen Keller for me and her howls of 'Wa-Wa!' fairly shook the rafters."

"So, how'd you hear about me?" Joe asked, standing up.

"Calvin Wirt."

I waited for a reaction and got one. His brow tensed and his eyes retreated behind his nose.

"He *recommended* me?"

"He said you were a genius."

He frowned, trying to process this.

"You seem surprised," I said.

"Let's talk." He turned to Molly and pointed. "You sit over there like a good little girl. Don't you move, okay?"

Without hesitation, she walked over to the plastic chair, sat, and did not move a muscle. Like most abused children, she was submissive to a blood-chilling degree.

Joe led me through a black curtain into a thirty-odd-seat theatre with auditorium seats of tattered, red plush. The floors were black and dusty. On the small stage stood a bedroom set with French doors that opened onto a veranda hung with plastic magnolia blossoms. I guessed a Southern drama. *Katz on a Hot Tin Roof?*

"Mind if I smoke?" Joe asked.

"I insist."

We lit up together—I, my twentieth generic of the day; he, a delicious name brand, the favorite of cattle ranchers everywhere.

"How do you know Calvin?" he asked, pushing smoke through his fine nostrils.

"I directed him in a play."

This surprised him as much as Calvin's recommendation had.

"What play?" he asked.

"*Twelfth Night.* He was my Malvolio."

Silence.

"Where was this?" he asked.

"The Starlight Dinner Playhouse of the Ozarks, in Elmer's Junction, Arkansas. I'm the Artistic Director."

"Was he any good?"

"His gangly limbs and doleful countenance were ideal for the role."

"Yeah, sure, but what about his acting?"

"Abysmal. When he entered in his cross yellow garters,

red chiffon tam, and green plaid sporran, the laughter was so tumultuous that he immediately dried up. He needed a half-dozen prompts just to make it through the scene."

Joe relaxed a bit; this was clearly the first thing I had said about Calvin that matched his expectations.

I leaned forward in my chair. "Just between us, Joe, impresario to impresario, how did *you* find his work?"

"God awful."

"But you straightened him out, right? Taught him a thing or two?"

"Here's the story, Max." He stretched out his slender legs. Around his girlish wrist he wore a yogi bracelet. Considering how dismally the cowboys treated the coolies, it made no historical sense whatsoever.[13]

"A pal of mine sent Calvin over," Joe explained. "Said the kid wanted to be an actor, but he didn't think he had what it takes."

"Monstrous self-regard?"

"Talent."

"That's what I meant."

"He said if Calvin was no good, I should tell him so. I said 'You bet.' See, that's my whole method, Max. It's what I'm known for. I'm a straight shooter."

"So you filled him fulla lead, huh?"

"Well, here's how it went—" He pinched his tawny filter and sucked deep. "The kid comes in, and he's nervous as hell. I gave him sides to read. From a classic."

I assumed he meant a classic of the English or American stage, but he meant a classic film—a comedy only twenty years old.

---

13 They shot them for sport.

"His reading was poor. I'm not even sure he understood half of what he was saying. I told him so. I said, 'Kid, you got nothin'. And, even if you did, you're ten feet tall, wear a wig, and weigh a hundred and twenty pounds. What the hell are you gonna play? A god-damn flamingo?'"

"Oh, dear."

"He took a swing at me."

This was a side to Calvin's nature that I had never suspected. If there was one word to describe the young man I had known for ten hours, it was "gentle."

"What happened next?" I asked, at the literal edge of my seat.

"I hit him back. Didn't want to, but the way he was swinging at me . . . . I socked him once is all. In the only place I could reach. The breadbasket. He fell like a bale of hay." He pointed his cigarette to the floor at the foot of the brass bed. "Right there. His wig landed over there. I felt terrible. He cried like a baby, saying how he wanted to be an actor more than anything in the world, and how he'd kill himself before he'd quit. Let me tell you, I felt lower than . . . than—"

"A rattlesnake's belly?"

"Whatever. The last thing I wanna do is drive some poor kid to suicide."

There was that word again. Was it possible that Calvin had merely killed himself? Could it be that terribly simple? This would require serious consideration.

"How did you leave it with him?" I asked.

"I helped him to his feet, dusted him off, and told him that if he really wanted to be an actor, then he shouldn't listen to me or anyone else. I said, 'You get out there, kid, and prove me wrong!'"

"Did he buy it?"

"Oh, yeah. Charged outta here full of piss and vinegar."

"Phew."

"Now he's callin' me a genius? I don't get it."

"You must have worked some magic."

"I reckon I did, Max."

I went to fetch Molly, but she was no longer in the plastic chair. I banged on the restroom door. No reply. I dashed outside, heart racing, afraid that a passing pervert, spying her through the window, had beckoned her with penny candy. Thank heaven, I found her laughing with Jesus on the hood of his truck, slurping a can of orange soda. She looked happier than I had ever seen her. It grieved me to tear her away, but I had promised her mother that she would receive a free hour of instruction, and I am, if anything, a man of my word.

Verdict

After an hour, Jesus and I returned to the lobby and found Molly waiting for us, unblinking, in her plastic chair. A moment later, a toilet flushed and Joe Kenny emerged from the restroom again. I suspected an irritated bowel, born of a lifetime's worry that photos of his lavish Bar Mitzvah would be leaked to *Variety*. He threw me a look that said he needed to talk to me alone. I passed the look onto Jesus, who in an instant was out the door, carrying Molly.

"Well, pardner, what's the verdict?" I asked.

Joe shook his head as one does after witnessing a fatal rodeo spill. "Oh, she's good, Max. *Really* good. I've never seen anything like it."

This was not what I had expected.

"The kid's got it!" he kvelled. "I gave her a monologue from *Double Trouble* and, damn, if she didn't nail it to the wall."

"What's *Double Trouble*?"

"A screenplay I wrote. About a governor's twin daughters who get kidnapped by terrorists. Only the twins're scarier than the terrorists. It's pretty darn hilarious."

"Sounds it. So you think she might have a future?"

"Maybe I'm not making myself clear. This is the most talented kid I've ever come across. And she can take direction, too. I told her to do it three different ways, and every time she nailed it."

"To the wall?"

"Every time. A little prettying up and two hours a week with me, and she'll be getting work in no time. Damn, I sure wish I'd seen that *Miracle Worker*."

"I'll get you a video copy. She was superb. She won the Golden Armadillo. Our version of the Tony."

"I'm not surprised."

"Thank you so much for this, Joe. I'll pass your recommendation on to her mother. How much do I owe you?"

"Two hundred. That's my rate."

"I see. I hope you aren't saying all these nice things about Molly simply to exploit the situation financially. Because if you are, I must tell you, it would be most cruel. Her mother's fresh off the worm farm. To afford your lessons, she'll have to beg, hook, and steal."

"I don't need money, Max. I've got students coming out my ass. Molly's the real thing, simple as that."

I forked over ten of Calvin's twenties, and departed with the promise that I would do everything in my power to make sure that Molly's mother followed through on his plan.

Back at the Palms Plaza, I found her rubbing suntan oil on her white, bony legs. She flipped coquettishly onto her side, like an odalisque.

"Well?" she twanged eagerly.

I sent Molly inside for a nap.

Before delivering Joe's verdict, I stared at the woman long and hard. In every crease of her hangdog face, in her sharp, glistening eyes, in her hungry smile, I saw, writ large, the hardscrabble poverty of her childhood, the domestic labor that had robbed her teenage years of all delight, and how she, too, had endured an unwanted caress or two, or ten, from a neighbor or uncle, until they weren't unwanted anymore (or if they were, she had forgotten), and how all the misery born of these trials, rather than soften her to compassion, had hardened her for revenge, not only toward men, but toward all the living world. She was stupid, cruel, slothful, and cash-hungry. The moment she learned of Molly's huge talent, her nipples would harden and dollar signs would quiver to a stop in her eyes, like lemons in a slot machine. Oh, she would do just as Joe had instructed, and when her money ran out, she would do anything to stick to the plan, even if it meant renting herself, or even her daughter, to smelly strangers. So what if it stole the last of her own dignity or the last of Molly's innocence?

Molly *would* be a star, I knew it. Treading the boards? Of course not. *I* would have made a better Helen Keller. But Hollywood was a different matter altogether. Making movies was about creating images that lived in the unconscious mind long after the story was ridiculed or forgotten. No surprise then that, since the birth of cinema, those most able to flourish in the enterprise were those whose childhoods had been so appalling that they lived in dreams themselves. One only had to think of, say, Miss Norma Jean Mortenson, alias Marilyn Monroe. Born to an insane mother, raised in foster homes, molested as a teen, and passed around like a sperm cookie by the studio moguls, Marilyn ended up a desolate, pill-popping, baby-talking nymphomaniac—and the greatest international sex symbol in cinema history. Of course Molly would become a star; she had all the prerequisites. She would do as she was told, twisting herself into any shape that directors demanded, and if she, too, became suicidal in the process, who would notice or care?

"She's dreadful," I declared. "One of the *least* talented children Mr. Kenny has ever had the misfortune to meet."

The woman was stunned. Her jaw eased open, and I beheld a lode of mercury fillings.

I showed no mercy: "Molly is without poise or grace. Her diction is rotten and her voice grating. But he did concede that she is highly intelligent. He suggests you whisk her back to Fayetteville at once, so that she might apply herself to her studies and perhaps one day become a doctor or a lawyer, both of which are highly lucrative professions."

This inspired a flicker of hope in the beast's eye, which she took with her as she returned to Room 13.

Lying in bed that night, I questioned what I had done, examining it from both sides. In the end, I decided that it was the right thing. I had given Molly her last, best chance at a normal life. But would her mother go along with it? I got my answer the next morning when I awoke to her screaming: "God damn it, girl! You forgot to pack your culottes! Here they are, right under the bed!" A minute later, she swore up a storm as she lugged something from the room. Molly whimpered an apology. The gate tinkled and slammed. No more voices. Tires crunched the gravel. The engine roared as tires hit the street.

I learned later, from an irate Tupta Parween, that Molly and her mother had left without paying the bill and that their credit card and license plates were stolen. I wished that, overhearing their getaway, I had stepped outside or at least cracked the blind. Surely Molly had turned around at the gate, hoping to see me one last time.

Through a Wine Glass, Darkly

Day was night and night day, waking dreaming and dreaming waking. The only interruptions to my delirium were bouts of midnight smoking, a burst of rain, and an occasional agitation of gravel which told me that another delivery boy had arrived to break my fast, slake my thirst, or fill my lungs with ash and embers. No sooner was the meal devoured (dinner was breakfast, breakfast dinner), the bottles downed, or the carton dented, than the cycle began again: dawn was dusk, dusk dawn, and when I woke up from my hagridden sleep it was always with a deadly fear of waking. I felt that I was rolling in the pitch dark, down the torrent of a terrible fate, and that nothing could stop it. My stomach toiled and moiled. A most unexpected depression, it was, but its source was no mystery.

A venerable, old meaning of the word *clew* is "a ball of thread." No surprise, for it is a ball of thread that enables Theseus to escape the labyrinth. Expanding on the metaphor, my emotional collapse was a result of being lost in a maze, clueless.

Desperate to escape, but lacking the crucial ball of thread, I longed, simply, to disappear. I lifted the phone three times to call Amtrak, but each time I slammed down the instrument, unwilling to abandon Calvin. Good God, this was not astrophysics, it was detective work, and if I wasn't up to the challenge, then how on earth had any mystery *ever* been solved? How many flatfoots on earth were even half as clever as I was?

I had learned somewhere that the cornerstone of investigative work is rarely the application of the deductive mind to a set of observable facts, but, rather, blind luck and tips from anonymous do-gooders. As I was the beneficiary of neither, whenever I found the will to resume my investigation, I had no other option but to call Calvin's customers again. They knew my voice by now, so no matter what name I used, they hung up immediately. Twice I called Gin Reinheimer, to make sure that Calvin had not turned up and she had forgotten to tell me. Calvin was still missing, she said, and his room, painted buttermilk now, was occupied by Anson Diamond, who had been kicked out of his residential center for sexual misconduct—a common occurrence among the mentally retarded as they storm, slobbering, arms windmilling, toward puberty. What a ménage! Gin, a dozen dogs, Anson, and a kilo of locoweed. I prayed that I would not be spending Christmas there.

Whenever my telephone rang, which was rarely, it was always Jesus checking in. I was too ashamed to tell him the truth, so I told him that there had been some very interesting developments in the case and that any day now I would be requiring his services. I am not sure if he believed me, but his credulity was certainly challenged one Monday morning when he dropped by to collect his previous week's wages. He was alarmed by both my appearance and that of my room, with its overflowing ashtrays, wastebasket filled with empties, and on every surface the oily remnants of take-out meals. I told him not to fret, that detective work required fierce focus and that I was on the verge of a breakthrough. I almost believed it as I said it, but he did not. He insisted that I bathe.

The thought of exposing my stinking corpus and drunken brain to water was almost unbearable, but the man would not take no for answer, so I forced myself into the spray with all the poise of an alley cat. The run-off from my bulk was of a greyish-green hue, which even today I gag to recall. Despite its first shock, however, the shower proved to be refreshing, and I stepped from it with enough sobriety to trim my beard, eyebrows, nostrils, and ears. When I reentered the room, naked as the day I was born, Jesus did not interpret this as a come-on, but rather with the clinical cool of a nurse. He handed me a pile of not-so-dirty clothes. I threw them on and, when I saw myself in the mirror, I did not look half as repulsive as I had feared. Again, I had lost plenty of weight. My bosoms had shrunk and my cheekbones could have cut glass. Jesus took me by the hand, quite literally, and walked me to his truck.

"You been eatin' junk food," he said.

He sped me not to American Hamburger, as I demanded, but to a health food restaurant, where he ordered me a breakfast entree that resembled a boiled Earth Shoe on a bed of lawnmower clippings. It was not tasty, but I doubted that it was meant to be. As I grazed, we discussed the case. I shared with him the meager fruits of my logic: Calvin had died in an accident, been murdered, killed himself, or simply walked away from his life. If it was the last, then he had done it either against his will (amnesia) or willfully (selfishness). Of all the possibilities, this seemed the least likely. No one simply drives into the sunset without his money and phone. It would have cost him nothing to return home instead, eat a hunk of cake, and then, upon waking, grab his few belongings and drive into the sunrise. Amnesia, too, seemed unlikely, as it was the stuff only of bad fiction and the best television. Had there been a car accident? A fiery wreck that had left his body too charred to be identified? No, because The Wine House was only a few blocks away; we would have heard the sirens.

What of suicide? It was not out of the question. While reason says that he would have simply returned home, waited for his guests to leave, then hanged himself in the closet or driven off a cliff into the wild, black yonder, reason has no portion in suicide. I have known in my rich and varied life many instances where suicide defied all logic: a psychiatrist that jumped out the window with a sniveling client clutching a tissue not ten feet away; a father who blew his brains out on Christmas morning after filling his triplets' stockings; even a manic-depressive bartender who swallowed poison in the middle of a rollicking dance floor. In short, the impulse to self-slaughter often comes on like a gang of crazy clowns.

Perhaps, puttering down the block toward The Wine House, Calvin was suddenly seized by the desire to die (a desire which, if Ted Sommers was to be believed, he knew quite well) and had simply driven on and on until there was nothing but the dark road ahead and the moon above. He yanked a sharp turn onto the chaparral, and, when his tank was close to empty, he stopped, stuffed his shirt into the tailpipe, and lay down in the back seat to meet his Maker and Émile Tonkin. This would explain why his body had yet to be found except, perhaps, by a pack of clever coyotes who had managed to open the back door.

Jesus nodded sagely. "Yeah, it's possible."

"But you don't think so?"

"No," he said, "I don't."

"What *do* you think?" I asked. "Was he kidnapped? And, if so, why? He couldn't be worth much as a sex slave."

Jesus gathered his noble brow. "Mr. Troop, Calvin liked to make people happy. He was always doin' nice things for people. Once Mrs. Reinheimer wanted a burrito, but it was rainin' very hard. Calvin, he goes out to get it for her, even though the wipers on his car are broke. I told him, I said, 'Calvin, that's stupid. You don't go out in the rain like that with no wipers. It's too dangerous.' He says, 'But she was hungry.' That's the kind of person Calvin was."

"Yes, I know. He ran out to fetch me wine coolers in the middle of his own birthday party."

"Sometimes Calvin would have a date, but if Mrs. Reinheimer needed somethin', he'd cancel the date. That's why he was so poor, why he never bought a house."

"A house?"

"That was his dream, Mr. Troop. A little house. But he never saved enough money, because he was always doin' things for people. After my accident, he gave Maria a thousand dollars. He said, 'I don't care if you never pay me back.'"

"So how does this relate to his disappearance?"

"I don't think he would just drive away. Or kill himself. Not with a party goin' on. He'd move out first . . . pay his rent . . . say good-bye to me and Maria and the boys . . . then maybe he'd do it."

"So what *do* you think happened?"

"I think maybe he saw someone in trouble. Maybe a guy whose car was broke down. He helps him. He couldn't call and tell you because he didn't have his phone. So Calvin gave this person a ride and this person killed him."

"You think he's dead then?"

"I think so. He's been gone a long time."

"What do you think I should do?"

"Go home. If one day Calvin comes back or they find his body somewhere, I'll call you. But you got a family, right? Many friends? I think you should go home. Have a good life."

His argument was faulty only in that I did not have a family and many friends. I presided over a house of young artists who enjoyed my low rent and aesthetic guidance, but who deemed me a cumber and a nuisance. The only exception was, of course, Adrian and even his patience I sorely tried. I might have told Jesus this, but I avoid self-pity whenever possible. Instead I said, "I have a better idea. Let's pop by the morgue."

Open Sesame

"Department of the Coroner."

"Yes, hello. How are you this morning?"

"Fine, sir, how are you?"

"Unwell."

"I'm sorry to hear that."

"I would like to visit your morgue today."

"I'll connect you to the P.O."

A couple of rings, then a deep, mellifluous voice: "Captain Kelly."

"Hello, Captain Kelly, I would like to visit your morgue today."

"What for?"

"A friend of mine has gone missing, and I fear he's dead. I'd like to take a look at your unclaimed corpses."

"I'm sorry, we don't do that."

I detected a hint of hostility.

"That's ridiculous. A young man has gone missing and—"

"Listen, friend, I've got three hundred Does here, wrapped and tagged. We start *unwrappin'* 'em, we'll be at it all day."

"So even if I were the boy's mother, you'd refuse me?"

"I'd show you some photos."

"I'd like to see photos, please."

"You're not his mother."

"How do you know?"

"'Cause you're a male."

"Touché."

He laughed. He appreciated my wit. There was hope.

"Here's the situation, officer. His father is deceased and his mother's serving time in Alaskan state prison for drug dealing. Which means that no one on the planet cares where he is but me. I owe it to him to find out if he's dead."

"Did you file a missing persons report?"

"Of course, but the cops with whom I filed it were, pardon my candor, imbeciles. Real mouth-breathers."

"Listen up now. Every missing persons report is sent to us, and we do our best to match 'em to our Does. If there's no easy match, we run the prints through the state computer. If the Doe has a criminal record or even a California license plate, that'll come up, too."

"But with so many carcasses in your freezers, surely the system isn't foolproof. An occasional stiff slips through the cracks, no?"

He exhaled wearily. "Sir, I've got no time for this."

"Fine, fine. Let me speak to your superior."

"He's in a meeting."

"Well, then, please have him ring me. The name is Troop. B.K. Troop. I'm staying at the Palms Plaza Hotel. The number is—"

"What did you say your name was?"

"B.K. Troop."

He went falsetto: "Get out!"

"Why?"

"The writer?"

My heart skipped a beat.

It had long been a secret hope of mine, since the publication of *Christopher,* that I would one day be recognized by a random member of the reading public. I had always pictured it taking place in a crowded bistro or night club. I would be sipping a cocktail, hear a gasp, and look up directly into the saucer-eyes of a pretty stranger who hardly dared believe that he was beholding in the flesh his literary hero. I might feign annoyance for a minute or two, so as not to seem too easily won, but then I would invite the boy to sit down with me. For the next ten or fifteen minutes, he would lavish me with the most excessive and sincere adulation, and then, when it was time for me to toss him back into the great swamp of anonymous humanity from which he had crawled, I would give him whatever he wanted—an autograph, a hug, even a long soul kiss. Although this fantasy had played out in my head a thousand times, no version of it had ever starred a Los Angeles cop working the morning shift at the Los Angeles morgue.

"In the flesh," I purred.

Modesty forbids me to share what came next, but I will say this: he was most articulate in his conviction that *Christopher* was a high-mark of twenty-first-century fiction. (Even though the century was still young, I still took it as high praise.) He had read the book twice, in fact. My only disappointment— and this was another departure from my fantasy—was that the second time he read it, it was in bed, aloud, to his *girlfriend.* I'd always wondered if there might be a heterosexualist or two among my fan base and at last I had found one. It could not have happened at a better time or in a better place, because his worship triggered a small miracle. Just as the red-velvet ropes of the world's most glamorous discotheques are unclipped for

VIP's, so, too, the heavy granite doors of the city tomb were flung wide open for little old me.

A Second Digression

As the winsome, bug-eyed genius, Mr. Laurence Sterne[14] once said, "digressions are the sunshine of life." Which says as much about the rarity of sunshine in England as it does about his fondness for digressions. It also explains why life in sunny Hollywood sometimes seems to be nothing *but* digressions. It's not true, of course. All it takes is for a genuine digression to appear and one realizes that one's life in Los Angeles had been advancing all along. One *did* have a goal. One was not merely chasing one's tail in the noonday sun.

An ideal time for a second digression! The drive to the morgue was worse than the drive to Sun Land. Bumper to tailpipe we crawled, a million sorry souls, down Highway 10. It was a full hour before we even spotted the office buildings of downtown, towering like a tiny chunk of Manhattan against a blanched sky. We chugged onto another highway that cut into the thick of the action, but it only led to another highway, which led to another, which led to an exit labeled Mission Drive. We drove along this

14 It must be noted here, given the placement of this mention, that when Sterne died, his corpse was stolen by medical students and dissected.

road for a mile or two, into a district dominated by shops selling Hispanic auto glass. Everywhere I looked there were unsightly signs and billboards, and, running below us like a river,
another clogged, dismal highway. If I were a city planner and
needed a spot to dump my dead, this would be it.

The long drive, rather than a barren gulch in the desert of
my investigation, proved to be an oasis, because Jesus seized it
as an opportunity to talk about himself. It all started when, after a long swig from my flask of strawberry wine, I asked, quite
perfunctorily, where he was from.

"Juchipita Zacatecas, Mexico," he said.

"Is that a large city?" I asked, trying not laugh at the funny
name and the funny way he said it.

"Maybe 50,000 people. We were very poor."

"Yes, I assumed as much."

"My father wasn't like a father. He was like a general. Very
mean. When I was a boy, he'd tell me, 'I've got nothin' to give
you. All you get when I die is what I teach you. And all I can
teach you is how to live.' So he was always tellin' me things,
like, 'Make sure the ground is strong before you take a step' or
'Never spend one penny more than you have.' Things like that.
Life lessons."

I remained uncharacteristically silent.

"When I was twelve years old," he continued, "he sent
me to live in the mountains. With an eighty-year-old man.
He said, 'If you survive there, you survive anywhere.' Once a
week he brought us food. But sometimes he would forget to
come, so we'd eat rabbit, and seeds from the trees. Oh, I was
very sad, Mr. Troop. Lonely. I thought he didn't love me. One
winter, he didn't come with the food. For one week . . . two . .
. three. The old man and me, we walked down the mountain,
and when we got to my house, we found out that my father

was dead. No one told me because no one knew where I was."

I was interested now.

I rolled down the window and flamed a cigarette.

"Go on," I said.

"I was fifteen years old when I came to Los Angeles. I came with my sister Norma. She was seventeen. We had papers to go to school. Very soon she met a rich man and married him, but he was very mean. He drank too much and didn't like that she had a brother. When she saw me, it had to be a secret, and she was afraid to give me money, because if he found out, he'd beat her up. I only stayed in school for a little time, because I had no one to support me. I was all alone. I worked as a janitor. I cried, Mr. Troop. I slept in a car and I cried every night."

He took a difficult breath.

Who would ever have imagined that beneath this man's placid demeanor there lurked such a tortured history? I thought of Mr. Alexander Pope and his depiction of the young scholar, climbing the mountain of knowledge, who, when he has reached what he believes to be the summit, looks up only to see that "hills peep o'er hills, and Alps on Alps arise!" But I was not looking up at peaks. I was looking down fathoms into a man's most painful memories. And there were more to come.

"Then I met a man," Jesus continued. "I met him when I'm cleanin' his office and he said he felt very sorry for me. He said, 'I'll make a deal with you.' He said if I come and took care of his garden, I could sleep in his garage, and he'd teach me English. I was very scared, but I said yes. Today, I call him my guardian angel, because he taught me how to dress, how to speak English, how to be with people. He said, 'When you talk to a man, look him in the eye. Don't put your head down. Don't be afraid. And when you shake hands, do it strong, because you're as good as he is.' For four years, I worked in his garden. I learned how to take care of flowers . . . plant vegetables . . . trim trees. Soon, I worked for his friends, too. I made good money. I found a little house. The man said, 'You're not a gardener no more. You're a landscaper now.' He told me how much money to charge for my work. Every day, he taught me new words in English. When he died, I went to his funeral. I wanted to say something, because this man was my hero, my guardian angel, but his children, they said I couldn't talk. No time."

"Bigots!"

"But I'll tell you, Mr. Troop, my father is also my hero. I have children, so now I understand that he loved me very much, but he was poor, and he wanted my life to be better than his. He wanted to teach me things to help me survive. He would have done anything for me, just like I would do anything for my sons. Anything to protect my boys."

Listening to this, I thought how curious it is that most of us secretly believe that negative ethnic stereotypes are grounded in some truth, and yet positive ethnic stereotypes (the all-forgiving Christian black grandmother; the taciturn, noble Yankee doctor; the snide but golden-hearted piss-queen; the eager, happy Chinese waiter) we dismiss out of hand. Yet here I was, face to face with a bona fide Mexican laborer-saint. And his name was Jesus!

When he had finished his story, he asked me about *my* life, something that almost never happens. I told him a great deal, but not too much, suggesting that it would save us both a lot of time if he simply picked up a copy of *Christopher*, and, eventually, of *The House Beautiful*. He was wildly impressed to learn that I was a novelist and promised not only to read both books himself, but to pass them on to his wife, Maria, as well, who was an avid reader.

No, Jesus was not wealthy, and, yes, he had a painful bone

chip in his neck that forced him to squire me around, but he was a lucky man. He had a loyal wife who adored him and three sons whom he cherished—he lacked for nothing essential. By what possible measure could I be considered his superior? Yes, of course, I had read a few thousand more books than he had and logged far more sensual adventures, but so what? I spent most of my waking hours trapped in a lonely daydream, and when I *did* confront the truth of my existence, it was almost always against my will and at a tremendous outlay in terms of mucus and tears.

At last, Jesus turned the wheel into the grounds of the coroner's department. To our left was a gorgeous structure of red brick, the most wonderful building I had seen since leaving Union Station, but the guard told us that this was not our destination. He pointed to a dreary, institutional-looking building in back. We found a spot next to a phalanx of bright white cars whose doors were marked "Coroner." Strolling past us were two men dressed like ice cream vendors. The sawbones of the dead!

Walking up to the front door, Jesus eyed me as I stole one last snort of wine.

"Why do you drink so much, Mr. Troop?" he asked.

As hard as this might be to believe, no one had ever asked me this question before.

Deflecting it, I said, "Because I'm so often thirsty."

When he did not find this amusing, I told him that his question was serious and deserved a serious answer and that as soon as I had one, I would give it to him. He seemed content with this, but I was not. He had set my noggin spinning. But not for long. I had a more pressing mystery to solve.

Teeth and Tongue
Will Get You Hung

The scarred, indigenous creature behind the dirty glass at the Los Angeles County Coroner's office handed me a nametag and Jesus a parking pass. A moment later, an electronic door clicked open and Captain Kelly strode in. He was a black man with skin the color of perfect wheat toast. His bearing was aristocratic. He wore a fancy gold badge at his waist and a tiny facsimile of the same on his lapel. His face brightened when he spotted me.

"I'm honored to meet you, Mr. Troop," he said as he shook my hand with his much larger hand.

"Same here, Cap'n."

He examined me from head to toe, smirking amiably. "I must say, you're not what I expected. The picture of you on your book—"

"Yes, it was an old one. A daguerreotype."

He burst out laughing, then, patting me on the back, walked me through a security door into a fluorescent-lighted hallway, where he immediately launched into another glowing appraisal of my work. It was hard to enjoy, however, as the corridor stank of disinfectant and noxious gases, which made no sense. The crypt was upstairs. We were passing mere administrative offices.

"What on earth inspired you to pick up my book?" I asked when I was sure that he had finished praising me.

"My brother's gay."

"Ah!"

"Now, like I said over the phone, I'll be happy to show you the photos, but first maybe you'd like to take a look around."

Lately I had devoted so much of my time to The Case of the Missing Calvin that I had sorely neglected my novelistic duties. A morgue tour would expand the range of my experience. It might make for an excellent chapter, if I ever wrote about my trip to Los Angeles.

"O, Captain, my Captain, that would be lovely."

The elevator climbed three floors.

When it stopped, Captain Kelly looked me in the eye and whispered: "Death has a smell."

I knew that he had delivered this warning before, but that did nothing to lessen its power. The doors parted, and we emerged into a corridor whose stench can only be described as that of the devil's toilet. The soy and weeds in my guts expanded, begging for one last round of chewing. I swallowed hard and followed my guide into a supply closet, where he fitted me with a pink breathing-cup.

"Inhale through your mouth," he instructed.

The vault was like a huge icebox, stacked from floor to ceiling with plastic-wrapped cadavers, whose skin colors ranged from yellow to green to violet. My eyes bounced everywhere, looking for one that was gangly and bald. After a few futile minutes, I noticed a cardboard Santa taped to the frosty wall, and my stomach began to seize up again. The Earth Shoe stomped all over the dandelions in a frantic effort to escape. I told Captain Kelly I had seen enough, and he hurried me out.

Our next stop was an empty autopsy suite. The operating beds were made of stainless steel and the tiled floors were fitted with generous drains. He showed me where the dead were photographed and where their clothes were hung for safekeeping. He walked me past laboratory after laboratory in which blood was centrifuged, livers deli-sliced, and "tool-marked" stiffs inspected to determine just what sort of tool had administered the fatal blow. On television these labs would have been decked out in lurid neon, with gorgeous young things hunched over fancy computers. In reality the linoleum was chipped, the equipment colorless, and the technicians pimply. It was the dullest place on earth.

When the Captain offered to show me "Decomp and Skeletal," I politely demurred.

We tossed our masks and descended to the ground floor.

I thought, *I will never, ever write about this place.*

In his small cluttered office, Captain Kelly wheeled his chair over to three shoeboxes filled with snapshots. The first was marked "Jane Does," the second "Baby Does," and the last "John Does."

He laid the Johns on his desk.

"It's chronological, so start with the day your friend went missing and work forwards. If you'll excuse me, I've got to make some calls."

As soon as he was gone, my fingers stepped into the gallery of horrors. Most of the victims looked as though they had been trounced to death, their livid faces as bent and loose as discarded rubber masks. I saw the photo of a black boy who had blown his own face off, the word "self" scrawled along its border. An Asian man, his face purple, had been garroted by an electrical cord, which he still wore, like a winter scarf.

As I flipped faster, past face after face, I was sure that at any moment I would see Calvin's gray eyes staring back at me, but when I reached the present, I still had not found him. To this day, I don't know what possessed me, but I suddenly threw myself into the past, flipping back weeks and months at a time. A teenager with an open neck. Another missing an ear. An old man with eyes open wide and a black hole in his temple. On and on it went—reminder after reminder that we are nothing more than briefly animated meat.

I stopped short, my heart rising into my throat.

There he was.

I must have made a sound, because Captain Kelly strode into the room.

"You found him?"

"No, no, someone else." I pointed a shaky finger at the face of Émile Tonkin, just as Calvin had described him—thick neck, handlebar mustache, teardrop tattoo—only he was missing his teeth.

The Captain calmed me down, allowing me to smoke, then he asked me to tell him everything I knew about the Doe. Before I had finished, the Captain was parked at his computer terminal, typing quickly. A long list appeared on the screen. He moved through it.

"Here it is," he said, and then he smacked a few more keys, and began to read aloud: "The Los Angeles County Department of Coroner is seeking the public's help with the identification of an unidentified Caucasian male. He is approximately six-feet, two inches tall, and weighs approximately 220 pounds. He has brown-gray hair and brown eyes. His age range is believed to be between 35 and 45 years of age. He was found, beaten and dismembered, teeth and fingertips removed, on February 20th at approximately 7:00 a.m., floating in the ocean near 235 Marina Place Gangway #14, in the Long Beach Marina. He was pronounced dead at the scene. No wallet or identification papers were found. Scar: None. Tattoos: facial teardrop. Jewelry: none."

"I know why they did this to him," I blurted. "He'd stumbled upon a white-slavery ring, operating out of a local strip club. He went to the police to report it and never came back. The only thing you have wrong is his age. He was in his mid-fifties."

"How well did you know him?"

"We never met."

"But your friend knew him?"

"They were lovers."

I longed for the quiet and safety of my motel room, but Captain Kelly whipped out an official form and demanded that I start at the beginning.

The Process of Elimination

That night, lolling before a television crime show with my great pal Nick O'Teen, a jug of red wine, and a bag of cheese crisps, I reflected on the life and death of Mr. Émile Tonkin. If Calvin was to be believed (and I saw no reason to doubt him), Émile had driven off one morning to deliver to the Hollywood police evidence of a white slavery ring and had never returned. Now I, quite by accident, had discovered why. He had been butchered. But by whom? Who had felled this fine man as he performed his civic duty?

I knew the slavers could not have done it, for there was no way they could have learned so quickly that he had found their files, miraculously unburned, among the charred wreckage of the strip club. The only ones who knew this, aside from Calvin, were the police themselves. So, by the process of elimination, I concluded that Émile had been butchered by the police themselves—not all of them, of course—but by a corrupt unit within the squadron, working in cahoots with the slavers.

On the heels of this deduction came, as thunder follows lightning, another deduction, far more ominous. At the morgue, Captain Kelly had said that he would pass my testimony to the Hollywood Vice and Narcotics Unit, and that they would conduct a thorough investigation. What I had told him included, naturally, my room number at the Palms Plaza. It had seemed like a good idea at the time (there might be a medal coming my way, or a reward), but now it struck me that if I were one of the crooked cops who had chopped up Émile and word reached me that some do-gooder named Troop had put on yellow wings and sung, would I wait around for him to repeat his story under oath? No, I'd jump into an unmarked police car, and, under cloak of darkness, pounce on the old snitch and slice a second mouth into his windpipe. Or, even better, I'd blast his squealing brains all over the rainforest wallpaper.

I snapped off the television set and torched a shaky fag. If I were, indeed, to be slain by the same men who had slaughtered Émile, who would bring them to justice? Was there a second B.K. Troop out there willing to drop his own life in order to unriddle the mysterious end of mine? The answer was a shrill "No!" In fact, there were only three people in the world who would even be remotely *curious* as to who had killed me: my old friend Cassandra, retired now and frying in the Arizona sun; Adrian, the tender-hearted poet, safely tucked in my garret, and, of course, Jesus, my trusty squire. Of the three, only Jesus had the stubbornness and moxie for detective work, but he also had a wife and three boys to support. Placing his own life in jeopardy would be the height of irresponsibility.

Then, heartbeat erratic, I realized something even more terrible. It was unlikely that anyone, including these three, would even learn that I was dead in the first place, let alone murdered. The killers would certainly remove my fingertips and teeth as they had Émile's, and, when I had checked in at the Palms Plaza, in order to discourage bill collectors, I'd given Tupta Parween a fake Manhattan address, a fake Social

Security number, even a fake name[15]. This meant my carcass might very well go unidentified. It would lie on ice for months before being shoveled into a pauper's grave or fed to the hungry saws of a medical college.

Horrified, I jumped to my feet and almost immediately sank to the floor. I was farther behind the cork than I had thought. I clambered up, weaved across the room, and began to barricade my door with every available stick of furniture. Then I stopped. It was a ridiculous waste of time. If an old dainty like me, cross-eyed and spindle-armed, could move the furniture so easily, then a sober, young triggerman could do it with his breath. I staggered to the closet, yanked down my bags, pulled out my trunk, and began to stuff them with everything in sight. When, ten minutes later, eyes bulging, cheeks red, I barged into the motel office, Tupta Parween cried out and reached under the counter for his pistol.

"Sorry to startle you, my friend," I gasped, slapping down my room key, "but I must have a new room. I've just gotten word that my ex-wife has discovered my whereabouts and is on her way over. The woman's a drug-addled firebug. If she finds me, she'll burn the place to the ground."

He grimaced at me as though I were insane, so I laid it on thick (as the boys at the Carnegie deli say), stacking anecdote on anecdote to prove my ex-wife's dangerous pyromania. As every good novelist knows, falsehoods live or die in the details: "And then she drenched a roll of pink toilet paper with lighter fluid, torched it with a navy-blue lighter, and tossed it into the driver's seat of a Lamborgini XZ-48!" And: "A church, Tupta! The one where she was baptized! Can you imagine anything so barbaric? Everything reduced

15 Brian Kyle Troop

to ashes, but the piscina, the reredos, and the sacristy!" And then to rouse his Hindu ire: "She threw the burning match right into the hay loft! Thank heavens the farmer had moved all forty-three of his Guernsey calves to the teething shed the night before or he would have lost the whole herd!"

There was only so much of this he could take before his smile turned queasy and he was forced to ask himself: *What if this madman is actually telling me the truth? It is unlikely, of course, but what if? Do I really want the destruction of the Palms Plaza on my head?*

He slid a key across the counter. Room 13. Molly's old room. I slapped a tenner into Tupta's surprisingly pale palm and made him promise that no matter who showed up—my ex-wife or even her hired henchmen—he would never, ever reveal my whereabouts. He agreed. On my way out the door, he handed me three phone messages, my first since arriving the previous month. They were all from Willow Stetz. What on earth did that trollop want? I bunched them up and jammed them in my pocket.

A grueling hour later, I was safely tucked into my new room, fully unpacked, and ready to pick up where I had left off. I threw back the Tahitian comforter and, by accident, threw back the sheets as well. The mattress bore a urine stain the size and shape of a catcher's mitt. Was this the spill of an ailing pensioner or a cry for help from an anguished, little actress? I would never know. As I laid out my fags and wine, I scrawled a drunken mental note that it was time to move out. Tomorrow morning, I would find a proper hotel.

Fully dressed for a speedy getaway, I slipped beneath the covers with my pockets full of Calvin's cash. I torched up, took a mighty gulp or two, and snapped on the TV set. Who was I kidding? I was far too agitated to watch TV or even to read a book. I closed my eyes. I would lie motionless instead and soothe myself with reason. I began with the following comforting fact: I had spent most of my adult life in a state of panic, conjuring images of impending doom, yet never in all those years had the worst come to pass, or even the third worst. Rather, I had enjoyed a fairly safe and secure existence.

Why was I such a scaredy cat then? Was it merely a function of my narcissism? I mean, did I honestly think that corrupt vice cops had nothing better to do with their nights than hunt me down and kill me? Was my testimony really such a threat to them? Of course not! It was mere hearsay. If anyone's testimony was a threat, it was Calvin's—he had actually *seen* the incriminating files. Did this mean they had killed Calvin, too? Oh, dear. No, I mustn't entertain the thought, not tonight, not when I was already so jittery. I opened my eyes and introduced a long smoky tendril of Medusa-hair to the shears of the ceiling fan. Meditation wasn't working.

Perhaps a wank.

Hours later, my eyes flew open.

What I heard stalled my blood: steps on gravel, the clank of the gate, and the tinkle of the bell. I lunged at the wicker. Outside was my nightmare come to life. Was I still asleep? Was this really happening? A huge man in dark clothing stood with his back turned, banging hard on my old door.[16] When he got no answer, he rattled the knob and found it unlocked. He entered the room and flipped on the overhead light. My reaction to this was more slapstick than melodrama. I ran in ten directions at once, arms flailing as though I were being attacked by hornets, and while I did not scream, I certainly squeaked. Thankfully, some long-dormant knack for derring-do took

16 Today, in my mind's eye, he stands seven feet tall and seven-feet wide.

hold of me. I threw on a blazer, stuffed the pockets with cigarettes, lighter, and telephone, then grabbed my crime journal
and bolted outside.

When I reached the gate, I dared a glance back and saw,
in my old window, the outline of the man shaking his head
with frustration. I smothered the bell, eased open the gate, and
to avoid the gravel, fell into the shadows of the flowerbed. I
crawled on my hands and knees around the parking lot. The
earth was smelly, wet, and soft—had it just been fertilized?
When I reached the sidewalk, I turned back. Peeping out between blossoms, I watched the killer stride with great purpose
into the motel office. I bolted again. Unluckily, I tripped and
skidded, palms first, into the pebbles. The office door banged
open at my cry. I found my feet and sprinted.

Rather than try to outrun my pursuer, which would have
ended with either a cardiac event or my being walked down
and shot dead like a lame dog, I fell into the shrubbery and
curled myself into a tight ball. I heard running footsteps. Certain that I was about to die, it took all of my courage even to
crack an eye. When I did, I saw, through a throng of cactus
paddles, the triggerman hurrying past. His rugged features
were indistinct in the glow of the streetlight, but not their
murderous expression. I listened as his hard soles slapped into
the distance. The ruse had worked. The last place he would expect to find me was back where the pursuit had begun. Just to
be sure, I remained absolutely still, throat closed, lungs heav-
ing, guts unfastening. Was I about to soil my pants? I prayed
not. I would hate to be delivered to Captain Kelly that way.

Eventually, the galoot trudged back into view, winded and
demoralized. There is nothing a cop hates more than to be out-
witted by an amateur. He stopped to consider his next move.
He must have heard a noise of some sort (my fart?) because

he whipped around and stared straight at me. I shut my eyes, ostrich-like. Seconds later, he gave up, walking back to his un-marked police car and driving off.

I waited a full twenty minutes before emerging from my hiding place. Only then did I feel the cold that had turned my joints to rusty iron. I attempted a stretch, but the pain was too much for me. Good God, I would die of pneumonia out here. Teeth chattering, I looked up and down the block. What now? Where to? I might go back to my room, but what if the thug had given Tupta Parween *two* tenners to call him as soon as I returned? No, impossible, too risky. Despite the late hour, I had no choice but to call my squire.

Viva Mexico

When Jesus and I arrived back at his home, his children were asleep, but, thankfully, his wife Maria, like every good mother, slept with one ear open. Within moments of Jesus pouring me a big glass of Guadalupe Red (leukocyte forward; hemoglobin back), the fine woman emerged, tying a fuzzy yellow bathrobe around her big bosoms and offering to feed me. She was a gorgeous creature, this Maria Cabrera, the quintessence of Mexican womanhood, except that she was not even remotely squat. She was, in fact, a towering five-foot-five and exceedingly well spoken.

"Mr. Troop, I've heard so much about you," she said, stunning me with her mastery of the present perfect tense.

"Likewise, my dear." I lowered my tumbler and wiped away the bloody mustache. "If only we could have met under happier circumstances. I've just narrowly escaped being murdered by a policeman."

"Oh, no!"

"I'm afraid so."

"Sit down. Please."

Seated at her dinette table, scarfing down a dish of spicy

beans in egg yolk, I told her the whole grim tale, including a few stray details that I had forgotten to share with Jesus on the drive up. She could not stop shaking her head, and who could blame her? Here I had tarried in Los Angeles to solve a missing persons case, and now I was at the center of a police corruption scandal, which, quite frankly, I wanted nothing to do with. Some things are eternal. Police corruption is one of them. Another is prostitution. Another is the grisly demise of anyone who thinks he can put a stop to either. Just ask Émile Tonkin.

"I'm no hero," I concluded. "I am, in fact, a giant coward, but one who happens to believe that when a friend goes missing you don't rest until he's found, and that means no matter what. The unfortunate thing is, I had expected the police to be my ally. Now I find that they are allied *against* me. But I won't give up. I feel a bit like the Spartan commander who, when told by his Persian enemy that their arrows will darken the sun, replied, 'Very well, then. We will fight in the shade.' So shall I. I will find Calvin, even if I have to do it alone."

"Calvin is an odd man," Maria sighed, "but always sweet to me. And very kind to my boys."

"Yes, he was always good," Jesus concurred, sadly dropping his eyes.

For the next thirty seconds, the three of us sat in silence, each remembering Calvin in his own way. I think we might have remained silent longer, but my belly spoke up.

"More beans, please?" I said, holding out my plate.

As the sun rose, Maria led me through the living room, where an artificial Christmas tree blinked by the fireplace. It was decorated with simple ornaments of blue, gold, and red, and three big white bows. On the mantel sat a modest nativity scene made of clay. Joseph wore a sombrero: Mary had a faint mustache. I wondered if the Cabreras were going to invite me to stay for the holidays.

"I hope you'll be comfortable, Mr. Troop," Maria said, as she led me to the den. "The couch is pretty small."

"It's a damn sight bigger than a slab at the morgue, which is where I was headed if your husband hadn't rescued me."

The den was cozy, filled with paperback books, framed photographs, video games, movies, spelling trophies, a sewing machine, and a rocking horse. At the window, I touched aside the curtain. Gin Reinheimer's house was on the other side. Thank heavens. My sleep would not be disturbed by barking pups.

"Oh, I am weary, Maria," I breathed, "and wish to lie down."

She yanked the plaid sofa into a bed. When she turned her back to pull a pillow down from the closet, I stripped to my boxers and wifebeater and slipped between the sheets. Staring up at Maria's broad, smooth, full-lipped face (characteristic, I believe, of the Olmec tribe, or perhaps the Mayans), I wanted her to kiss me good night. Silly, yes, but an old man is twice a child. The good woman must have read my heart, for she met me half way, laying her cool palm against forehead and murmuring, "Sweet dreams, Mr. Troop."

I did just what Mommy told me, because the next time I opened my eyes the room was sunny and bright and three little boys were smiling at me. They were lined up youngest to eldest, each with an identical haircut, fashioned, it seemed, from cereal bowls.

"My mom said you'd better get up soon or you'll never be able to sleep tonight," the eldest said.

"What time is it?" I asked.

"Four o'clock."

"In the afternoon," the youngest whispered.

I noticed that the middle boy, who had yet to speak, wore red velour sweat pants, white ballet slippers, and a glittery T-shirt. He held a little suede purse on a golden chain. So this was the sissy. In cases like these, nothing is more important than that the boy's uniqueness is affirmed by a sympathetic adult. An adoptive aunt of mine had done this for me in her yearly visits from Hibbing, and it had made all the difference. Yes, I would show the lad special attention, but first I had to wake up. I flung aside the covers. All eyes widened at my paunch and pouch.

"Excuse me, guys," I said. "I have ablutions to perform."

I showered and shaved with vigor, but my gladness to be clean again was dampened by the fact that the only clothes I had were those that I had brought with me, and they stank of manure. When I emerged from the bathroom, however, I discovered that Maria had laundered them for me. They sat in a neat pile on the bed.

"Hello, Mr. Troop," she sang, as I entered the kitchen. "Well, don't *you* look handsome."

That voice, that smile, those red lips! If my adoptive mother had possessed even half her beauty and charm, I would have attended her funeral.

"Oh, Maria, you're a dear, but I'm afraid the last time I was considered handsome, Johnson was president. *Andrew.*"

I grinned, waiting for laughter. When none came, I reminded myself that no one is perfect, not even Maria. She lacked a sense of humor.

"Boy, you sure can sleep," she said.

"Yes, I sleep brilliantly, but you'll find I eat even better." I moved to the stove and sniffed. "What's cookin', good-lookin'?"

She smirked at me strangely. I didn't blame her. No one likes a terminal dose of the wisecrack.

"It's a specialty from the part of Mexico where I was born." she explained. "It's called—"

She rattled off a foreign name, then removed some of the sauce with a wooden spoon and let me slurp.

"*Delixioso*," I declared.

"It won't be ready for two more hours. Why don't you relax, watch some TV?"

"I'd rather play with the boys, if you don't mind."

She shot me a worried glance. Perhaps she was afraid that I might say something hurtful to the sensitive one.

"You have nothing to fear," I murmured. "I'll handle him with kid gloves."

I gave her a reassuring wink and off I went. I found Jesse and Omar, the eldest and youngest, in the driveway, playing basketball with a miniature ball and hoop. To show that I was not playing favorites, I fell to the pavement and executed a few whirly slam-baskets. They laughed themselves sick, which made the damage to the knees of my linen trousers well worth it. Then I pleaded shortness of breath and slipped around back, where I found Domingo all alone on a plastic swing. His purse dragged in the dirt and there was a far-away look in his eye. What visions danced in the lad's lonely brain I have no idea, but I would have bet a million against a fig that they were tinted lavender and trimmed with lace. I took the swing next to him, but the apparatus creaked and sagged, so I was forced to sit on the thick, green grass instead. While lack of funds had stopped Jesus from planting new grass everywhere, the part that was finished looked good enough to graze.

"Lovely," I said, rolling my fingers through it.

"It comes in rolls," the boy said. "Like carpet."

"Gorgeous flowers, too," I said, surveying the garden.

"White hawthorn. Pastoral eglantine. Fast-fading violets. And mid-May's eldest child, the musk-rose."

He looked at me like I was insane. I am no botanist, you see, so whenever I'm in a garden, I always say the same thing, words lifted from Keats. Not once in all the years I had used the trick had I been caught. Few know anything about flowers. Unfortunately, this boy did. Beaming with pride, he pointed out each type of flower to me, naming it and telling me how best to keep it from dying. Rather than tease him about his expertise, I pretended that his was normal, boyish know-how.

"Any other hobbies?" I asked, patting his bony, little back.

"Wanna see my collection?"

"You bet I do!"

He led me inside. What was I was about to be shown? Dolls? Costume jewelry? Turn-of-the-century porcelain toe shoes? Nothing could have prepared me for what he dug out of his closet. A sneaker box filled with baseball cards. Maybe there was hope for him yet. He fanned some down on the carpet.

"These are from the late '70s," I said.

"Calvin gave them to me."

Sure enough, when I looked closer I saw that the lion's share of the cards were Seattle Mariners. So Calvin had tried to butch him up a bit. Not a bad idea. I would support his efforts.

"I commend your red-blooded interest in our national pastime, Domingo. Baseball is a wonderful sport. Rockwellian, in the only good sense of the word. Perhaps one day you'll play the game yourself. You're built like a utility infielder."

Domingo touched a player's face with a tiny, translucent fingernail.

"He's handsome," the boy whispered.

It was an Aryan mook with a crew-cut and a big, white Evangelical smile.

Calvin's efforts, it seemed, had failed.

"So is this one," Domingo continued, showing me a black pitcher with wiry limbs and a well-shaped head.

"Is he your favorite?" I asked.

He flashed a naughty little smile and nodded. Oh, how the world had changed! When I was a boy, no matter how much you adored an athlete, or any other male for that matter, to declare it would have been unthinkable. Yet, here was a boy, not yet ten, revealing his crush to a complete stranger. Was it only because I was a fellow traveler on the Yellow Brick Road, or did he confess it to everyone?

"Let me ask you something, boy. Do you tell your friends at school that you think these players are handsome? Or do you keep it a secret?"

"I don't really have friends."

"I'm sorry to hear that. Why not?"

"They call me names."

"Proud Mary, tush-tangler, girl's girl, Faggoty Andy, things like that?"

He looked bewildered, if not crushed. "They call me stupid."

"Oh, I see." I was embarrassed. I would have to correct my mistake, and fast. "But you aren't stupid. Not at all. You're smart and special. I think so, and so does Calvin."

"Is he coming back soon?" he asked me.

I told him the truth, that I had no idea.

Dinner proved to be a most spirited affair, with all three boys talking at once and Maria displaying remarkable patience and generosity of spirit. As Jesus was running an errand, I was left to play Daddy, a role which, I must say, I enjoyed tremendously.[17] I corrected their manners, their utensilship, their grammar, but always in the most gentle way. I served them vegetables and helped them cut their meat. I sang of the virtues of cleaning one's plate, what with so many children starving to death just down the block.

As strange as it might sound, what I found most enjoyable about the meal was the noise and chaos. Almost every night of my adult life, I had dined alone, and the quiet was nothing short of funereal, but I had always told myself that this is how I liked it, that silence was integral to my sense of well-being, and that without it I would go mad. This meal, however, revealed the lie. In fact, I liked the clamor, especially when all the children talked at once. (Even shy, little Domingo chimed in, complaining that a girl at school had pulled his hair.) The louder the chatter, the more at peace I felt.

Just as Maria was about to serve us a traditional Mexican pudding (flange, it's called), a car drove up.

The boys cheered and raced for the window, crying "Papa, Papa, Papa!"

Moments later, Jesus entered, smiling ear to ear, dragging my carry-ons. My steamer trunk stood in the bed of his truck.

"How did you get into my room?" I cried.

"No problem," he said.

"No one interfered?"

"Only the manager. He asked me who I was and I said I

17   This was my first family dinner since the death of my adoptive parents, and
     what an improvement. At every meal from my birth until junior high school,
     I had cried at least once. My adoptive father would criticize me into a heap
     then berate me for slouching. Within weeks of my refusing to cry anymore,
     I developed an ulcer. Had not both my adoptive parents died blessedly early,
     I'm certain that it would have eaten clear through my spine before my twenty-
     first birthday. Instead, it magically lost its appetite when the last shovel of dirt
     hit the old man's box.

worked for you and that you broke your leg and that you were in the hospital, so I needed to pack your bag. He said, 'Okay, but you tell him some guy came by and left a note.'"

"The man who chased me!"

"He went to get the note, and I tell you, Mr. Troop, I was scared." Jesus laughed. "I packed fast."

"Did you escape before he came back?"

"No, he came back too quick. Here's the note." He dug into his flannel pocket and pulled out a piece of paper.

It said "Call Willow," followed by a phone number that I had never seen before.

Maria looked at it, too. "Do you know someone named Willow?"

So my midnight visitor had not been a crooked cop, after all, but a messenger from Willow Stetz. How ridiculous I felt. I had run for nothing. All of the night's terrors had been self-inflicted. I was reluctant to admit my mistake to my hosts, of course, for I had not only ruined their sleep, but also made them believe they were my saviors. I couldn't bear to burst their bubble. Although, in a way it was still true, wasn't it? Only it was not death they had saved me from, but loneliness.

"She's one of the dirty cops," I replied.

Oops

After dinner, I threw on a tweed jacket and excused myself for a smoke. The sky was low on stars and plumb out of moon. A burst of laughter exploded from Gin Reinheimer's house. I stopped at her gate, wondering whether or not to investigate. Just as I had decided to move on, the front door opened and a dozen barking puppies spilled out.

"Eddie, I thought that was you! What ya doin' out there?"

There she was in all her unsightly glory.

"I'm staying with your neighbors," I replied.

"The Cabreras? Oh, yeah, they're good ones, all right. Come on in. I'm havin' a Christmas party. I made some eggnog."

Only because I love eggnog, I opened the gate, and, kicking aside pups, made my way through the potty field. The smell was indescribable, so I won't bother. When I reached Gin, I saw that she was wearing a rhinestone snowman at the waist and a panel of red mesh at the cleavage. I averted my eyes and walked inside. There were only two guests: Rowdy Diamond and his son Anson.

"Santa Claus is coming to town!" the boy cried.

"Have you been a good boy?" I asked.

"You bet he has," Gin interjected. "Except for the dust-up at the center. And that wasn't his fault. Little slut was teasin' him bad."

"Santa Claus is coming to town!" Anson roared, so loudly that I almost plugged my ears.

"Still haven't found Calvin, huh?" Rowdy asked.

"No, I'm afraid not. But I found the dead body of his ex-boyfriend in cold storage at the Coroner's office."

"Which ex-boyfriend? Gin asked.

"The one who took Calvin in when he first arrived in Los Angeles. A body builder with a teardrop tattoo and a heart the size of the Grand Canyon. Émile Tonkin was his name and he—"

"You mean *Emil*," Rowdy said. "Emil *Tolkin*."

"No. Are you sure? You knew him?"

"Sure I'm sure. Emil was a good buddy of mine. He used to hire me to work night security. That's how I met Calvin. After Emil got whacked, the kid had no place to live, so I introduced him to Gin."

"That's me," she said, raising a lumpy hand.

Eager to know more, I pushed aside a dog and plopped down next to Rowdy. "Tell me, how old was Emil when he died?"

"I dunno. 60, 62."

"No! Are you sure?"

"Sure I'm sure."

The Coroner's Office had estimated the dead man's age at 35-45. Had Calvin lied to me about Emil's age, or was my memory really as bad as all that?

"What did he look like?" I asked.

"Well, he was about six-four, I'd say, lots of muscles, mustache, white hair, lots of tattoos."

"Are you sure? I thought he had just one, on his cheek. A teardrop."

"Oh, no, he was painted up good. He had a fuckin' dragon on his back."

No doubt about it then. The cadaver I had identified was not Calvin's lover. I wanted to slap myself senseless.

"You found his body, huh?"

"I . . . I don't know, Rowdy. Maybe not."

"What about Calvin?"

"Calvin's a naughty boy! A naughty boy!" Anson sang.

"No luck," I muttered.

"Doesn't surprise me. Kids like Calvin, they're like tumbleweeds. They roll in from nowhere, and then they roll out again."

"So you don't think he's dead?"

"When they found his car, I pretty much figured, yeah, he's dead, but now I dunno. I think maybe he just—"

I had reacted as though jabbed by a hat pin. "What? They found his car?"

"Gin didn't tell you?"

I glared at the human mudslide.

She shrugged. "Couldn't find your phone number. He probably *ate* it." She pointed to Anson, who was, indeed, nibbling the edge of a reindeer napkin.

"Cops found it a few days ago," Rowdy explained. "Traced it to a chop-shop not a mile from here. The owner says he found it parked in his lot the morning after Calvin disappeared. He figured it was a gift."

"Now I'm really confused."

"It doesn't mean the kid's dead," Rowdy said. "Maybe he'd had enough of this place, dumped his car, stuck out his thumb, and blew out of town."

"Without his money or his telephone?"

"Huh." That got Rowdy thinking. He lit up a cigarette.

"Here you go, Ed," Gin muttered, handing me a big glass of eggnog. "Looks like you could use it."

"Indeed," I said, taking it. "Right now, all of Los Angeles looks to me like a tired, old whore."

"Easy now," Gin snorted. "I never took a penny from no one."

"You took free dinners instead," Rowdy countered with a smile.

"A lady's got that right."

"Calvin's a naughty, naughty boy!" the half-wit cried again.

I couldn't take another minute of it. I downed the nog in three huge gulps.

"I must get back," I said, standing. "Jesus and his family will want to sleep, and I don't want to wake them with the doorbell."

"You can sleep here if you want," Gin said.

"No, I must get back."

"How long you stayin' over there?" she asked.

"I don't know," I answered, drifting to the door.

Later that night, as I lay wide awake, memorizing the ceiling and reflecting on the meaning of Calvin's abandoned car, Jesus came into the den, his brow troubled. He sat down beside me on the edge of the foldout bed.

"I been thinkin'," he said. "You're a good person. And Calvin was not."

"What do you mean? You sang his praises."

"I was showing respect for the dead. He was a *joto*, Mr. Troop. He charged money for sex. I think maybe you are doing too much for him. You're not happy here. You're smoking and drinking all the time. You're an old man now. You should take care of yourself. I think it's time for you to go home."

Negative Capability Revisited

Who was Calvin Wirt? What had I learned about him in my investigation? He was a boy who—Wait, untrue. Even though in my mind's eye he was a boy, and I referred to him as such, he was twenty-nine years old. Why did this fact continually elude me? Was he extraordinary, this young man? Worthy of a place in my heart at the right hand of Christopher and Adrian? Of course not. He was uneducated, freakishly tall, bald, morally bankrupt, and, worst of all, egregiously untalented. Yet I had promised to stay in town until the mystery of his disappearance was solved, and I hated to break a promise, particularly to myself.

If I did stay, what would be my next step? The Cabreras had not invited me to join them for Christmas, so I would most likely return to my motel and pass the holidays alone. A dismal prospect. When New Year's came, then what? Back to the case. But there was no case! I was groping in darkness. Like what? A tapeworm? A mole? The miner who digs his hands raw to line a rich man's pocket? No, no, I was laboring in the dark *exactly like an artist*.

"We work in the dark," Henry James affirmed, and hadn't dozens of other artistic giants, trying to explain to the amateur what creation is like, said virtually the same thing? Wasn't it always compared to a leap in the dark, an oarless venture into night, a blind exploration guided by faith and instinct and little else? And wasn't that precisely what I had been doing in Los Angeles? Groping blindfolded into tomorrow, sniffing out my next move from the rear end of the unknown? B.K. Troop, conducting himself like an artist? Who would have thought such a thing possible? I wasn't cut out for it!

Yes, of course, Gentle Reader, I know what you're thinking. I had written two excellent books. How could I disparage myself this way? But they were memoirs—no, even worse than that, they were memoirs based on theft. *Christopher* I had cribbed in large part from an unpublished manuscript that the boy had left behind when he escaped to start graduate school. *The House Beautiful* was based on an unpublished manuscript written by one of my most brilliant lodgers, a manic-depressive who I knew would never press charges, for the simple reason that she was either dead, homeless, or chewing lead paint off the radiators in a mental hospital. This meant that when I sat down at my desk to write these books, I never stared at a blank page, never faced the void. There was always a pre-existing text. This alone had given me the confidence to proceed.

Mr. Gertrude Stein once said something like this: *You write a book and you're ashamed because everyone thinks you're nuts and yet you write, and you know that you will be mocked and ridiculed, and you have a sick feeling you don't know where you're going, and yet you go on writing.* This is precisely how I felt about my investigation. I had no idea where it was going and wished I'd never taken it up in the first place.

It was these reflections and more that persuaded me that it

was time to give up. Detective work was a mission of instinct. I was a man of reason who belonged at home in bed. So few of us know how to grow old! It was time for me to return to The House Beautiful, to burn old wood, drink old wine, and read old books. There I would recline and wait for Death, whose clip-clop carriage I fancied I could already hear, coming closer and closer, making its patient way to eternity.

A Second Lunch
with Lucifer

I f, before calling Amtrak to reserve my place on the Southwest Chief, I had not finished off the last of the Guadalupe Red, then the remarkable events that followed would never have taken place. I would have boarded my train at the appointed hour and returned home a failure. Thankfully, I *did* drain the pitcher, and then, half-cocked, wrote down my ticket information. A few hours later, I stood over my hosts' bed, where they lay sound asleep in darkness. I jostled my squire awake, and he let out a scream.

"*Pardona, amigo*," I whispered, "but I need you to drive me to Union Station. My train leaves in ninety minutes."

Because he was still owed a week's wages, my sleepy squire had no choice but to stagger into his dungarees. While he brushed his teeth, I poked my head into the next bedroom, where Jesse and Omar slept in twin beds, smiling like angels. I bid them a silent, dizzy farewell. In the next room, I found Domingo dreaming under pink sheets. I hoped that he would remember me forever, as one who had not judged him.

"I'm happy you're going home," Jesus said, as we sped down the dark highway.

"If the French have taught us anything," I replied, "besides the value of rich sauces on rotten meat, it's the upside of surrender. I know when I'm licked."

I slept the rest of the way to the station.

When we jerked to a stop in the cold dark, I checked my roll. Because I had stiffed the motel of three days' board, I still had a full six hundred dollars of Calvin's money left. I kept a C-note to pay for my travel incidentals and gave the rest to Jesus—a hundred more than I owed him. He was most grateful and offered up only the feeblest of objections.

"Nonsense," I said. "With the exception of your wife, you're the finest Los Angeleno I met. I wish you only the best. Here's my phone number. If you're ever in Manhattan, or if Domingo ever makes his way out to audition for a musical, and I'm still alive, you must allow me to repay your hospitality."

At the curb, we shook hands like men.

Following the porter and my luggage to the station door, I looked back for one last glimpse of my friend, but his truck was already gone. Either he was not as sentimental as I or else more so and did not want me to see him cry.

At the gate, I was reminded, once again, of the price one pays for a too-greedy belting of the grape. My train, did, indeed, depart at 6:45, but p.m. not a.m. I had a twelve-hour wait ahead of me! Stifling a sob of self-pity, I checked my trunk and bags, and set up base camp in the waiting area. I drank coffee, slipped outside to smoke, and read the last of my local novels[18]. By mid-day, I was so hungry that I would have stolen a chop

18 Mr. Evelyn Waugh's *The Loved One: An Anglo-American Tragedy.* As subtle as a
    bull terrier. I could have told it better using only half the alphabet.

from a dog. I looked around for a vendor of some sort. That's when I spotted a familiar backside, checking bags. Was it possible? What were the odds?

"Jimmy!" I barked.

Jimmy D'Anunzio turned around and did not recognize me.

"B.K. Troop," I said, "we met last month on the Three Rivers."

"Oh, yeah, yeah," he said, his black eyes darting away. "How ya doin'?"

Did he remember our tussle in the couchette? Was he filled with shame? Lust? He was so distracted that it was hard to tell.

"I'm heading home today on the Southwest Chief," I explained.

"That doesn't leave till tonight."

"I like to check in early, to make sure that my bags clear customs."

He took me seriously and did not laugh.

"Are *you* heading back, too?" I asked sweetly, hoping to put all the bad blood behind us.

"Yeah, I'm taking the Sunset Limited to Houston. At 2:30."

"You have some time then. Let's grab a bite. I'd be more happy to blow you to a B.L.T."

Unfamiliar with this innocent Jazz-Age idiom, which means nothing more than to "treat," he stared at me for a long time, then shrugged his shoulders and gave in. On our way down the block to find a restaurant, I regaled him with the highs and lows of my stay. Something in what I said must have struck him, because he stopped walking and asked me to hold on a second. He jabbed at his cellular phone, then turned his back on me. Speaking to someone, he waved his arms in a comically Italian way. When the call was finished, he spun back around, smiling wickedly, and said he knew just the place for us to eat.

Cabbing it there, I told him about a few more of my adventures, and although he did not say a word, I sensed that he was deeply impressed that I had applied myself with such dedication to The Case of the Missing Calvin. (Perhaps because he had never applied himself devotedly to anything except the rape of virgins.) Finally, we came to a stop outside a pub called O'Brien's—the sort of place where an off-duty fireman might buy a secretary a burger and six pints of beers before luring her back to his apartment for a minute and a half of violent intercourse and twelve hours of sleep. When I entered the dining area, I was not surprised to see a bowl of pickles on every table. It was hideous and dispiriting. Why Jimmy had chosen it, I couldn't imagine, so I asked him.

"*I* didn't pick it," he explained. "My buddy Scotty did."

"Scotty? Who's that?"

"My buddy. He's gonna be here any minute to make you an offer you can't refuse."

"What sort of offer?"

He smiled that same wicked smile. "A movie offer. That's what you want, right?"

We fell into a booth by the window. While Jimmy made a few more telephone calls, I contemplated what was about to take place: my second lunch with Lucifer. More than likely its origin was something like this: One morning, sitting over an Etna of barbiturates, Jimmy had told his friend Scotty all about the pitiful, old queer whom he had met on the train ride out and how he had written a "fag novel" he was hoping to sell to Hollywood. When Jimmy told Scotty the name of the book, Scotty leapt up, screaming, "Are you kiddin' me? I love that friggin' book! The film rights are still available? I want 'em!" Jimmy told his friend, an up-and-coming producer, that this was impossible. The rights were already spoken for. But even if they weren't, he had no way of finding the old flamer. Now, as chance would have it, I had turned up again, and my Los Angeles narrative had jogged Jimmy's memory of the preceding drug-addled conversation. That is why he had stopped dead in his tracks and placed the urgent phone call. Scotty was hightailing it to the pub now, clutching his checkbook, hoping to seal a deal.

My hopeful reverie was interrupted by the grumble of a Mustang outside. The car's license plate read "FLMFLM." Film Film? Flim Flam? A hideous creature emerged from the vehicle. He had curly hair mounded on his head like whipped cream and a sawed-off nose the size of a knuckle. He wore the smug smile of a life-long brat. He strode into the place with great purpose.

"Scotty Fleemer," he said, holding out a hand.

"B.K. Troop," I replied. "But I'm sure you already know that."

I grinned like an old fool, blushing a bit, fully prepared to be drowned in applesauce.

Instead, I was sickened by a proposition.

"There's this old dude," Scotty said, a minute later, crunching down a dill. "Lives up in Calabasas. He's seventy if he's a day. He stars in these homemade videos. Doesn't cost him shit. Maybe five hundred bucks to hire the actor. Anyway, he shoots about six of these videos a year, sells 'em online, and makes a shitload of money. So I was thinking, why don't we do the same thing? I've got a company, Fleemer Films. I've got a camera, a house with a pool. We'll split everything in half, 50-50, down the middle."

"I didn't understand a word of what you just said," I replied. "What sort of films are you talking about?"

"Porn," he replied, with a smirk. "Think about it. You get to screw hot young studs and get paid for it."

Blood boiling, I jumped to my feet and threw Jimmy a murderous glare.

"You're loathsome," I declared. "Even more despicable than I remembered. You insult not only me, but serious artists everywhere. I hope that you overdose and die!"

I strode out of the place. I had no idea where I was going, but I didn't care. All that mattered was that I never saw either of their imbecilic faces again. My resolve was stronger than ever. It was time to escape this Parking Lot of the Gods! I turned a corner and saw an old man wheeling a shopping cart, his very own prairie schooner, with a little wind-twirler at the helm. His eyes were deep and knowing, and his beard was thick.

"My good man," I said, "Do you know the way to Union Station?"

"That away," he said, pointing a leprous finger. "Two miles."

I had hoped that the long walk would calm my nerves, but, instead, my agitation only increased with every hot, miserable step. It was not rage I felt. No, no, it was something far more profound. It was *rebellion*, against every degradation that I had endured since my arrival. How had I let this tawdry town defeat me? And defeat Calvin as well? Now he would be just another Doe. His life unnoted and unremarked, as insipid as an animal's. When I died, I would leave behind two books. But where were Calvin's footprints in the sand? I felt like crying. How could I do such a thing to the gentle, wounded boy who had left his chewing gum on my TV and his cash on my nightstand? By the time I reached the station, I had reversed myself entirely. I would stay in Los Angeles until the mystery was solved! If I found Calvin alive—happy day; if he was dead, I would see to it that his killer was punished. Then at least the world would know that once upon a time there lived a young man named Calvin Wirt, and this is who killed him and why.

After canceling my ticket, my hands still atremble at my bravery and high integrity, I opened Calvin's telephone to call Jesus, but I stopped. I could not bother him again. The good man had given enough. But where else to turn? Calvin's cash was almost gone. If I stayed in another motel, I would be forced to raid my own savings. I could call Christy Winkler, but we were too fat to share close quarters. There was Ben Fuchs, but I hardly knew him. Eduardo Wiggins and I had developed something of a rapport, but his affectations drove me insane. Who did he think he was, the Queen Mum? And what of Gin Reinheimer? No, the thought of seeing her again made me want to find the ocean at last, and dive in.

I remembered something.

I dug frantically in my pockets and found the note that Willow Stetz's messenger had left with Tupta Parween. I dialed without thinking. A young girl answered. It took her a full minute to get Willow on the phone, which gave me time to light up a cigarette.

"Finally," she said.

"You called?" I purred, as though nothing at all was the matter.

"Yeah, like ten times. Why didn't you call back? I had to send someone to your motel."

"Yes, I know. I've been busy. Ever since Mr. Shipp and I broke off our talks, Hollywood has beaten a path to my door. I'm in demand."

"Well, that's sorta why I called. Remember that part you had for me in your movie? My new boyfriend wants to talk to you about it."

"Why?"

"His name's Frank. Frank Yehudi. He's a famous movie producer. He read your book and liked it. He wants to talk to you about it."

"When you say 'movie?' What do you mean exactly?"

"He makes *movie* movies, you dick."

"You say he adored my book?"

"I said he *liked* it. What's the matter with you?"

"So many things. And what did *you* think of it, if I might be so bold as to ask?"

"I didn't read it. I'm dyslexic. It takes me to read forever."

"Was that a joke?"

"Yeah, and it was funny, you wiener. So, anyway, you should totally take a meeting with him."

"But I'm totally at the train station. I'm totally heading home in a few hours."

"God, I hate you. Cancel your ticket. We're having a Christmas party tonight. You're invited."

"Where will I stay? Is there a youth hostel or a YMCA campsite near your house?"

"Hint-hint. Fine, stay with us."

"Oh, I couldn't possibly. Are you sure?"

"Yes, asshole."

As the porters attached my trunk to the roof of a taxi, I was filled with terrifying hope. Was I about to pluck victory from the jaws of defeat or would this be just one more cruel cosmic joke?

Private Dick

The journey from the Sunset Boulevard exit of Highway 450 to the Hombly Hills estate of film producer Frank Yehudi would have been the aesthetic high point of my stay had I not been continually distracted by the oncoming traffic, which at every sharp curve seemed headed straight for my lap, and by the taxi meter whose clicks sickened me like drops of my own blood splashing my loafers, and, worst of all, by the driver, a heavily cologned Serb named Svetozar Uljarevic, who insisted on playing tour guide.

"Big houses der," he said, jerking a thumb over his hairy shoulder. "Playboy house dat way. See dat der? Dat is Belair. Dat way is college. Big one. ACLU."

"I believe you mean UCLA," I said, exhaling smoke and scribbling his name in my crime journal. "Don't tell me you're dyslexic, too."

"No, I from Smederevo."

The oaf pulled the steering wheel to the right, screeching on two tires up a sweeping bend, and then he yanked it the other way, hurtling us across the boulevard. We bounced, scraping the undercarriage of the car, and roared down a shady lane. Behind us an angry driver held down his horn. We slowed to a crawl in cool shadows. Svetozar squinted to read the addresses bolted to brick walls and ornate iron gates.

"Fency," he muttered.

"Yep, and schmency."

He jerked the steering wheel and came to a squeaky stop just inches from the gates of the Yehudi estate. He reached out the window with a long arm, as hairy as a chimp's, and pressed a golden button. Moments later, the same girl who had answered the phone when I'd called Willow asked who it was.

"Yellow cab," he growled. "I got old man."

"Mr. Troop," I whispered.

"Mr. Scoops!" he barked at the intercom.

"*Troop*," I corrected.

"Troops!" he barked.

A click, and the gate swung open. We glided down a driveway flanked by towering evergreens, huge ferns, and exotic plants bearing gigantic blossoms. Remarkably, I saw no sign of human habitation anywhere, only the fence of a tennis court. That it was possible to live like this in the heart of a major international city said everything about what made Los Angeles so appealing to the rich and famous, and the agoraphobic.[19]

Eventually, we reached the front door of an English manor house, a glorious structure of medieval stone and primordial ivy. The entrance porch was a full two stories high and faced with decorative crenels. The slate roof, bearing a half-dozen chimneys, was a splendid bedlam of juts and gables. Two towering windows bore blood-red coats of arms; behind them, set into small recesses of the roof, stained-glass windows depicted

19 I, however, could never live in a place where at any moment a band of hippies could break into my property, disembowel me, and not be overheard. In cramped Manhattan, you can hear your neighbor snore.

scenes from Chaucer. This was clearly one of the great architectural wonders of the town. One could only hope that it was registered as a historical landmark; otherwise, like everything else west of the Mississippi, it was just one parvenu away for the wrecking ball.

Willow Stetz appeared on the doorstep, smoking a skinny brown cigarette. Although it had been only four or five weeks since our dinner, I hardly recognized her. She was still boulder-bosomed and sausage-lipped, but she had put on some good weight, and her complexion had regained its old, innocent paleness. Her hair was better, too, cut like Jean Arthur's and dyed a warm, pleasing blonde. In her chic black-and-white cocktail dress she would have been right at home in the more exclusive country clubs of South Hampton or Johannesburg.

"You made it," she said, as I spilled out of the car.

"You don't miss a thing, do you?" I replied, swatting ashes from my thighs.

"Don't be a jerk."

"I can't help it. You disinvited me to Thanksgiving dinner. It was unforgivable."

She smiled at me through her smoke, then laid a hot moose-eye on Svetozar, who was pulling down my trunk. When he saw her gawking, he flexed his biceps and grinned back in a way that said, "If only we had met under different circumstances, I and my friends would have made love to you at bayonet point."

"Pay the man," Willow said. "And tip like a human being for a change."

Resenting the implication that I was penny-pincher, I gave Svetozar his thirty-two dollar fare, plus an additional four bucks. The stunt made me want to scream, but when I saw the look of astonishment on Willow's face, it was worth it. As the creature drove off, I reached for my bag, but found only air.

Willow flipped her brown fag-end over my head.

"He beat you to it," she explained.

I spun around and saw a white-haired Filipino gent gliding my trunk and bags on a big dolly through a garden door. Bless my beard, but he looked familiar.

"Who's that?"

"Gabriel. Frank's butler. He's the one I sent to your motel."

Clearly, my drunken terror had lent the old man additional height and girth, because he was no taller than five-foot-seven and not at all menacing. In fact, he was a bundle of sticks in a bag, and yet I had fled him. What was the matter with me? I really was a huge girl. Willow snapped her stubby fingers at me. One bore a diamond as big as the Palms Plaza.

"Come on. Frank's waiting."

She walked indoors, head thrown back, swaying her little rump from side to side. She was an imperious thing. From the cocky smile on her face as she spun around in the entrance hall, you would have thought that she had designed the place herself, if not actually mixed the mortar. Why was it so easy for these young actresses, within minutes of landing a rich man, to take on his possessions and accomplishments, even his very past, as their own? Acting schools really ought to teach a course in shame.

The Yehudi home was breathtakingly beautiful. Peaked archways in both directions led to grand rooms laid with rich Oriental carpets and gleaming American antiques. The heavy, old sconces and chandeliers rivaled those of the Union Station. To my left, the grand staircase was hung with WPA oil paintings, which, next to the Ashcan, is my favorite school of American art. During the tour that followed, I was thrilled to discover that Mr. Yehudi's art collection was not only vast, but devoted entirely to such works. Everywhere I looked I saw railroad yards, weary hoboes, black jazzmen, subway riders, fleabag hotels, laundry lines, summer stoops, Hooverville sluts, shoeshine boys, apple vendors, and union strikers. How could a man of such exquisite taste in art have such poor taste in women?

When we entered the living room, Mr. Yehudi stood up from a settee with a hand extended. He was short-legged, pot-bellied, potato-nosed, and close to eighty.

"Frank Yehudi," he said, giving my hand a solid shake, "pleasure to meet you."

His voice was deep and manly, and he looked me square in the eye. I liked him already, but I knew that I must not show it. This was a business meeting not a sewing bee, and this was Los Angeles not Fargo, which meant that every seeming benefactor was, in fact, an exploiter. The pain and humiliation of the Harry Shipp fiasco was still fresh. I would not allow a repeat.

"Bryce Kenneth Troop," I replied coolly. "Call me B.K."

I sank into a silken armchair near a grand piano laden with Mr. Yehudi's family photographs. He had been married twice before and had produced, by my count, six children, all of whom had inherited, to varying degrees, his tater nose and dinky legs. Both of his ex-wives were the epitome of elegance and sophistication. Behind the piano were French doors that opened onto a lawn as long and wide as a football field. A massive swimming pool sparkled bluely in the afternoon sun.

"Willow, get your friend a drink."

"Yes, my tonsils *are* a little dry," I said, smiling superiorly at her.

Oh, how it galled her to be forced to wait on me.

"Whaddaya want?" she snarled.

"A Galloping Ghost," I replied. "Straight up. Two onions."

"What's a Galloping Ghost?"

"The same as a Pollywog, only with Vermouth instead of pear juice."

She threw a hand on her hip. "Do I look like a *bartender*?"

"You did before your boyfriend bought you that swell dress."

Much to his credit, Mr. Yehudi laughed. Oh, how he roared! Willow's eyes narrowed with hatred as she raised a fist over her head. "Dude, you better knock it off."

"Fine, fine," I twinkled. "Bring me a gin and tonic."

Willow padded out of the room, still sulking. Her shapely calves were tanned and smooth, but the bottoms of her feet were black.

"If you don't mind my asking," I said, turning my eyes to the window, "how big is your property? I've yet to see a neighbor."

"Six acres."

"Two and a half hectares. Most impressive. But not as impressive as your art collection."

"Oh, you like it?"

"I'm a huge fan of the Great Depression."

"Is that right?"

He found this amusing, so I explained: "It was the last epoch in our history during which it could be said America possessed a soul. No surprise, it gave birth to a style of painting utterly indigenous, untainted by the affectations and airs of the Europeans."

"You're a pretty smart guy, aren't you, B.K.?"

I blushed to my eartips. He was flattering me and I loved it. In danger of losing the negotiation before it had even started, I battened down the hatches.

"Smart enough to know when I'm being cornholed. Let's talk flickers."

"*What?*"

"Movies."

"Yeah, okay." He sat back and crossed his hands over his third-trimester tummy. "Willow tells me you came out here for a movie deal, but it never materialized. How come?"

"Well—"

Willow appeared with my cocktail. I took it, torched a fag, and, although determined to play hard to get, told Mr. Yehudi everything. I mean everything. I spilled every last bean, pausing only to light another cigarette or to allow Gabriel to refill my glass. It took me two full hours. I cannot say why I did it, except that I trusted the man. Also, like every truly interesting person, he was truly interested, and that is no small thing to someone like me, a natural-born storyteller to whom few ever listen. I shared with him nothing less than the whole sorry saga of my journey westward, just as it has appeared in these pages. I left out only my Amtrak tussle and my bouts of despair.

Darting her eyes around the room and bopping her head to music that only she could hear, Willow spoke not a word. Mr. Yehudi interrupted only to ask an occasional question or offer up a relevant personal insight, such as: "Harry Shipp? That's who brought you out here? Shit, no wonder the deal went south. He's a liar and a drug addict. It's a miracle he's still alive." Or this delicious tidbit: "Ted Sommers hired the kid for sex? Jesus, I knew he was a sociopath, but a *fagela,* too? Sick fuck, he had it all. Head of a studio before he was thirty, and now he's cold-calling strangers, asking for handouts. *I* gave him one a few years ago. That's fifty grand *I'll* never see again."

When I was finished, I sat back, winded. Mr. Yehudi asked me why, if I still didn't know what had happened to Calvin, I'd been so close to leaving town.

"Because I've been miserable here."

"Yeah, I get it."

"Although at this moment I'm not."

"Why's that?"

"Splendid home, yummy cocktails, a gracious host."

"Well, that's very kind of you to say." Mr. Yehudi tucked his creamy silk shirt into his belt. Then he hoisted the belt a bit, revealing bare, white legs above his dress socks. He was vaude-ville-adorable and the thought of him making love to Willow was oddly titillating.

"Let me tell you a little bit about myself, okay?"

"Please." I lighted up again, most keen to hear.

"I make movies."

On the word "movies," Willow snapped to.

"I don't make as many as I used to," Mr. Yehudi explained. "Maybe one or two a year. Usually, I make 'em with the studios, but every now and then a project comes along that's too small or too smart for them, so I finance it myself."

"Bravo."

"Enter Willow. Romantically, I've got nothing to offer her. I'm seventy-eight years old and been widowed twice. My heart's held together with staples and string."

"At least you *have* a heart to hold together."

"Doesn't matter. Willow's not interested in it. Like every young actress, she's out to advance herself, and I don't blame her. For these girls, every year's like a dog-year. Youth and beauty is all they have. It's their only currency."

"I saw her play Catherine the Great once. In a Shaw one-act. She was quite good, actually."

"I was the bomb," she said.

"Anyway, Willow wants to be in your movie. Play the role you suggested—Divina, the whore with the heart of gold.

So she gave me your book. I read it and, I gotta tell you, I couldn't put it down."

"You're too kind."

"Wonderful story. Just wonderful. And beautiful prose. But there's a problem."

"Yes, I know. The narrator. I suppose he *could* be made into a woman."

I was so startled by what I'd said that I clapped a hand over my mouth. A month earlier, the very same suggestion had flung me into a rage, and now here I was suggesting it myself! Was *this* how it happened then? The artist arrives in town, imbued with the purest sort of idealism, and a few hard knocks later, he's crawling around on all fours, wiggling his rump like a poodle in high rut? I remembered the wisdom of Swift: "Climbing is but horizontal crawling."

"You're talking like Shipp now," Mr. Yehudi huffed. "That's one of the stupidest ideas I've ever heard."

"Thank heaven you said that," I gasped.

"No, the problem is, there's no character named Divina in your book. There *is* no whore with a heart of gold. Only a black street hooker with stretch marks!" He burst out laughing, deeply, from the belly. I inwardly cringed, remembering that I had lied to Willow about the role, assuming, quite correctly, that she would never read the book.

"I never said there was a character named Divina," I insisted. "Willow must have gotten it mixed up. Or maybe I did. My memory isn't what it used to be. You see, Divina appears in my *second* novel, which isn't out yet."

I looked over to see if Willow was outraged by my duplicity. When our eyes met, she silently mouthed the words, "You're drunk."

"I know," I mouthed back.

"Anyway, doesn't matter," Mr. Yehudi said. "'Cause, honestly? I'm not the guy to make it, anyway. It's an indie. Find a wunderkind out of NYU to shoot it on the cheap. With the right cast, you'll make back three times your investment, I guarantee it."

This was not what I had expected to hear.

Once again, my hopes were dashed.

I could not hide my disappointment.

Mr. Yehudi chuckled: "Don't pout. Let's talk about this *other* story of yours. Maybe *that* could be a movie."

"*The House Beautiful?*" I asked, brightening a bit.

"What's that? No, I'm talkin' about this kid who disappeared. Calvin. Why couldn't that be a movie? An arty, little mystery, with lots of style and humor. Willow could play herself."

Not even for an instant had it occurred to me that my West-coast adventure might one day become the basis for a book or film. The reason was obvious.

"But there's no ending," I said.

"You're a writer. Make one up."

"Oh, no, I couldn't possibly. I'm not imaginative. I have no daemon. I drop a bucket into my unconscious and it comes up empty. All my books are based on fact."

"Oh." Mr. Yehudi looked over my head at nothing at all, then his eyes returned to me. "Guess that means *we'll* have to solve the case together."

"How?"

"You got that crime journal of yours?"

"It's in my bag."

"Gabriel!"

His butler manifested in the blink of an eye. Had he been hiding behind a pillar or a hunk of drapery? Mr. Yehudi asked him to show me to my room. I eagerly stood up and instantly sank to the floor.

"Jesus, you're down with the fish," he laughed.

"Sometimes when I overdo it, my knees go dicky."

"I'll say."

Gabriel took me by the elbow and escorted me out. I did not feel drunk so much as I did old. I remembered my adoptive grandmother being helped to and from the potty in the very same way.

"Slowly, slowly," Gabriel giggled, as I mounted the stone stairs one jellied knee at a time. His voice was high and dulcet. He was the girl from the intercom.

"I believe I owe you an apology," I said. "You came to my motel room to give me a message."

"You ran away so fast," he sang, with a warmth that bordered on flirtation.

"I'm sorry. I thought you were a corrupt cop come to kill me in my sleep. But I didn't really run away. I hid in the bushes."

"That was you? I heard you in there."

"Yes, a nasty case of the collywobbles, I'm afraid."

"What's that?"

"Borborygmus."

"I don't understand."

"Gas, gas!"

In my room, which was four times as large as my New York bedroom, I found my bags and trunk sitting on the floor next to the sumptuous king-sized bed. After a moment to take it all in, I pulled out my crime journal. On the way back downstairs, Gabriel, guiding me with his small, warm hands, asked if I was a homosexual.

"So far" was my honest reply.

"Me, too," he whispered.

I looked at him. His smile was pretty. He was the antique version of my type.

Back in the living room, Mr. Yehudi opened the journal. The very first page stopped him cold. His brow gathered in knots. "These are the kid's regular customers?"

"That's right. Movie people. 'Big shots,' he called them. As you can see, I have their initials, phone numbers, and home addresses."

Mr. Yehudi turned the page.

"Ted S. is Ted Sommers?"

"That's right. It's the only set of initials I decoded. I did it with the aid of a google computer."

"Did you call the whole list?"

"Many times. They want nothing to do with me. Mr. Sommers only agreed to talk to me because I showed up at his house posing as a homicide detective."

"Let's find out who they are," he said, reaching for the telephone. "If they're film people, I might know them."

"Who are you calling?"

"Buddy of mine. A private detective."

Come Let us Adore Him

Lying in an Eden of happy thoughts, drifting toward desperately needed sleep, a serpent slithered over and whispered in my ear: "Gratitude is merely the secret hope of further favors." I was unsure who had coined this nasty apothegm, but I suspected that he wore tights and spoke French. *But was it true?* I asked myself, suddenly alert. In a mere few hours, my host had already filled me with expensive spirits, listened with rapt attention to the saga of my investigation (as though I were a person of moment), and hired a top-notch private dick to give my saga a proper finish. If generosity so lavish did not inspire genuine gratitude in me, then what on earth was I? Nothing but a leech, a cannibal, a vampire. One of the bad guys. A Harry Shipp.

I snatched the serpent, swung it over my head until it snapped, then tossed it away like a used Johnny cap. No more French cynicism! I would not question joy. I closed my eyes more tightly and settled more deeply into my bed of grass and blossoms. Life was good. The sky was blue as only a sky can be. The breeze was temperate and fresh. And I was safe. Yes, indeed. Nothing to worry about, nothing to fear. The future was my friend; Mr. Yehudi my hero.

Suddenly, raucous laughter shattered my reverie. My eyes fluttered open. The room was pitch black, and at my side there was no burbling brook, just a clock radio blaring a pop tune. Four hours earlier, I had watched as Gabriel set the alarm for six o'clock so that I would have an hour to dress before dinner. Now the clock glowed 7:14. How was it possible that an hour and a quarter of bad radio had not roused me? Then I remembered that I was old and weary, that health and wealth had missed me, and that the bed linens were made of Egyptian cotton into whose soft folds my swollen manhood was buried like a dagger. The laughter I heard was that of arriving dinner guests. I would be unpardonably late! I thought: *So what?* My eyes fell shut and my worries sank under a swell of oblivion. I was adrift in Lethe.

"I think you'd better wake up now," Gabriel piped, five minutes later. "The party has started."

"Down in a jiffy!" I hollered back, but then I realized that he was not outside my door, but standing right above me.

To the sound of his sweet giggling, I popped up, much refreshed, and, cupping my manhood so as not to clear an end table, I scampered into the bathroom—a showplace of mocha granite, greenish glass, and shiny chrome. The blast of the shower nearly knocked me over. As I lathered myself, I hummed an unknown disco ballad, learned by osmosis while I slept. The water was magnificently hot and the milled soap smelled of spice. What a blessing! Just the night before, I had bathed in the Cabreras' peeling pink shower with a scrap of scentless lard, and now look at me! My lodgers had been right. In Hollywood, at any moment, all of one's dreams could come true.

With Gabriel's help, I retrieved my best ensemble, which happened to be the same one I had worn to my lunch with Mr. Shipp: blue zibeline blazer, yellow linen trousers, a white short-sleeve, and a black neck tie. (My burgundy scarf was still in his clutches.) A superstitious man would surely have gone in a new direction, but I, a man of reason, thought otherwise. What better way to defeat the past than to relive it with a better outcome?

Minutes later, every hem and hair in place, I was escorted by Gabriel down the staircase. I glided with a crooner's grace. I felt every inch the debonair, old bachelor. "Who is this dashing stranger?" the guests all wondered as Gabriel swept me into the living room. "Who is this latest protégé of the great Frank Yehudi?" Because the dinner bell clanged immediately, the introductions were hurried. I never did properly learn, and thus could not record in my journal, all the names of those present. As we made for the grub, Gabriel took me once more by the elbow. Clearly, he had been assigned the task of keeping me on my feet.

With its high wooden ceiling and leaded-glass windows, the dining room recalled the good olde days when jesters performed capers and tricks between courses, and dogs were used as napkins. The gleaming twelve-foot table was laid with sterling, crystal, and poinsettias. High above it hung a primitive iron chandelier the size of a lunar module. We took our seats according to place cards. Mine was next to the roaring fire, which spat and crackled in a hearth so tall that I could have stood up inside it without bumping my head.

Because it had been decades since I had been invited to a proper sit-down dinner, I felt uncharacteristically bashful and did not speak a word during the first two courses. I was content to observe and listen. The holiday menu was first-rate: squash soup, artichoke salad, Cornish game hen stuffed with scallops, new red potatoes, cranberry sauce, pickled white asparagus, and, for dessert, homemade chocolate-mint ice cream. The wine was an out-of-this-world Oregon Pinot Noir, as complex a vintage as any I had ever tasted (black cherry and tar aromas with an overnight surprise of toadstool, an underhand lob of honeydew, a spadeful of mulch, and a finish of fleas.)

The stereotype that all Los Angelenos do is sit around talking about movies is hogwash. I am happy to report that the conversation that night was as spirited and articulate as any one could hope to find in Manhattan. Its subjects ranged from movies to books, back to movies, to politics to money to real estate, and back to movies again. I was still fairly sleepy, but it did not stop me from smiling and nodding in all the right places. No one noticed my silence. I think this was due mostly to the great fun they had when they spoke themselves.

When my attention wandered, it was toward Delmore, Mr. Yehudi's godson, and the only male under forty. An associate professor of Latin at one of the better local colleges, he was quite tall, with Elvis Presley sideburns, blue-black eyes, and a voice so deep that I would have laid a bet on four testes. He was an overserious lad, who had clearly spent far too many hours harvesting the Groves of Academe and not nearly enough on his belly in bed, screaming uncle. I suspected a firm derriere and tiny mulberry nipples sensitive to cold.

Next to Delmore sat Little Al Goetz, a movie producer of my age and height, who weighed well over four hundred pounds. He was a grumpy-looking fellow, impeccably dressed in a gigantic, red cashmere sweater-vest and green flannels. His gold wristwatch sparkled with diamonds. Like Mr. Yehudi, he was semi-retired now. He preferred to stay home with his cats, he said. The conversation took a perilous turn when he stabbed a spear of asparagus, wagged it at Delmore, and said, "So, Doc, what do you think of these wars we're fighting?"

Delmore decanted upon the conflicts in a most original

fashion, using quotations from Thucydides *Peloponnesian War* and Ovid's *Art of Love* to attack both those who had launched the Iraqi and Afghan enterprises and those who conducted them today. When he was finished, the table erupted with such vehemence that one would have thought he had sparked dissent, but, in fact everyone agreed with him. What followed was a half-hour assault on the Pentagon and all three branches of government. Curious, I thought, how those who have no more power over our national affairs than do the homeless (i.e., one vote) think that if they voice their outrage with enough clarity and passion, they are somehow doing their part to change the world.

To my left, Ellen somebody, a scrawny psychotherapist, was giving me the hairy eyeball—quite literally, for she was egregiously beetle-browed. My first thought was that there was nubbin dangling from my nose or beard, but then I realized that she was simply mesmerized by me. She reminded me of Dr. Gaby Geitman, a no-nonsense Jungian from Great Neck, Long Island, who had saved my life in the early 1980's, after a terrible week that had begun with my flushing my lithium down the toilet, taken a downward turn with my staggering out in my pajamas in search of an affordable rooftop hibachi, and ended abruptly when I slapped a Puerto Rican cop across the face.

"You're awfully quiet," she said to me. "Don't tell me you're a Republican."

"Quite to the contrary," I purred, speaking for the first time and commanding immediate attention. "In fact, I'm a life-long supporter of Mr. Arvo Halberg, also known as Gus Hall, the president of the American Communist party. May he and *it* rest in peace."

She frowned as though her palate were smeared with manure, but everyone else roared with laughter.

Sensing that I might be on the verge of a roll, I continued: "Truth be told, these days I eschew politics altogether. It's become a carousel without horses. More hard cheese than soft soap. A cretin's lullaby."

Fourteen eyeballs blinked in slow motion at me.

So much for my roll.

"An obscure quotation," I explained, my scalp tingling with embarrassment. In fact it was not. I had made it up. I would certainly have done better had I not been, for the second time today, rotten with alcohol. Already! How was it possible? Not my style at all. I was a tippler not a guzzler. What had changed? Was my intake on the rise or my tolerance in decline?

Eager to change the subject, I turned to Delmore: "Good Schoolmaster, you mentioned that you recently earned your doctorate. What, pray tell, was the subject of your dissertation?"

"The crisis of the male in late Republican Rome," he replied.

"It was delivered slowly," I'll bet. "The carriers waylaid by the Visigoths and Ostrogoths?"

"Not m-a-i-l," he laughed. "M-a-l-e."

"Oh!"

Everyone guffawed. If I had not been soused, I would have been mortified. Instead, I smirked and tipped an invisible hat, as though I had been joking.

"During the death throes of the Republic," Delmore explained, "male members of the elite faced a crisis of masculinity and—"

"Elite male members?" I cried far too loudly, hoping to turn things around. "Oh, this is getting *good!*"

When no one laughed, I coughed, pretending some wine had gone down the wrong pipe.

I forget what Delmore said next, because I was gagging and

he said it in Academese, a language as pretty as German and as accessible as Cheyenne. The next morning I did, however, take the time to record the following: *Delmore . . . sideburns . . . bass voice . . . four balls . . . used big words . . . must remember never to look them up: occult countercultures . . . Cosmopolitanization . . . performative scripts . . . transformed valences of value terms . . . haruspicy . . . neo-Pythagoeranism . . . oneiromancy.* As the egg-head banged on, puckering our brows and making us sleepy, all I could think was how desperately he needed a sound spanking followed by a long, hot bath followed by another sound spanking. I wanted to scream, like Molly Bloom: "O rocks, tell us in plain words!" The only person who didn't seem bored by his high-falutin' blather was Willow, but only because she was chewing her food so loudly that she couldn't hear it. At one point, I saw a shard of hen fall from her lips directly into the chasm of her décolleté, and she did not even notice.

Soon, the discussion returned to motion pictures. There were four film professionals present—Mr. Yehudi, Little Al Goetz, Julian Lowry (a screenwriter wearing a white ski sweater under a wrinkled corduroy suit), and an octogenarian movie director I'll call Deaf John. Deaf John was Ellen's father and the director of B-movies in the 1950s. He was vaguely senile and full of indiscreet asides made even more indiscreet by his inability to control his volume. "Ginger Rogers fucked the town flat!" he shouted. A minute later: "Laurence Harvey drew the line at goats!" Neither of these revelations surprised me, but his description of one of my favorite post-war teen starlets making love to Walter Brennan on a pile of coats at a party made me want to plug my ears and wail like a fire engine.

The four wise men explained the difference between old and new Hollywood. In the old days, it seemed, a film had one or two film producers and the function of these film producers was to produce the film. Today, there were thirteen producers, most of whom did nothing. The few that did something, mostly did damage. Whatever dismay the old-timers felt for this new method was small change compared to the rage felt by Julian, the screenwriter. His scorn was not, however, directed at the studios, but at today's movie stars.

"They're insane children, entirely dysfunctional human beings, but they get *script approval*. They ruin the movie before it even starts and no one stops them. And the public has no idea! They think movies stink because we're all a bunch of morons, when it's really because a group of overpaid, insecure mental patients has the keys to the kingdom. It's a scandal, the ugliest trade secret we've got, but no one has the guts to talk about it!"

His high dudgeon would have been more impressive if it had not been painfully obvious that he would have given his right leg for the privilege of having a movie star destroy one of his scripts. He was like the stripper who grouses about her customers not two minutes before showing them her ovarian walls. Either quit screenwriting or shut the hell up, that was my opinion. Then again, I was biased. Lately, I wanted nothing more than to sell out. What did I care if the movie was good or not? I would be dead before the premiere.

While Julian used his mangy corduroy sleeve to wipe the foam off his mouth, Deaf John looked at Mr. Yehudi and screamed, "Why'd you invite this schmuck?"

Everyone nervously laughed.

Mr. Yehudi grinned and slapped Julian on the back. "What can I tell you? I get a kick out of him. Besides, he's right!"

To move things along, I said, "I think we all agree that Hollywood is *a ass*. Now let's talk about me."

Frowns all around, except from Ellen, who asked. "So, Mr. Sloop, what's *your* interest in the movie industry?"

"*Troop.* Well—" I pointed at Mr. Yehudi with my fork. I had forgotten that it held a new potato. The tuber flew, ricocheted off Mr. Yehudi's shoulder, and struck a seventeenth-century tapestry. Everyone laughed good-naturedly, except Willow, who narrowed her eyes at me and mouthed the words "You're drunk again."

I decided then and there that once the Calvin Wirt project was off the ground, I would demand that Willow be required to audition for the role of herself, and then I would personally see to it that she lost the role to a younger, prettier girl who treated me with respect.

"B.K. wrote one helluva novel," Mr. Yehudi intervened. "We're trying to make a deal right now. But not for the book. A different story. A true story."

"Let's hear it," Little Al said, removing a cigar from his blazer pocket.

"It's about a friend of mine," I began eagerly. "A young man who disappeared into thin air. His name is—"

"Oh, no you don't," Mr. Yehudi snapped. "Not till the deal closes. It's bad luck."

Guests moaned, insisting that no one present would think of stealing it. From the way Mr. Yehudi stared at me, I could tell that there had been more to his silencing me than the reason he had given.

I wisely clammed up.

While the dishes were cleared and the tablecloth scraped, Ellen peppered me with more questions about myself. The next thing I knew, I was sharing my psychiatric history with the entire table, conjuring for all present the breathless ride of my fast-changing moods and ten-gear cycling, and naming what I believed to be its tandem sources: my genetic make-up and my adoptive father's molesting of me until I was nine years old.

"So you self-medicate with alcohol," Ellen noted.

"It's curious," I replied. "I've lived in New York City for almost half a century and no one has ever mentioned my drinking to me, but you're the second Los Angeleno to do so in the past two weeks."

Ellen's response was original. She said that centuries hence, when our empire had disappeared into the sands of time, and the world looked back on the United States, we would be remembered for only two things: Hollywood movies and the 12-step approach to conquering addiction. While both originated in other states, they had reached their apotheosis in California, so was it really any mystery that the locals were reaching out to me about my alcoholism?

I flinched at the word and fully expected someone to scold the woman, informing her that it was highly unprofessional to make such a grave diagnosis without more evidence, but no one did.

To defuse the tension, I lifted my wine glass and said, "Do I suffer from alcoholism? I don't know. I do know, however, that I suffer from an insuperable proclivity to wine. Are they one and the same? Perhaps. Cheers!"

No one even smiled.

"But why?" Dr. Ellen asked softly. "Why do you drink, when it's so obvious that it's killing you?"

Everyone stared at me, waiting for my answer.

I stammered, at a loss for words.

Finally, I found some.

"My wound is great, because it is so small," I said.

I wasn't even sure what this meant, or even who had first said it, but it did the trick.

Everyone but Ellen nodded, fully satisfied.

Dessert was served, coffee poured.

Delmore, raising his cup, toasted our host, thanking him for the "Lucullan feast." We all clinked glasses and sipped. Then the young professor noted that as it was Christmas Eve (this was news to me; I had thought it was still a few days away), so wasn't a holiday toast in order? Although everyone agreed, no one volunteered to lead it. I looked around during the awkward silence, trying to decide which Gentile ought to do the honors. Delmore was out of the question; he would lecture us on the Yule log, the red-eye flights of Odin, the sodomy of the Saturnalia, the birthday candles of Mithras, and Aesthetic Responses to Epistemological Cockney Crises in works of Mr. Charles Dickens. Willow was unfit to lead anything, except, perhaps, a good man to gonorrhea. Julian, a miserable cynic, would bring us all down. Thus, it fell on me. I cleared my throat and lifted my glass.

"Let us remember the ancient proverb," I declaimed, "'Better is a dinner of herbs where love is, than a stalled ox and hatred therein.'"

Everyone stared.

I coughed a few times to gather my strewn wits and began again in a more heartfelt way:

"As one gets older, without children, without grandchildren, and with one's old friends and enemies dying daily, Christmas becomes increasingly lonely. One reaches the point that one cannot even look at a glass of eggnog or a red-nosed reindeer without breaking into tears. A mere twelve hours ago, I thought that I would spend this holiday night on a train, lonely indeed, a defeated man, rattling across the Arizona desert. Instead, I am here breaking challah with all you wonderful folks, on the brink, perhaps, of my very first movie deal. What I am trying to say is, Santa Claus does exist and his name is Frank Yehudi. Come let us adore him."

As I extended my crystal, the tapestry above the side-board flew upward, and I realized that I was falling. My head hit the base of the hearth with a monumental crack, and my last thought before the world went hot and black was that Julian, whose grubby desert boots might be the very last things I would ever see, was Julian L. from my crime journal. That is why he had been invited to dinner and why Mr. Yehudi silenced me as I was about to utter the name Calvin Wirt.

The Real Calvin Wirt

awoke in a dark chamber and did not know where I was, or even what day it was; what I did know was that I was very cold and my right temple felt as though it had been punctured by a knitting needle. When I sat up, the darkness shuddered and swooned and I landed on my side, sucking air like a baby seal. When would the bad men come back? Would they be swift in their carving? Who would wear my snowy pelt? My breathing grew faster and faster. My gorge rose.

Next, I was staring at scarlet numerals, and I realized that I was in my big soft bed at Mr. Yehudi's house. He was my hero and we were going to make movie magic together. 1:41 said the clock. Day or night? I slapped the radio. Right on cue, the disc jockey said it was Christmas morning. I had not been asleep long. Was I still drunk? Who had carried me to bed? Who had stripped me? Had Gabriel sneaked a peek?

2:21. A baritone was singing about a frosty chap who had died of sunshine. Thumpety thump thump, thumpety thump thump, look at Frosty go. Thumpetty thump thump, thumpety thump thump, over the hills of snow. Would I die that way, too? I rolled over. Just inches from my nose, I made out a glass of water and a bottle of aspirin. Gabriel was a magician. American women expect from their husbands a perfection that English women only hope to find in their butlers. Who said that? I crawled to the pills. Somerset Maugham? P.G. Wodehouse? Maybe I said it.

2:56. Sitting up on the edge of the bed, staring into the shadows, I remembered those arty photographs of Somerset Maugham, where he's wearing a bowler hat and holding a cane, lifting a bushy eyebrow at the spectacle of a young man's naked bottom. Poor Old Willy, all those years of playing it straight tossed away like a handful of confetti. Weirdo that Maugham. Short. Nasty underbite. Wait, who was singing now? Oh, yes, Dino. Handsome and tall. No underbite. Baby, it's cold outside! Why was I awake? Must sleep away this pain. Even if it takes forever.

Looking back today from the comfort of my summer desk, I would love to think it was some sort of Sherlock Holmesian sixth sense that inspired me not to sink back into sleep and instead to walk downstairs, but I confess it was something far more mundane: I was famished. When I had fainted, I was only halfway through my ice cream. The thought of all that minty cocoa deliciousness left uneaten nagged at me like a bad loan.

"I am owed," my stomach grumbled.

Suddenly, my bare feet were slapping down cold stone steps. I wore a gigantic, fuzzy, pink bathrobe (think Mrs. Claus). The fact that it was the witching time of night and I was moving through a strange mansion in search of ice cream seemed like the most natural thing in the world, and yet, strangely, when I reached the kitchen, I swept right past it. I was suddenly keen to investigate the voices I heard, or fancied I heard, coming from the far edge of the world.

I peeked into an open door and saw a wood-paneled den.

Willow lay curled up on the bearskin rug, sound asleep, looking surprisingly innocent and sweet. I stepped in and noticed that in the valley of her hard cleavage sat a gold chain, bearing her initials. A Christmas gift from Mr. Yehudi? Only then did it strike me: why was Willow asleep on the floor? Was she dead? The tiny stem of a goose feather poked out of a nearby pillow. I plucked it, knelt, and held it beneath her nostrils. It stirred! Good news. What was *not* good news was that I noticed a dab of white powder on the tip of her upturned nose. Good heavens, who would ever have imagined that Willow Anne Stetz, who had arrived at The House Beautiful fresh off the farm, smelling of new-mown grass, averse to anything stronger than a cough drop, would one day use cocaine? Was it a mere dalliance or was she already deep in its abominable, snowy thrall?

Many footsteps later, I entered the living room, where I found Mr. Yehudi and Julian L. sitting together, sipping liqueur by the dancing fire. When they heard me, they turned their heads at the same time and broke into simultaneous laughter.

"Hey, how about a little modesty?" Mr. Yehudi said.

I blinked like a sleepwalker. What on earth was he talking about? I looked down and saw that, through a gap in my fuzzy robe, my privates dangled like fruit bats. I yanked it shut.

"What're you doing up?" Mr. Yehudi said, walking over. "That was a nasty fall you took."

"I was hungry," I replied, "but . . . but for some reason not anymore."

"Probably the sight of your own nuts," Julian muttered.

Mr. Yehudi escorted me to a love seat. "Here, take a load off."

I fell into it.

Gabriel materialized at my side, holding out a glass of fizzy water. His smile was maternally kind. If I had been able to stand up, I would have hugged him.

"You're a splendid man," I sighed. "If only you had a great-nephew."

Gabriel smiled and vanished like the Cheshire cat.

"I've got some bad news about Calvin," Mr. Yehudi said.

My face heaped. My eyes rounded with horror. In my very marrow, I knew the truth.

"He's dead," I whispered. I pointed a shaky Zola-like finger at Julian. "And this faggot killed him."

"Christ, you were right," Mr. Yehudi said, frowning at the accused. "We *should* have called a doctor. He's lost a few marbles."

"And he didn't have many to spare," Julian smirked.

"Oh, shut up, ugly man!" I shouted.

It was childish, yes, but I don't fancy being insulted by strangers, especially when I am concussed and they're wearing corduroy to a Christmas party. Fighting tears, I gulped my fizzy water. Mr. Yehudi watched me drain the glass before he explained. He said that during my afternoon nap, he had received a fax from his private dick, who, using the addresses and initials, had come up with the names of all of Calvin's customers. They were entertainment people: agents, actors, studio executives, a stand-up comic, and a producer of a kids' show. One name, however, had caught Mr. Yehudi's eye: Julian Lowry.

At last, I had been correct about something!

"Julian pitched an idea to me a few years back," Mr. Yehudi explained. "But I hadn't seen him since. So I called him up and invited him over. I told him I had a project I wanted to discuss. I figured he'd say forget it, it being Christmas Eve and all. I assumed he had plans."

"I did," Julian confessed, with a wormy smile. "I was throwing a dinner party, but after you called I canceled it. Work comes first."

I shivered at his professional desperation.

Back to the bad news: When the dinner party was over, Mr. Yehudi sat down with Julian and told him that he knew he was pals with a two-bit bangster named Calvin Wirt. Mr. Yehudi handed him a glass of peppermint schnapps, and said, "Tell me everything you know about him." Because Julian was unaware that Calvin had gone missing, and that he himself, like all of Calvin's other johns, was a prime suspect in his murder, and because he still hoped that there might be a job in it for him somewhere, he spilled every last bean.

Julian had met Calvin the previous August, on a night when he felt especially vulnerable. He had just finished writing a speculative screenplay for an epic film biography of Alexander Graham Bell. (The shocking twist was that Bell does not invent the telephone; he steals it from a poor Italian immigrant.) Because the script was "total fuckin' genius," he knew the odds were high that it would join the seventeen other unsold total-fuckin'-genius screenplays moldering on his shelf. In serious need of a morale booster, he dug out a triple-X newspaper. His eye landed on Calvin's ad. Although Julian preferred black bucket-queens, there was something in the boy's eyes that touched him. He looked like the only human being on earth sadder than he was. He picked up the phone and dialed.

Because Julian was by nature less sentimental than I, and because Calvin let slip that he "didn't mind it rough,"[20] Julian did not squander his hour with the boy as I had, dispensing grandfatherly advice and hugs; instead he took out on the boy all his hatred of Hollywood and the way it dishonored the

20 News to me.

most crucial member of the collaborative team. At one point, going too far with a clamp and an orange, Julian feared that the neighbors would overhear and call the police.

However badly he had mistreated Calvin that night, all was instantly forgiven when Julian, an amateur photographer, learned that the boy was an aspiring actor and offered to take his headshot for free. Calvin accepted, loved the results, and, in the weeks that followed, they met constantly, always off the clock, for a cup of coffee here, some career counseling there, and even, two or three times, a quick hour of Thai Leapfrog.

Everything changed Labor Day weekend, when Julian was invited to a party at the home of Rick Alvin, a celebrated television director. Rick's sprawling hacienda was one of the most glamorous in a posh enclave of Malibu called—and I am not making this up—Point Doom. Among the estate's many glories was an Olympic-sized, black-tiled swimming pool, in which Rick intended to whip up a batch of "man soup." To support the effort, each of the middle-aged guests was required to bring with him a young man to whom he was not romantically attached. Julian thought of Calvin. Julian would feed his chum to the sharks (pun intended) and he was sure to be repaid in spades (pun intended).

The weekend started off with a 1970s poolside disco dance, complete with bad music, poppers, pooka shells, and a vintage strobe light. Sure enough, Julian quickly found a silver-haired rogue for Calvin to boogie with, and the rogue's dusky· date quickly attached himself to Julian. Just before dawn, the two friends reunited, happy, sore, stoned, wet, and tired. They fell straight asleep. All through the night, Calvin squeezed Julian's hand, like a child clutching his teddy. When Julian awoke at noon, he felt strangely protective toward Calvin, even a little bit in love.

Everything turned ugly two hours later, during the barbecue, when Julian, who had been put in charge of the weenie roasting, noticed that Calvin had gone missing. Julian abandoned the grill and went inside to look for him, expecting to find him happily hanging off a shower rod with a wiffle ball in his mouth. When he did not find him inside, Julian took to the beach, walking for a full half-hour before he noticed, poking over a rise in the sand, a shiny cowlick, which he identified at once as the cutest part of Calvin's toupee. He found the young man sitting in a tide pool, holding hands with a boy who could not have been more than eleven years old. The look the little boy threw Julian was beseeching and terrified.

"Hotdogs are ready," Julian said.

The little boy jumped to his feet and dashed away. He did not stop running until he was almost out of sight.

Heading back, Julian wanted to grab Calvin by the nape of the neck, force his head under the surf, and hold it there overnight, but instead he kept his cool and told Calvin he needed serious psychiatric treatment and that he would gladly help him pay for it. Calvin agreed, almost eagerly, which surprised Julian and allowed him to enjoy the rest of the weekend.

A few days later, when Julian called Calvin to arrange for his first visit to the shrink, Calvin did not answer the phone. Julian called every day for the next two weeks, leaving messages each time, but he never heard back. Julian was so furious that he would have called the police, only he had no idea where Calvin lived and wasn't even sure about his last name.

Two months later, out of the blue, Calvin called and apologized. He said that he'd known if he was ever going to get better, he'd have to take full responsibility for his own cure. So he'd found himself an awesome therapist at a local free clinic. Although he was taking it one day at a time, he was pretty sure he'd never act out again. Oh, and another reason he called? His twenty-second birthday was on Saturday and he was having a party and he wanted all his best friends to be there. Would Julian come? He didn't have to bring a present or anything. Julian replied that he didn't believe a word Calvin had said, that he didn't believe he was seeing a doctor or even that he was twenty-two, and that he wanted nothing further to do with him. Before he could hang up in Calvin's face, Calvin hung up in his.

Julian shrugged at me. "That's it. That's all I know."

I didn't know whether to laugh, cry, or throw up. I had learned nothing about Calvin's fate, but far more than I wanted to know about his character. The time I had wasted on him! Whether he was alive or dead, I no longer cared. Good riddance! I rued the day I had ever ventured to Sun Land.

"Well," I whispered, looking over at Mr. Yehudi, "I have my ending. Only this is no murder mystery. It's a tragedy. For all concerned. With a bit of farce thrown in for good measure. I'm afraid we'll make no movie magic together. I have an artists colony to get back to. I'll be leaving tomorrow on the Southwest Chief."

Dark Epiphany

As though the universe were seconding my decision to flee Los Angeles, I awoke Christmas morning to a sound that I had rarely heard since my arrival—the pitty-pat of rain. Lying in bed, looking out the window, the pitty-pat soon turned into machine-gun fire and then, abruptly, an all-out blitzkrieg. The trees shook like the heads of keening madwomen, and water came at the glass in buckets. I might have been afraid, but the ancient house, standing since the days of Chaplin and Roach, had already withstood the worst that nature could bring. I smiled and rolled over for a cigarette. Thank heavens for the nasty weather. It made leaving just that much easier.

Two hours later, during brunch, the storm bestowed upon me a second gift, because it gave Willow something to talk about other than herself. If I sound bitter, it was only because I was down on L.A., and Willow, more than anyone else, had come to typify the place for me. Unfortunately, listening to her expound on the scarcity of rain in Southern California, as though it were a startling scientific observation sure to land her the Nobel, proved to be only marginally better than listening to her bang on about her hopes and dreams. It was enough to make me wish that Julian were there to jam a tangerine in her mouth and slap on some duct tape.

When Willow abandoned the rain and set to telling us what she thought was the "coolest thing about Porsches," Mr. Yehudi cut her off and brought up a fresh topic which I found absolutely delightful: my future. *Whither B.K. Troop?* is essentially what he asked me, chewing his sesame bagel.

I told him I had absolutely no idea. I was drained, dejected, and damned by dollars. Never in all my life had I felt so close to death, and my desire to write was less than nil.

"Well, you've got to do *something,*" he chewed. "You can't just crawl into a hole."

"He can if he finds one big enough," Willow muttered, lifting her screwdriver with a cocked pinky.

So that's how it was going to be. Now that I had no film in the offing, it was open hunting season. I resisted the provocation.

"Well," I sighed, with a hint of martyrdom, "I've always wanted to learn Greek. And the publisher of *The House Beautiful* will expect me to promote it. Then, of course, there are my lodgers, to whose needs I must continually tend."

"Yeah, right," Willow scoffed. "Their only needs are toothpaste and soap. I used to hide in my room, just so I wouldn't have to smell their bad breaths and B.O.'s."

It was one thing to insult me, and quite another to insult my charges. Although I was keen to fight back, out of respect for my host, I smiled and spoke with forced patience.

"My dear, hygiene and genius are not even kissing cousins. Which ought to come as no surprise to you, as you take four showers a day."

"Those idiots in your house are *geniuses?* Please. They're total phonies. They talk about art all day, but it's such bullshit.

They're totally lazy. They have no commitment to their craft. You should kick 'em all out. They all hate you, anyway—except that pathetic little poet guy. They just like the cheap rent."

I was aflame with indignation.

"How dare you?" was all I managed. And then I huffed: "Such ingratitude!"

"I should be *grateful?* For what? You're nuts!"

"Kids, kids," Mr. Yehudi interrupted, laughing. "Come on, play nice, it's a holiday."

"Grateful for what?" she continued. "Living in the H.B. was the worst six months of my life."

"Is that why you only paid for *three?*"

"I paid for six!"

"I never got the check!"

"Well, the money left my account, so either someone forged your signature or you cashed it when you were drunk and forgot!"

"Coke addict!"

"Fat, ugly faggot!"

My eyes closed as though I had been pepper-sprayed. I should have known better than to corner an unemployed actress the morning after a coke-bender. Sooner ask a grizzly bear to dance. My hurt was so profound that I was not able to speak for several minutes. When I finally found words it was only to lie about the departure time of the Southwest Chief.

Five full hours before I needed to be at Union Station, Gabriel set my trunk and bags into the spacious rear of a gleaming black truck, next to a suitcase I did not recognize.

"Look at it come down," Mr. Yehudi said, smiling up at the rain from beneath the arch of the entranceway. "Could be worse, I guess. Could be snow."

I pumped his hand and thanked him for everything.

As ever, he looked me squarely in the eye.

He told me not to mention it.

"Oh, but I must," I replied. "Since arriving here, I felt at times like a latter-day Diogenes, the great Greek cynic who lighted a lantern in the sunshine and walked the streets of Athens looking for an honest man. Only I was looking for an honest producer. Just as I was ready to give up, I met you, and I knew that my search was over. Only you are more than honest, sir. You have the soul of a gentleman. You're civilized."

I heard a sound. I looked over and saw Willow wagging her head and snapping her fingers to music from a pair of headphones. I decided to take advantage of her deafness and ask the question that had nagged at me since my arrival. I chose my words carefully, so as not to anger Mr. Yehudi.

"Please, sir, tell me this. Why would a man with such exquisite taste in art, choose for his mate such a vulgar beast?"

He stared at me, surprised. Had I gone too far? No, thank heaven, because he laughed. But not so loudly that Willow removed her earphones.

"Listen," he said, laying a hand on my shoulder. "I've got over fifty years on the kid. Even if she *weren't* who she is, what the hell would we talk about? And you know what? I've got plenty of friends to talk to. I've got my kids and *their* kids. But there's only one Willow. I mean look at her. She's gorgeous. If I said no to that body, it'd been a crime against nature, right?"

Yes, of course. Why hadn't I seen it? For a man pushing eighty with a potato nose and short legs to lie every night next to a body as delicious as Willow's, and be permitted to poke around inside it whenever he chose, was, indeed, a victory of Austerlitzian proportions. Who on earth was I to judge? What did I know about human relations, anyway? I had just wasted precious weeks, loyal to a pedophilic pavement-princess, and the only two men I had ever loved were partial to women.

My host and I shook hands again, and because I was suddenly feeling a smidge sympathetic toward the beast that shared his bed, I surprised Willow with a kiss to the cheek. She smelled of bubble gum and greed. As I stepped away, I noticed something that froze me. Chiseled in the stone at the side of the doorway's ancient timbers were the words "Anno 1974."

I breathed a mournful sigh. The house was no landmark, merely a flight of fancy. Was nothing in this town what it appeared to be? Was it all just a conjurer's trick? I felt like Alice down the rabbit hole or Dorothy up in Oz, only I would not magically wake up in my own bed; first I had a three-day train ride.

As the truck glided away, I could not bring myself to turn around in my seat and wave good-bye to Mr. Yehudi. I was still shaken by own gullibility. I might cry and then learn later that he was, in fact, a robot or a creation of the studio prop shop. I fumbled for a cigarette. At least in New York what you saw was what you got—never better, never worse.

Driving through a torrent of cleansing rain, looking out with loneliness at the glittering mini-malls and up at the chalky sky with its invisible poisons and ten million wires, and straight ahead at the myriad cars, whizzing past, wipers working, and then, closer, at the tiny, white hairs at the nape of Gabriel's smooth, brown neck, I thought of all that had transpired since my arrival. What if I had not answered the phone the day that Mr. Shipp had called? Or what if I had simply told him that my words were not for sale? Would I be better off today? Without thinking very hard, I knew the answer was no. Every artist needs to enter the marketplace even if only to reject, in the end, its vanities and shams.

All my life when people asked me why I disliked L.A., my

answers had been nothing but the paraphrased wisdom of others: "Because there are so many beautiful people in Hollywood that beauty starts to look ugly." (Fitzgerald); "Because the soul evaporates in too much sunshine." (Huxley); and my favorite, "Because Hollywood is the place where one morning you fall asleep by the swimming pool and wake up thirty-five years later to discover that you are an obese laughing stock." (Orson Welles). But now, *now,* I could speak from experience about its allergens, its dirty skies, its paucity of books, its encroachment of cars, and the blank looks you get whenever you say something sarcastic. And, most damning of all, I could speak of its widespread mendacity and corruption.

"We're almost there," Gabriel murmured.

"Excellent," I replied.

I flipped my second butt out the window and resumed my ruminations. Yes, I had learned much, but had it really been necessary for me to stay as long as I had? Hadn't I already known by the morning after Thanksgiving all I needed to know about Los Angeles? What if I had not let Calvin persuade me to stay? What if I had told the little pintle-twister that I had better things to do than attend his birthday party? What would have been the result? I would have come home just as defeated and not one bit wiser. But, alas, I could not resist him. That undersized head, the endless abdomen, those sad, gray eyes. And he had invited me so sweetly, as though his whole happiness depended on it. I recalled what he had said to Julian Lowry: "I want all my best friends to be there."

It was then that I was struck by an epiphany so unexpected, dark, and violent that I cried out like a schoolgirl at a mouse.

I had cracked the case!

I knew that Calvin was dead, and I knew who had murdered him and why.

Because my train did not leave for hours, I had time to confront the killer.

"A change of plans!" I cried to Gabriel.

As he turned the steering wheel, pointing us due north, I whispered to myself, "Well done, old feller."

The Ending

itful winds blew the stink of wet fur and feces about the muddy yard. A dozen shivering Jack Russell pups, bigger than before, and the proud authors of bigger piles of dung, went berserk at the sight of me, hoping that I might lead them back inside, where it was warm and dry. The ever-vigilant Gin, having heard Gabriel's engine, peeked out the front window. I could barely make out her chins through the marijuana smoke that gushed from her mouth. When she saw me, she cocked her head from side to side like one of her Jacks. A few seconds later, the coughing face of her roommate popped up next to hers. The last thing Anson needed was a contact high. It was a recipe for geriatric rape. What a pair they made! Were she alive today, Diane Arbus would have refused to photograph them on the grounds that they were too depressing.

I surprised them both by walking away.

I strode to the next house, opened the screen door, and knocked. Jesus could not have been more surprised to see me. Not only should I have been long gone by now, but it was Christmas morning, hardly an appropriate time for a pop-in visit. Over his shoulder, I saw Omar and Jesse sitting on the living-room shag beside the tree, surrounded by toys and books. Neither looked as happy as Domingo, who sat on the sofa, squirming his new doll into spangled pedal pushers.

"I need to talk to you," I said. "Alone."

He found a smile and whipped around. "Boys, look who's here!"

Six black eyes lighted up. They could not have been more pleased to see me if I had sported a white beard and carried a red sack. Maria, entering from the kitchen, greeted me with a big, bosomy hug and a brandy-touched kiss. She eased away, still holding my elbows, and studied my face. Her eyes gleamed as though by firelight, but there was no flame, only a loving heart. I had come on grave business, but I was unable to refuse her offer of my favorite holiday drink.

"Coming right up!" she sang, as she went to fetch the nog.

The first cup coursed through me like a promise of happiness, the second made my toes curl, and the third I carried with me untouched down the hallway for my private talk with Jesus. It was too wet to speak in the backyard, so we chose Domingo's room instead.

"Was it always painted this color?" I asked, eyeing the rosy walls.

"I painted it last year."

"And were there always stars on the ceiling?"

"Yes."

"Funny, I didn't notice that before. And what about the mannequin? Was she always here?"

"No, he saw it yesterday in a dumpster at the mall. He asked if he could keep it."

"Did he dress it himself?"

Jesus smiled with sincere pride at the boy's talents. "Yeah,

Maria doesn't like it. She's jealous. She says it looks better in her clothes than she does."

"Impossible. Your wife is a great beauty."

Smiling, he crossed his arms and sat back on a little chest of drawers covered with floral decals. "So, Mr. Troop, what are you doin' here? I thought you went home."

"I'm here because my Hollywood business wasn't finished," I said, walking to the window. "In the process of trying to close a movie deal, I happened upon some information about Calvin that I thought you'd like to know."

I turned and studied his face for a reaction.

Nothing.

"He's a pedophile," I blurted, hoping to catch him off his guard.

Again, no reaction.

"What's that?" he asked.

"He touches children," I said.

At last it came, the reaction that I had been expecting. The gentleness drained from his face. Fear took hold, stony and animal. He knew precisely why I had come, but he wasn't going to make it easy for me.

"You're sure about that?" he said.

"Yes, and so are you." I turned back to the window. "You've known he was sick since the night of Calvin's birthday party. You were invited, of course. So was Maria. Maybe even the boys. He wanted all his closest friends to be there, and how could you not be counted among them? But just as you were about to head over, Domingo seemed withdrawn, sad. Perhaps he'd developed a rash or a strange infection. You pushed him for an explanation and, at last, he told you what Calvin had done to him. Or maybe I have it wrong. Maybe you found toupee hairs in the lad's underwear. It doesn't matter. What matters is that you learned the truth of the crime, and your Latino blood caught fire. You paced the living room like a caged jaguar. Every cell in your body cried out for vengeance. You wanted him to pay in blood! Maria begged you to calm down, not do something you'd regret. Then you heard Gin's door slam. You ran to the window and saw Calvin heading to his car, and before you could stop yourself, you ran outside to confront him.

I turned and looked at him again. He stared back at me with unrepentant eyes. This was no saint, but a flesh-and-blood father.

"He hurt my son, Mr. Troop."

I had my confession, but it was no time to celebrate. I wanted details. I needed them. I deserved them. I crossed over to the twin bed. The room shifted a bit. The nog had done its happy work. I sank onto the lavender comforter and something poked me. A high-heeled shoe. I tossed it into a basket of stuffed animals.

"Tell me everything," I said.

He shifted his weight, kept his eyes glued to the floor, and spoke softly. "Domingo said, 'I don't want to go to the party, Daddy. Calvin's not my friend.' I said, 'What do you mean? He is your very good friend.' And he said, 'No, not anymore.' I was worried. I said to him, 'I'm your father. I love you. You can tell me anything. Tell me why you don't like Calvin.'"

Jesus struggled to hold back his tears.

He was a proud man.

I could not bear to make him say it, so I interrupted: "After he told you what Calvin had done to him, you heard the door open and close next door?"

Jesus, sniffling, nodded.

"You hurried outside?"

He nodded again.

"Calvin told you he was just dashing out to get some wine and that you should go inside and enjoy the party, but then he saw the expression on your face, and he knew that you knew. He backed away in terror, but you jumped up and caught him by the neck with both hands and you squeezed. He couldn't scream. His bulging eyes begged for mercy, but you thought of your sweet, defenseless son and you squeezed and squeezed and squeezed. He sank and sank until you were the same height and his knees fell at last into a heap of dog shit."

Jesus, fighting tears, nodded again and again, tortured by my vivid depiction. He had suffered enough. His only sin was loving his son too well.

"And then you let go of his throat," I whispered. "Calvin fell at your feet, gasping for air. He told you how sorry he was. He begged for mercy and you granted it."

Jesus stared at me, astounded by this bizarre twist in my narrative.

I walked back to the window. "A lesser man would have killed the monster. A lesser man would have stowed his body in the garage and dumped his car at a local chop shop, and then, later that night, when all of Gin's lights were out, dragged the corpse into his backyard and buried it. Right there." I pointed out the window. "Where that new sod has been so conspicuously laid." I turned around with a glad look. "But not you. After he crawled to his feet, you said, 'Get lost and never come back. Leave your car, your phone, your money, and go. If I ever see your face again, I will report you to the authorities.'" I paused dramatically. "That *is* what happened, isn't it?"

Jesus stared at me with wonder, open-mouthed.

"Very well," I chirped, "there's no law against that. You did exactly what I would have done. If only you had told me so the morning we met, you would have saved me an awful lot of bother."

He looked so ashamed that I took it right back.

"No, come to think of it," I said, patting his strong shoulder, "then I would never have met your charming family and experienced so much of Los Angeles. My next book would have ended before it started."

We returned to the living room and were met by a wild, frightened look from Maria.

"Is something wrong?" she asked.

"Yes," I replied. I turned my cup upside down. "I'm nogless."

Relieved, she flashed that dazzler of hers, took the cup, and ran off to the kitchen. I took out my wallet, walked over to the boys, and gave Jesse and Omar five dollars each.

"Ho, ho, ho," I said as I forked it over.

They were happy, of course. When I got to Domingo, employing sleight of hand, I swapped his five for three twenties. It was the last of Calvin's money. Why not?

"Buy yourself something pretty," I breathed.

He grinned at me with special knowledge. My cheeks burned with love for the boy and with sorrow for all that he had endured. Maria reentered with my fourth nog. I drained it in one big gulp, waited for it to kick me in the groin, then I hugged her, shook Jesus's hand, and headed for the door. Once there, I spun around on my heels, almost falling over, raised a big hand and exclaimed ere I walked out of sight—"Happy Christmas to all, and to all a good night!"

Adieu

The storm advanced like portable midnight. Driving to Union Station, staring up at the menacing gray, I thought of all the abused children in the world, millions upon millions of us in every corner of the earth. Little Molly. The boy on the beach. Domingo and all other boys whom Calvin had introduced to shame. (Was Anson among them? If not, how did he know that Calvin was a "naughty boy"?) Down at the morgue, there was an entire shoebox full of Baby Does. None of them had come into the world looking for trouble. I could only hope that one day Jesus would find it in his heart to plant something hopeful on Calvin's grave. An orange tree, a tomato vine, a seesaw.

"Gabriel, do you mind if I ask you a question?"

"No, sir."

"Before we left, I noticed that you packed a suitcase that doesn't belong to me. Whose is it?"

"Mine. I'm going on vacation now. I have a week off."

"You're leaving today?"

"Right after I drop you."

"Where are you going? Back to the Philippines?"

"Philippines?" he cried, falsetto. "Man, I'm Chinese!"

"Oh, I'm sorry. I don't know why I thought that."

In fact, I knew exactly why: his bone structure and scent.

"So you're going back to Hong Kong then?"

"Nope, never been. I was born in Fresno. I'm going to San Francisco."

"How wonderful. I think it's the most beautiful city on earth."

"I agree."

"I've been only once. In 1958. In fact, I still own a pair of wooden shoes I purchased there one drunken afternoon. I told my Beat pals that I was going to start a bohemian book club called the *clognoscenti*. I wasn't serious, of course."

"Why don't you come with me?" he said, throwing me a coy, little smile.

"What?"

"I have a wonderful hotel room. I'll drive you back to Union Station on January first."

"Oh, I couldn't possibly!" I tittered.

The prospect of joining Gabriel on his trip made me blush like a naked debutante. Imagine! Sharing a room with a man I hardly knew, and not just any man, but one roughly my own age. Not since my early thirties had I come within a country mile of a contemporary. The thought of it was absurd. I remembered Dr. Gaby Geitman telling me that my preference for the young was not conducive to intimacy. My reply had been something flip, along the lines of "Precisely."

I lighted up and lowered the window, admitting some rain. What *would* it be like, I asked myself, to flop around in the hay with an autumn goat like Gabriel? Dull, probably. Then, again, one never knew. The first time I had slept with an Australian, I had expected great athleticism, but what I got was merely bumptious and passive. The opposite was true of my first and only Swiss. I had expected neutrality, but, my lord, how quickly he had taken sides! Setting the matter of sex aside, what would Gabriel and I do when the sun was *up*? I loathed sightseeing, and museums were only fun when you were alone and could leave in twenty minutes, but claim you had stayed for hours.

It was then that I remembered, with a sort of electric shock, that I had a friend in the Bay Area. Christopher Ireland was his name, and he was the eponymous hero of my first novel. He lived just over the bridge (or was it through the tunnel?) in Palo Alto, home of the dreaded Stanford University. For years, I had wondered if he taught there, but if he did, then why had his book, *Love's Sad Archery: The Allure of Heartbreak in Byron's Don Juan*, been published by another, less celebrated university? Was it because the book was mediocre, not up to Stanford's diabolical standards, or because he taught somewhere else in the region? The short biography under his photograph said that he lived with his wife Jill and three children.

The sky roared with thunder. Gabriel's wipers worked frantically to manage the deluge. I thought about what I had said the night before to Mr. Yehudi: "I have my ending." Even as I had said it, I had known it was a lie. I felt no sense of finality at all. But now everything was different, wasn't it? I had achieved what Dr. Gaby Geitman called "closure," hadn't I? How could it be otherwise? I had cracked the case, given away the last of Calvin's money, and bade the Cabreras farewell. My train left in two hours. What could be more final than that?

Yet, remembering Christopher now, and all that he had meant to me, and how little anything had meant to me since, I knew that this journey could not be finished. What, after all, was I running back to? As an avid reader, my days and nights were spent picking through the bones of the dead, and, yes, there was some pride and satisfaction in it, but what about the flesh of living? I had none in my life. I tended to my lodgers, but Willow was right: aside from Adrian, they mostly deemed me horrid. Was I actually unhappier than I knew? Was this why I had jumped the rails so eagerly when Hollywood called?

A week in San Francisco with a kind, capable man my own age—why not? A little high-powered necking never hurt anyone. It might even agree with me. And even if it did not, I would never regret the adventure, because one afternoon while Gabriel was out shopping for, say, ginseng, I would board a train, a bus, or a taxi and escape for a day trip to Palo Alto. I would find Christopher's college and walk down a long corridor, looking for the office whose number I had seen on the directory downstairs. Before I even reached the door, it would open and a young man would emerge into the hall.

Wait, no, not young. No longer young. Forty-five now. Good heavens. But even in the dusty, golden air slanting in from the leaded window, I would recognize those black, gypsy eyes, those fine, pretty features. When he recognized me, he would flash his pearly teeth. Would we return to his office? No, we would walk the quad instead and, as before, our conversation would come as easily as leaves to trees. We would remember and we would laugh. The hours would pass like minutes. When the sun fell, if he did not invite me back to meet his family, I would return to the hotel with hurt feelings, yes, but Gabriel would greet me there with a cup of tea. He would be most comforting. I might even fall asleep in his arms. Or perhaps not. When an old man lives with his heart wide open, sleep is not easy.

"Gabriel, I would be delighted to accompany you to San Francisco."

He made an odd, happy clicking sound and yanked the steering wheel, plowing us straight into a raging river that ran along the right lane, but the truck was safe and sturdy. Yes, Mr. Yehudi had been right, it was pissing rain. It was flooding the villas of the rich and the kennels of the poor, the Hombly tennis courts and the Brentwood swimming pools, the Points of Doom and the Plazas of Palms, drenching, too, the fresh green sod where Calvin Wirt lay buried, soon to be forgotten by everyone but me and a pack of wounded boys. What if it fell for the next forty days and forty nights? What would happen then? The great basin would fill, and when the very future of Hollywood was in doubt, what would the powers-that-be do? They would load a giant ark with cartoon animals. The written word would perish, but children's stories for adults would live on. I burst out laughing. My heart swelled with a sense of possibility and hope. I was ready to quit this mad place. My soul was still my own. And from the crown of my head to the balls of my feet, I was alive!